There was a young lady from Riga,
Who rode with a smile on a tiger.
They returned from the ride
With the lady inside
And the smile on the face of the tiger.

For Mum and Dad,
who did their bit . . .
and then a bit more.

ACKNOWLEDGMENTS

Many thanks to my team of first-draft readers (Jeannette, Clare, Ara, and above all, Bill), all of whom cheerfully subject themselves to acres of superfluous verbiage subsequently weeded out thanks to their wise advice. Thanks, too, to Uli, Inge, and Ant, who put me right on my linguistic infelicities, and Judy and Marty, whose continued support and encouragement is a very rare thing in the world of modern publishing.

There's three guys stuck in a lift, an Irishman, an Italian, and a German.

Sounds like a bad joke, doesn't it? Perhaps it was. Only the German was Adolf Hitler and the Italian was Benito Mussolini. The Irishman was nobody. The Irishman was me.

No punch line. Just one disgruntled daughter. Happened like this.

IN CASE ANYONE other than you, my dear, comes across these pages, this is the me that was: German mother, Irish father, studied history and modern languages at Trinity, fluent in French, Spanish, Italian, and German, and nowadays exiled so long that my native tongue sounds artificial, as if the tricks of translation have robbed me of my own true words.

I think that's it as far as identity goes.

Oh . . . and granny was English. But nobody's perfect.

Thus your motley lineage, my child: an Anglo-Irish-German-Italian Jewess, hopefully with a few other bits bunged in besides. I always had a soft spot for mongrels. We're all mongrels after a manner and the sooner our spatchcocked species accepts that fact the better. Not that I said as much to Hitler or Mussolini. Neither The Flatulent Windbag nor The Constipated Prick would have approved. But I take more pride in having fathered an Anglo-Irish-German-Italian Jewess than anything else in my footloose life. It is a superb hotchpotch, as good as it gets for anybody born outside Brazil before the advent of mass travel. Still, it does not make for a conspicuously placid temperament, not when the hotchpotch in question comes across a newspaper clipping showing her dear old dad hobnobbing with two of the century's most notorious dictators: "The Man Who Saved Hitler and Mussolini."

YOU DID WHAT?!

I appreciate that it must have come as a nasty shock for the daughter of a partisan heroine, but at least it has given you something to be angry about. I was always going to be a disappointing parent for one of your unruly generation. Kicking over the traces in the Colgan household must be like rebelling against melted butter. Never mind. Revolutions rarely matter as much as we think they do. Just get on with it, dear. Be kind. Have fun. Nothing else matters. And when those two imperatives clash, opt for the first. That's all you need to know.

So, how come I was on hand when Hitler wanted a guide to Italy's artistic treasures and some booby decided I was the man for the job? Well, my parents had died for one thing. As you know, it's something parents tend to do. We're obliging like that. Only mine were unusually ‘precipitate. Having lived long enough to bequeath me my linguistic heritage, they succumbed to the influenza pandemic. Thereafter, the best efforts of guardians and governesses notwithstanding, I developed into a remarkably feckless young man, given to roaming the Wicklow Mountains and loafing about the National Gallery. It was an education of sorts. Post commencement and loath to live in a Free State subject to the tyranny of men in black frocks, I took myself on a European tour and fetched up in Italy, thus joining the ranks of displaced Irish vagabonds dotted about the continent: Joyce in Trieste, Beckett in Paris, the other Joyce bound for Berlin, and Colgan in Rome.

The name is known now, the face more so. After we moved to France, I became a TV pundit, capable of delivering unrehearsed to camera however many seconds or minutes the producer requires on any topic pertaining to popular culture, politics, the arts, or the shocking shenanigans of my daughter's shrill generation. But back in the thirties, I was Europe's Least Promising Irishman, the last man whose face one would expect to see in the papers.

Short of funds, I cast about for a job that would not involve anything much resembling work. The gallery required an English-speaking art historian to be its new assistant curator. I was an historian with an eye for a painting. I only had to append an *Art* and I had a job. I did what was necessary.

THREE YEARS LATER, Hitler heads south, intent on visiting the monuments and museums of Rome and Florence. Benito is not a man for monuments and museums. Monumental women, yes. Just look at his principal paramour, that hapless flibbertigibbet Claretta Petacci. But statues and paintings are not his thing. A guide is required, one familiar with the works and fluent in German and Italian. Colgan gets volunteered. Who proposed me, I do not know. If I had, I would have had strong words with him. I didn't want the job. I never wanted any job, certainly not one that entailed being chummy with tyrants. But these things happen sometimes.

Admittedly, I had the languages and could prattle on about paintings. I even had a passion for mountains, a fact that might have been seen in a positive light by anyone familiar with those dreadful photos of the Führer in the Bavarian Alps, a faintly moist look in his eye, his stumpy little legs clad in lederhosen. But it still seemed unjust that a blameless individual like myself should have come to the attention of the diplomats, a class who can be quite pitiless when putting on a show for visiting bigwigs.

I told them the honour should go to an Italian. They offered me a passport. I smoked, I said, Herr Hitler hated smoking. I was informed that I would not smoke in his presence. I wasn't a proper art historian at all, I said. I knew the pictures, they said, I knew the history, the languages, that was enough. I even hinted that I was a pansy, but nothing put them off. You will not proposition our guests, they said. This without cracking a smile! Can you imagine? I mean, it's all very well being obliging to strangers, but the idea that even the most rampant homosexualist should have . . . have you seen these people? Göring? Actually he stayed at home to mind the shop. But Himmler? Hess? Ribbentrop? The mere thought makes me queasy. So I played my trump card, told them I was a notorious and ardent anti-Fascist. As it happens, I wasn't really an anti-Fascist, still less a notorious and ardent one, but I was desperate. The Duce, they said, can tolerate a little opposition. It was true, too. He even released the odd Communist on occasion. He wasn't really cut out for the dictating business.

Concerning my political credentials, I suppose that, insofar as I was anti anything, you might have called me an anti-Fascist, but to be honest I was more with Wodehouse on this one. What with the blue shirts and the black shirts and the brown shirts and the green shirts, I was looking forward to the moment when the fascistic movements ran out of different coloured shirts and started proclaiming themselves by the shade of their shorts. For my money, Fascism was typified by its first British martyr, a volunteer train driver during the General Strike who looked out the cab window and got his head knocked off by an oncoming locomotive. A minor inconvenience. The head, after all, is the last organ a Fascist requires. And the Fascist champion par excellence was Roberto Farinacci, the star veteran of Mussolini's Abyssinian venture, who achieved heroic status when he blew off his own hand fishing with grenades. One hardly needed to worry about a movement whose adherents were bent on dismembering themselves. And we haven't even got onto Hitler's monorchism yet.

If anything, it was the inelegance of the Fascists that upset me, not just sartorially (though it was hard to forgive that tassel on Mussolini's fez), but the vulgarity of their thoughts. Yet for all the triviality of my motives, when I accepted the inevitable and agreed to act as the dictators' guide, I knew that even a tepid anti-Fascist like myself ought to consider assassinating them. It's the done thing in these situations.

THEY'D MET TWICE before. The first time, four years earlier, had been a disaster. Hitler turned up in Venice, whey faced and lank haired, wearing a shapeless yellow mackintosh over the drab costume of a diplomat, only to find Mussolini had just got back from topping up his tan on the beach and was decked out in a uniform that looked like something out of *The Prisoner of Zenda*. Hitler wasn't happy. According to one journalist, he kept twisting his hat in his hands like a plumber holding an embarrassing implement.

Things did not improve when they got down to talks. They didn't agree about anything apart from not liking the French and the Russians, which most anybody would have agreed upon back then, including the French and the Russians, and they didn't understand each other, in no small part due to Mussolini's refusal to use an interpreter. He was proud of his gift for languages. He spoke German, English, and French, which isn't bad for a politician. Except Mussolini was a linguist like Hitler would be a military genius—a little early success had gone to his head with dire results. His speeches in foreign languages often left his audience confused, while he himself had difficulty following Hitler's heavily accented German. But being too proud to admit that he didn't understand, he lapsed into silence when things got too technical, a silence Hitler was all too willing to fill by reciting large chunks of *Mein Kampf*, blathering on about *Lebensraum* and the November criminals and his indomitable will and the superiority of the Nordic races compared to the dodgy ancestry of the Mediterranean peoples.

To cap it all, the conference was invaded by giant mosquitoes and coffee was served with salt instead of sugar. When I heard that, I wondered whether your mother hadn't been there. It was a bit primitive by her standards, but great careers often begin with unpromising premises. The upshot was that Mussolini dismissed Hitler as "a mad little clown" and Hitler went home feeling slighted. It was never a good idea to give Hitler the impression of being undervalued in any way. A month later, the Austrian Nazis tried their hand at a coup, one that failed but which did succeed in murdering Mussolini's friend Dollfuss, and that whilst Mrs. Dollfuss and the little Dollfusses were on holiday with the Mussolinis in Italy.

The second meeting, when Mussolini visited Germany in 1937, was everything the previous encounter had failed to be. Declaring that the Duce was not merely a partaker of history, but a maker of the stuff, Hitler laid on the full range of Nazi Speertacular, staging parades, flypasts, and military manoeuvres, showing off secret weapons, spanking new factories, and closely regimented party cadres, commandeering the population of Berlin to line the Wilhelmstrasse, and packing a further 800,000 into the Maifeld stadium to applaud the leaders' speeches, which they did, despite not having a clue what Mussolini was on about.

It was all goose stepping and gleaming steel, big guns and obedient bodies, the purpose of which was to persuade Fascism's founding father that the new kid on the block was coming along nicely, and it would be as well if Daddy Fascist put aside his scruples about Austrian independence and gave his approval to the *Anschluss* forthwith. The mad little clown was coming to town and he had with him a dazzling array of toys.

Duly dazzled, Mussolini returned home enthused with all things German, from disciplined subordinates to tall blond warriors, a class to which he concluded, the evidence of his looking glass notwithstanding, his own family undoubtedly belonged. There was a vogue for German cinema, German arts, even German food. Then the Duce decided the goose step was "the greatest thing in the world" and insisted, despite opposition from his generals and the king (a man not otherwise noted for his good sense), that Italian soldiers should adopt the *passo romano*, goose stepping being a Roman step seeing as how geese had saved the capitol in antiquity. This was not wise. You can't ask Italians to goose-step. It's like expecting cats to form a queue. And there was a fundamental difference between Italian and German soldiers. About eight inches to be precise. Getting the Italian infantry to do the Roman step resulted in what Marshal Emilio de Bono accurately predicted would be "a ridiculous show of mechanical dwarfs." I was tickled pink until my role in the fallout from the trip to Germany was revealed. Because it was as a direct consequence of that visit that Mussolini was set upon impressing Hitler when he next headed south.

GALEAZZO CIANO, THE Big Son-in-Law, was charged with organizing the jamboree. Poor Ciano. He was vain, idle, boastful, self-indulgent, pretentious, and sycophantic, but as I say, nobody's perfect, and there was a certain puffy charm about him. Moreover, this fickle *jouisseur* would surprise us all when they shot him, dying with a degree of courage and dignity few casual observers had anticipated. That's not why I felt sorry for him, though. There were two reasons, really. First, everybody hated him.

I mentioned a vogue for all things German. That was disingenuous, at least if "vogue" implies a spontaneous upsurge in popularity, because the Italians were wary of the Germans, and the Germans certainly didn't think much of the Italians. Bismarck said when Italy adhered to an alliance, it was already scheming to get out of it, dismissing Italian territorial ambitions with a withering, "Big appetite, bad teeth"; Houston Stewart Chamberlain called Rome the capital of chaos, Goebbels compared its citizens to a hill of beans, the beans getting the better of the deal, and Ribbentrop never tired of quoting the adage that Naples was the only African city without a European quarter, which was not intended as an anticolonial compliment. Italians were the eternal traitors, the Captains of Caporetto, *banditi* and *magnaccia*, vendors of ice cream, makers of macaroni, and players of mandolins, charming enough in small doses, but wholly unreliable. Later on, the Germans would tell the following joke:

> *German HQ hears that Mussolini has joined the war.*
> *"We'll have to put up ten divisions to counter him!" says one general.*
> *"No, he's on our side," says another.*
> *"In that case we'll need twenty divisions."*

Aspersions on the nation's martial qualities were bitterly resented, not least because many Italians had a nasty feeling they might be true, so there was never any easiness between the future Axis partners and the vogue for all things German was imposed from above. But there was one thing both Italians and Germans agreed on and that was the fact that Ciano was a waste of space, promoted to positions of power because he had sired the ducal grandchildren and was a first-rate toady. Another joke, this time Italian:

> *Is there anything Ciano can do well?*
> *Yes, he's an excellent cuckold, but even there he needs his wife's help.*

Truth be told, Ciano was more active on the extramarital front than Edda, and it was the appeal of the playboy that inspired my second reason for pitying him, because the only German who liked Ciano, and she really liked him, was Eva Braun. Reckoning Ciano was Rudolph Valentino, Errol

Flynn, and Douglas Fairbanks all rolled up in one handy package (women do get the strangest ideas sometimes), she would blush when he walked into the room and there were rumours she collected photos of him. I heard she even tried to get Hitler to dress more elegantly . . . "like Ciano." Not a happy suggestion. Six years later, the Germans insisted Ciano be shot for his part in the palace coup that had ousted his father-in-law.

In 1938 though, Ciano was Italy's foreign minister, and he was given the job of organizing what Mussolini called the return match. The glitz and pomp and ceremony of the German visit were a challenge that had to be met, regardless of expense—or taste.

NOTHING WAS TO be allowed to spoil the impression of a modern nation marching toward a bright future, no matter how makeshift the contrivances arrived at to sustain this illusion. New drains were dug and new plumbing installed to clear the pong that had pervaded Italian towns since medieval times (though Hitler would spoil that plan all on his own, *Hey up, Rover!*); pavements were laid, house fronts rerendered, buildings scrubbed cleaned, and even the kennels were daubed with slogans glorifying the dictators.

Fair enough. We all do a bit of dusting when a distinguished guest is due.

Except at the same time ancient stone was cut back to tidy up the facades of older buildings and marble parapets were covered with cement, as if the sheen of modernism might be tarnished by the time-weathered materials of antiquity. The vandalism was enough to make one appreciate the more ephemeral embellishments installed along the Führer's route, like the sheets of plywood and cardboard painted to resemble marble and bronze. Even the new railway station at Ostiense had a cardboard facade. The Fascists were fond of cardboard. A couple of years later when Italian troops were bogged down dying in the mountains of Macedonia, their government was pleased to send them a good supply of cardboard shoes.

The other thing that was never lacking in Italy were medals. Weapons might be scarce, but metal for medals was always available, as I discovered when I reported to the ministry. Everyone involved in the visit wanted a medal to wear. There were enough tinsel tits around to suggest the nation was staging a burlesque show and the chief of protocol was like a harried haberdasher's assistant dispensing rolls of military ribbon. He near kissed me when I told him I didn't want any decorations. But he couldn't help with the uniform. Everyone else was in a flurry of fittings, stitching as many trimmings to the basic outfit as they could get away with. It was like a tart's wedding and I wanted none of it, but I was told there was no way round it. Given the importance of my role, I had to wear the uniform of an officer in the *Milizia Volontaria per la Sicurezza Nazionale*, which is why I'm dressed as a bloody Blackshirt in that photo. Didn't matter that I wasn't actually a militiaman. Appearances were all. So I spent the best part of a week hunting out the shabbiest secondhand uniform I could find. I also got a pair of used cardboard shoes. And a threadbare fez that had lost its tassel. That would show them.

You'd have thought Italy would have had enough black outfits to be going on with, what with the priests' cassocks and the widows' weeds, but that fool D'Annunzio felt the black shirt was the very thing for promoting the paramilitary spirit. You probably haven't heard of him, in which case count yourself lucky. Gabriele D'Annunzio was a writer and war hero who combined the egoism of the first profession with the homicidal tendencies of the second to create a character of pathological narcissism. A prototype Fascist, he invented the rigmarole that Mussolini made famous: the straight-armed salute, the balcony harangues, the bovine chants, the pompous ceremonies, the secular religiosity were all dreamt up by D'Annunzio. He had a lot to answer for. But that he was responsible, no matter how indirectly, for me wearing a black shirt, that was unforgivable. I still feel quite bitter about it. Even standing on the platform at Ostiense, surrounded by scores of other men in the same dismal garb, was acutely embarrassing.

Why I had to attend was beyond me. I wasn't due to meet the Führer until the next day. But apart from the getup, I was not displeased to be there. Despite being an unwilling recruit, I was keen to see these people at close quarters. You can watch all the newsreels you want, read all the newspaper articles, but there is no substitute for actually meeting someone. That's why I'm going into so much detail here. Hitler and Mussolini are removed from you by time. They are removed from you by the medium of black-and-white film. Above all, they are removed from you by history, by a knowledge of what happened afterwards. You cannot see them because they are clouded by the crimes they committed. I saw them as people. Contemptible people. But people nonetheless. You should, too.

There's one of them now, all bumptious and pleased with himself, bobbing about like the cock of the walk. I wouldn't be all that surprised if he shook hands with himself. Let's see if I can't pop him on a postcard for you. I am, after all, an inveterate tourist, an outsider looking in, the perpetual expatriate. And what do tourists do? They send postcards to their loved ones, vignettes that try to fix a moment in time without pretending to capture the bigger picture. Moreover, the conventional concluding salutation of postcards is one that is close to my heart. I really do wish you were here, my absent, angry child.

POSTCARD FROM THE PAST #1.

Mussolini is standing beside the king, Victor Emmanuel III, a man I have not been able to take seriously since hearing that his hobby is collecting camels. I don't know whether this is true or not. But he looks like a man who might collect camels. The Duce is wearing his fez. I do wish he wouldn't do that. He's also wearing his Arse's Uniform.

Throughout this memoir, my dear, you will find a tendency to that infantile humour you loved when you were a child, loathed as a teenager, and have yet to grow back into as an adult. I had hoped to confine it to one or two pages, call them The Scatological Chapter, and have done with it, but it is too pervasive for that. This is not mere puerility on my part. There was something about Fascism that invited lavatory humour. This has not been the case with the century's other prominent dictatorships. No matter how despicable, Stalin in his time and Mao to this day do not lend themselves to smut, perhaps because the principle behind communalist thought is such an appealing one, an ideal to which we are bound to return regardless of how often it is abused and betrayed. But the others. Well, Mussolini, you only had to look at him. And Hitler, you only had to smell him.

Mussolini is wearing his Arse's Uniform. It is a style favoured by Fascists and Nazis alike: jodhpurs flared at the hips and jackets with immense ventless tails. And no matter how elegant the cut, no matter how slender the wearer, they always look like they have the most enormous bottoms. In this case, Mussolini's tight black boots and bulky corseted body mean he also resembles a sausage on a stick. And to crown it all, there are the narrow shoulders and the massive head. I'm not going to mention the fez anymore. It's too distressing.

It's worth dwelling on Mussolini's head, though. It was his most distinctive feature. When he was captured trying to sneak over the border at the end of the war, the partisan who recognized him shouted, "We've got bighead!" But it wasn't just its size. It was what he did with it. Mussolini was a vain man, never wearing glasses in public, faking stunts to emphasize his virility, staging appearances to dissimulate the fact that he was only five foot seven, and frequently having his photo taken beside the pocket-sized king. And he shaved his head to hide his receding hairline, and kept his jaw thrust forward to disguise his jowls, and he was always arching his neck as if balancing something on his chin or trying to touch his shoulders with both ears at the same time. He was all puffed up with himself and when he wore a helmet, well, my dear, there was no way round it, he resembled an engorged penis. He was dubbed The Phallus in Chief, in part for his notorious priapism, but also because he looked like a prick.

Hitler's train glides into the station. There's a swastika on the nose, like the locomotive is auditioning for a part in that book we used to read when you were a kid. Mussolini slips one hand into his pocket and touches his testicles to ward off the evil eye. My own eye is drawn by the sight of a young woman in a waitress's uniform slipping through the crowd. I only see her for a second, enough to know that she is uncommonly lovely, then she is gone. The king straightens his cap, Mussolini scans the passing rolling stock, the train stops, a flunky scurries forward, does the necessary flunking, and Hitler steps onto the platform.

POSTCARD FROM THE PAST #2.

For all the talk of his spellbinding presence, there was a puzzling anonymity about Hitler, and the man who alighted from the train was remarkably unremarkable. It was the first thing you noticed about him; there was nothing to notice. Big nose, perhaps? Silly moustache? I do remember the way he shook hands then abruptly saluted with his elbow bent, as if tossing the handshake over his shoulder. Also that he had a long body with short legs attached like an afterthought. He wasn't actually short. I checked the other day, five foot eight, above average for the time. Yet when he wasn't next to someone smaller, Hitler appeared to be short.

It's hard for your generation to understand how things have changed in this respect. Victor Emmanuel, Dollfuss, D'Annunzio, Goebbels were all five-footers; Franco was five foot three, Gandhi five foot four, Churchill, Stalin, Mussolini a few inches more. At six foot four, I was a giant, up there with Hindenburg, de Gaulle, and Mountbatten. I tell you this not because I am obsessed by height. Tall people aren't until we meet someone taller than ourselves, at which point we feel abnormally intimidated. But height is relevant to what happened afterwards.

Hitler stares into the distance in a manner calculated to convey a sense of destiny, but which also expresses a sort of pinch-lipped who-fartedness, a question I can answer from personal experience. His hips are wide, his shoulders narrow, the torso large and hollow chested. He looks flabby, formless, almost spineless. Yet this was the man who . . . well, you know what he did. We didn't.

What we did know was that war was imminent and that the available evidence suggested Fascism was the future. What this meant for the Jews was another matter. It would have taken as great an act of the imagination to predict the Holocaust from the Nazis' racial cretinisms as it does for you to imagine a time when the Holocaust was not the defining event of the century.

Can you conceive of this? Can you picture yourself in a time before? Or am I asking too much, succumbing to maudlin self-pity and self-justification, like my subjects? It's those hard words you used, storming out, leaving the lexis of accusation lingering in the air like something solid and indigestible.

It's probably futile, me trying to teach you lessons. You never could abide being taught something. Headstrong like your mother. I remember when you were about three you insisted you could swim, doing the breaststroke while paddling, or kicking your legs out with your hands down to prop yourself up. Bloody livid when I pointed out that this was not actually swimming. But at the risk of irritating you further, you shouldn't be too hasty to judge. When you get to my age, you'll realize everyone has accrued a quantity of guilt, that most people are broken somewhere inside themselves, warped by compromise and failure and inadequacy, and that a squeeze of the elbow is more important than pointing the finger. It's too easy to poke about until you prick a sore spot. I do feel guilty for what I didn't do when I had the opportunity. But these things happen sometimes.

POSTCARD FROM THE PAST #3.

The visitors descend from the trains. Trains, plural. Mussolini took a small team of ministers to Germany, a statement of personal austerity. But when a Mediterranean jamboree at the Italian taxpayers' expense was mooted, the Nazis were fighting to get their names on the list. And after years of scheming behind other people's backs, Hitler didn't want to leave a lot of conniving colleagues scheming behind his own back. So when the Italian ambassador's wife said, in what I suspect was a moment of misguided patriotic rhetoric, that "everyone" should see Rome, Hitler was all for it. And so were all the other Nazis. Göring was left in charge, presumably on the assumption that he would be so busy counting his medals that he couldn't do any damage while the boss was away. Göring liked medals, decorations, titles, and honorifics of whatever stripe. Hitler's favourite joke:

> One day, Mrs. Göring comes in to the bedroom and finds her husband waving his field marshal's baton over his underwear.
> "Hermann, darling, what are you doing?" she asks.
> Göring beams at her and announces: "I am promoting my underpants to overpants!"

He told that one a lot. It's not a bad joke, really, coming from a Nazi and what have you.

So, if *everyone* should see Rome, it was resolved that *everyone* would see Rome, and several hundred Nazis started packing their glad rags. It was an assassin's dream. All the top men came: Goebbels, Hess, Himmler, Heydrich, Ribbentrop, Rosenberg, Keitel, Amann, thugs like Sepp Dietrich, and that lunatic Karl Brandt, Hitler's doctor and a fantasist of the first water who actually believed the imbecilities of Nazi propaganda. I had hoped these people would have had the decency to be cynical shits coldly manipulating popular sentiment. The revelation that half of them adhered to the gibberish about the plot to vitiate Aryan purity through Jewish Bolshevik Christianity, Jewish Bolshevik Christian Capitalism, and Jewish Bolshevik Christian Capitalist Communism was an unpardonable lapse of taste. And there were four trainloads of people like this. Eva Braun came with a coach full of coiffeurs and minor functionaries nursing triple-locked briefcases, which I suspect contained nothing more important than a couple of cold bratwurst sandwiches laid in against the possibility that the Italian grub didn't agree with them.

Not only was the party numerous, they were humongous individually. Hitler's escort towered over the Italians like a bunch of blond, blue-eyed Brobdingnagians. I was cringing the moment they unfolded themselves from the train. As for the king, he looked like he feared they might pat him on the head and give him a boiled sweet. And they were all done up in elaborate uniforms the better to highlight Hitler's modesty.

As it happened, this wasn't necessary. You probably think of him and see the ranting, bug-eyed maniac, but in his dealings with ordinary people, Hitler was considerate and courteous. Unless you crossed him. But we'll come to that once I've introduced the rest of his entourage. Because it's not done yet. Not by a long shot. There were The Women, too.

They hadn't been invited. But once word spread that everyone should see Rome, there was no way they were being left at home. The boys could strut about all they liked, playing at politics, breaching international treaties, locking up people who looked at them in a funny way, but they weren't buggering off to Italy on their own, not when there were all those shopping opportunities, not to mention the Italian *signorine* with their dark eyes and swishy skirts and winsome Latin ways.

The *frauen* almost scared me more than Hitler's bodyguard. There was something at once voracious and venomous about Grande Dames like Magdalena Goebbels and Anna Ribbentrop, each of whom considered herself Germany's First Lady, and had the pointy elbows to prove it. They set the pace for the rest of the party, Magda playing the big Aryan blonde while La Ribbentrop carried on like a low-rent Katharine Hepburn, both of them patronizing poor provincial Ilse Hess, who could only look on envying the arrogance she mistook for elegance. Inspired by their doyennes, Margarete Himmler gave Hedwig Potthast the gimlet eye, while the wife of the Justice Minister resented the youth of the wife of the Head of Protocol, and the wife of the Secretary of the Foreign Ministry begrudged the glamour of the wife of the Undersecretary for *Frankfurter Würstchen und Westfälische Rinderwurst*, and the wives of the old-guard diplomats and generals despised the wives of the newly promoted Nazis. A nest of vipers, I'm telling you. Where was that lovely young woman in the waitress's outfit?

As for Eva Braun, she caused no end of difficulty flirting with Ciano, gadding about town buying enough alligator handbags to depopulate the Everglades, and getting her minders to take her dancing into the small hours of the morning, much to the irritation of her short-legged Lothario, which wasn't wise given what had happened with his niece. You don't know about Geli Raubal? I'll see if I can squeeze her in later. It's not a pretty story. Neither were The Women. Although I didn't have any direct contact with them, after a couple of days in the same country, I began to understand why Hitler was so obsessed with *Lebensraum*. Anyone shackled to one of those harpies would yearn for a little living space.

You must be fuming by now, my dear. You will say I am displaying that misogyny of which you so often accuse me, that this is "sexist." You may be right. I would like to think not. I certainly wouldn't want to insult all those young women who occasion such warm palpitations in the hearts of old farts like myself by burning their bras and liberating what your Tonton Jacques calls "free tits." But like most things I'd like to think, this is probably so wide of the mark that I've just put an arrow through the top of the head of somebody standing ten paces behind me. I appreciate that it is unreasonable to imply that the women were in some way worse than the men because the Nazi creed was a negation of life and any female supporting it was betraying the soft and fluffy baggage with which women have been lumbered. As it happens, I do half believe this. I am a man of my times. Even so.

But I'm getting ahead of myself. And talk of old farts reminds me that Hitler hasn't broken wind yet, at least insofar as I can tell from this distance. There again, maybe he has. The king and Mussolini both look a little strained. There is a moment's confusion. Hitler expects Mussolini to lead the way. But Mussolini is not head of state. The king is Hitler's official host, a fact that is to be the source of considerable friction in the coming days. Indeed, it may well have aggravated the Führer's meteorism.

Hey up, Rover! Time for some scatology and other lacunae of conventional history.

DIARRHEA CONTRIBUTED TO Napoleon's defeat at the Battle of Waterloo, Mozart wrote several canons to accompany the lyric *Kiss my arse,* Luther claimed spiritual enlightenment came to him when he was having a crap, Catherine the Great was not crushed by a stallion during an act of coitus as legend maintains, but died of an apoplexy on the toilet, First World War secret agents found that semen is an effective invisible ink (quite how I hate to think, but it confirms that all spies are wankers), while vibrators were invented by weary doctors worn out from provoking therapeutic paroxysms in hysterical women through manual asexual vulvular stimulation . . .

They don't tell you these things in history books, or they didn't in my day, and I doubt contemporary textbooks go into any great detail about the Führer's chronic and frequently uncontrollable farting. Yes, Hitler farted, as I found out, the hard way. *Hey up, Rover!* Certain digestive tracts should never be subjected to the strain of a vegetarian diet. Something to do with the enzymes I imagine. But after a few days in his company, I could understand why he used to wear those awful lederhosen: given his gastric affliction, ventilation was vital.

You may think that talk of Hitler's tummy troubles is a matter of the utmost irrelevance, but I can assure you, my dear, it is not. Indeed, you might not have existed had it not been for the Führer's flatulence. More than that, the fact that he was always breaking wind may have had a direct impact on the course of the war. And it is possible that the celebrated exploits of your mother's subsequent career as a partisan were as nothing to the sabotage in which she was engaged prior to the outbreak of hostilities.

You see, Karl Brandt was not the only doctor on the Führer's team. He had a rival, Theodor Morell, a purveyor of snake oil and dubious pick-me-ups whom Göring dubbed *Der Reichsspritzenmeister,* The Imperial Chief of Jabs. Morell dished out the drugs that kept the Nazi elite fired up for the next six years, dished them out with a liberality that would have put one of your rock and roll groups to shame. Come the end of the war, he would be treating Hitler with morphine, methamphetamine, cocaine, belladonna, strychnine, E. coli, potassium bromide, atropine, and other assorted barbiturates and narcotics, with essence of bulls' bollocks thrown in for good measure. I appreciate that you young people believe you invented everything. Every generation is persuaded of as much. But your famous drug culture is nothing new. Putting white powder up your nose has encouraged a fatal sense of invulnerability for more than a hundred years, methamphetamine has induced psychotic behaviour since the 1880s, and morphine has disengaged brains even longer. Hitler was always batting on a sticky wicket. If he hadn't been predisposed to flatulence and had your mother not been there to lend a hand . . .

The fact that the Führer was as high as a kite is something else you don't get in the textbooks. But I aim to tell you all the bits that books ignore. I want to capture Hitler and Mussolini, pin them down, and dissect them so that you can see what form of creature these mythological beasts were. This is an ethological endeavour, like the cetology chapters in *Moby Dick*, detailing the taxonomy and whale lore, describing the morphology and physiology of the leviathan. Cetology and scatology serve similar purposes. Postcards paint a picture. But the "ologies" dig down deep in the dirty bits and waste matter, the better to understand what's on the surface. We'll have more cetology later.

POSTCARD FROM THE PAST #4.

The Germans arrived midevening, but instead of retiring for a tête-à-tête with the Duce, the Führer was taken to the Quirinal Palace by the king. This was unfortunate. Hitler was uneasy among those born to privilege and hated the glacial protocol of the palace. Even Himmler, a man not famed for his effervescent vitality (there was always something disturbingly anaerobic about Himmler), said that at court one breathed the air of the catacombs. The courtiers treated their guests with maddening condescension, sniggering at their coarse manners and uncouth behaviour. That night, Hitler rang room service "for a woman." He couldn't sleep without seeing his bed remade, which is odd, but not necessarily symptomatic of untrammelled concupiscence. The story was too good to ignore, though. Within twenty-four hours "Hitler's woman" was the toast of Rome. As for The Women, prior to meeting the queen, they were given a crash course in etiquette. It wasn't kind. Trying to curtsy, they kept tripping over their evening gowns, and several bowed so low it looked like they were offering themselves up as a bicycle rack. One or two had difficulty getting up again. The dukes and duchesses nearly wet themselves.

The official agenda was taken up with diplomatic ceremonies, ministerial summits, military displays, conventional tourism, and cultural events. Despite my presence not being scheduled, I ended up attending a number of parades and war games. Not my sort of thing at all, I'm afraid, and memory has jumbled the pageantry into a homogenous muddle of tedium. I do remember admiring a squadron of planes flying past in swastika formation, but the same symbol had me biting my lip when it was etched out in the night by flaming brands beside others spelling HITLER, as if he might have forgotten who he was. Best of all were the soldiers in white uniforms goose-stepping their way through a rotating swastika. I did crack up then and had to excuse myself, pretending to an enraged Goebbels that I'd swallowed a fly. The motorcycle escort was priceless, too, weaving about like a bunch of armadillos on a trampoline, and the massed ranks of the military were always slightly skew-whiff, as if some giant hand had tilted the piazza so that the topmost soldiers were sliding out of line.

Under strict instructions to be nice to the natives, the Germans tactfully ignored their hosts' slapdash discipline. There were no snide asides or quips about soldiers with sunburned armpits. And they were genuinely impressed by the naval manoeuvres at Naples. These were at once monotonous and nerve-racking, since the sailor boys kept banging away with these bloody great guns, so that whenever one felt oneself slipping into a state of pleasant torpor another blast would bounce you out of it. The climax came when a hundred submarines dived then resurfaced in perfect unison. This was no mean achievement, not least because Italian submarines had a regrettable tendency to asphyxiate Italian submariners. Hitler gave Mussolini a look of such flawless envy that Il Duce nearly hugged himself with glee.

Behind the scenes though, the security people were frantic about a rumoured assassination plot. I could understand their panic. Everywhere we went, the streets were heaving and it would have been easy enough to take a potshot from the cover of the scrum, yet nobody tried anything. The crowds just carried on baying like a kennel full of dogs howling for their dinner. Later, the police had to round people up to greet visiting Nazi dignitaries, but in 1938 Hitler was welcomed with real enthusiasm. This must seem inexplicable to you, but there were good reasons for the popular acclaim.

As I recall, we got our first television set when you were five or six. You grew up with an understanding that drama was available in daily doses from a box in the corner of the room. We didn't have that in the thirties. We had to go somewhere for spectacle, to the cinema, the stage, the stadium, the street. So when the Fascists invented political theatre, we were vulnerable. We wanted both to celebrate and play a part in the performance. Well, I didn't. But not out of any nobility of spirit. I just couldn't be bothered.

The second thing was that people were trying to persuade themselves everything was all right, that their infallible leader hadn't just made the most monumental cock-up. Until then, Italians had considered Germans presumptuous barbarians, presumptuous because of their pretension to be following in the footsteps of Fascism, barbarians because . . . well, they *were* Germans. The Romans knew all about the Huns and the Goths and what have you. They had form. Now the Italians had to persuade themselves their new allies weren't so much a dog's dinner as the dog's bollocks. They were shouting loud to silence their own misgivings.

Finally, they were bowled over by Hitler. I was quite taken with him myself at times. Apart from the two occasions when he went off his head, he was Mr. Emollient, going out of his way to charm everyone he met. I repeat, he wasn't all bug-eyed ranting. He was quite a lot of bug-eyed ranting. But he could beguile as well as bully. That wise young bird Dietrich Bonhoeffer warned that this was less a *Führer* or "leader" and more a *Verführer* or "seducer."

I appreciate that this probably confirms your contempt for me and my generation, but you should be wary of condemning us. Few people are above compromising themselves. And once compromised, you'd be surprised how adroit we are at juggling moral qualms. In 1945, you'd have been hard put to find a Nazi in Germany, though how they filled all those stadiums is anybody's guess. France was positively teeming with men who had just realized they were Resistance fighters, most of them bravely wielding a pair of scissors and prowling the streets looking to prove their patriotism on some hapless woman without an alibi. And I wouldn't mind betting that among the people who abused the corpses of Mussolini and Claretta Petacci in the Piazzale Loreto, there were a good many who would have cheered rather than jeered a few years earlier. People of true conviction are rare. And they are not always the best people.

Looking back at the last few pages, I see that I began at court, drifted out to sea, and ended with a couple of cadavers hanging from the girders of a garage. I make no apology for such digressions. The pretence that life follows a strictly linear narrative is merely that, a pretence. Life progresses in fits and starts, backwards and forwards, taking shortcuts and slip roads, often as not turning circles like an inebriated tumbler; and an undisciplined memory like mine moves in the same way, back and forth and sideways. It's the only way I can get at the truth, sideways on. For what it's worth though, this was the schedule for my bit of the shindig:

> May 4th Rome. Pantheon (FW *Ein grosser*
> *Künstler*), Circo Massimo, Civitavecchia (CP
> sexually frustrated women / And if not?)
> May 5th Naples (MW! FW-CP Karl May / tie & tails!)
> May 6th Rome, Mostra Augustea della Romanità
> (*Cloaca Maxima*)—Palazzo Esposizioni
> May 7th Rome, Terme Diocleziano, Villa Borghese
> (MW more tart? / FW Sacred & Profane)
> May 8th Rome Musei Capitolini (CP Brutus), Castel
> Sant'Angelo, Colosseum (CP Foro)
> May 9th Florence, Uffizi, Palazzo Pitti, Boboli
> gardens, Palazzo Vecchio, Palazzo Riccardi

For what it's worth? You see what I mean about getting at the truth? I spent ages piecing that together, yet it tells you nothing you need to know. You've got to sidle up on life if you want to find out what it's about. Pretend you're not paying attention and follow the digressions. Facts don't get you anywhere. That was something The Flatulent Windbag didn't understand, as I was to discover at the Pantheon. But first, a bit of the sideways on stuff.

You see the parenthetical notes? They're memos to help me tell my story. You won't understand them now and you don't need to. Most will become clear as we proceed, but I ought to explain FW and CP. I think it's the second time I've called Hitler The Flatulent Windbag, but it's how I always think of him. It's not a tautology. Because as well as being a champion *pétomane*, he was also a shocking windbag, and I suspect that a good deal of his rise to power came about through his capacity for implacably crapping on until people were begging him to do a bit of world domination or whatever he damn well liked so long as he would please, please, please STOP TALKING!

Small wonder Rudolf Hess went round the bend. He was Hitler's amanuensis in prison. He typed the first draft of *Mein Kampf*. Imagine listening to that drivel day after day. *"In this little town on the river Inn, Bavarian by blood and Austrian by nationality, gilded by the light of German martyrdom, there lived, at the end of the '80's of the last century, my parents: the father a faithful civil servant, the mother devoting herself to the cares of the household and looking after her children with eternally the same loving kindness."* That fairy-tale opening alone is enough to have you sticking your fingers down your throat.

Even Mussolini, a man not known for his taciturn nature, was overwhelmed by the tangled verbosity of his guest's orations. For someone used to deferential idiots hanging onto his every word, it was an appalling position in which to find himself. But Hitler was merciless, going on and on like some Old Norse saga while his listeners engaged in an equally epic battle to stay awake. It was hypnotic. I don't mean that nonsense with the eyes. Everyone goes on about the magnetic quality of his eyes, but I never noticed it. The torrent of words, though, they could turn the world topsy-turvy. Never was so great a career constructed on so much wind. There's nothing superfluous about my term for him. Hitler was The Flatulent Windbag.

CP is Mussolini, The Constipated Prick. Poor old Mussolini. Anal retentives get a bad name, but it's the anal expulsives who worry me. They do most damage. And they get all the attention. That's why they smear their faeces all over everything in the first place. Retention has much to recommend it. It may not be healthy, but at least one tries not to shit upon others. In this case, despite pioneering populist right-wing politics, Mussolini is remembered as the second-string dictator, the sidekick struggling to keep up with his more volatile buddy, the stooge who was useless without his partner.

That's not how it seemed at the time. Many believed Mussolini was the greatest statesman of the age, the only man who might restrain Hitler. He thought so himself. But he must have been insecure from the start, fretful enough to strive to seem a bit bigger, a bit more martial, a bit more virile, a bit more macho. The fact that he ended up looking like an engorged penis was entirely predictable. And to add to the strain of tumescence, he had to contend with a painful stomach ulcer. In those days, milk was the mainstay of ulcer patients' diets. Mussolini drank six pints a day. As a consequence, he suffered chronic constipation.

So there you have it, The Flatulent Windbag and The Constipated Prick.

Make of me what you will.

"YOU DID WHAT?"

Oh, my dear, you and your sense of justice! Do you remember when that lad Arnaud picked on a Portuguese kid at school because he couldn't speak French properly? You were, what, six or seven at the time? Certainly no more than that. But you were so incensed that you grabbed the little blighter by the collar and hung him from a peg in the changing room, left him dangling there till he apologised. The head teacher didn't see the funny side of that, not when she called us in and told us what had happened, still less when I started chuckling. I'm not chuckling now, though. I'm wondering how long you're going to leave me hanging on the peg.

I don't doubt you will come back on one of your flying visits, probably with another exotic boyfriend in tow. I particularly liked that young chap from Ivory Coast, the one who thought so much (and, it must be said, spoke rather more) of Franz Fanon. You can bring him back from your Occupation Committee anytime you like. He was fun, corrupting the older generation. You didn't know that, did you? Well, he didn't smoke all that marijuana on his own, I can tell you. Whoever you bring back though, your old room is there when you need it. And I think you will need it from time to time. I appreciate that it's all part of the ethos, but a damp mattress in a defunct factory is no place like home, no matter how much autonomist bric-a-brac you decorate it with. That sort of rebellion gets wearisome after a while. But that's not the reason you'll come back. Personal comfort never compelled you to do anything as far as I could see. Quite the contrary. No, you'll be back because of your indefatigable curiosity.

You always did need to know, to understand the whys and the wherefores. You didn't like being taught, but you wanted answers to your questions. You were forever asking me "why" when you were a kid. Why this, why that, why the other. Why is the moon round, the sky blue, water wet? Why do frogs croak, wasps sting, dogs die? It was exhausting. There was no stopping you, though. When you asked me why it rained, I said it was because I'd turned on the windscreen wipers. Pointed out that every time I turned them on it started to rain. Ergo, it rains because . . . You nearly believed me for a moment. I nearly believed myself come to that. I always had a problem with cause and effect. But teasing didn't deter you. The torrent of whys continued, wearing me down till one day I could take no more and I said, "Look, I don't know 'why.' I don't know everything!" You were appalled. "So who does know everything?" you asked. "Does Mum know everything?" To my shame, I said, yes, she did. She didn't, of course. Just acted like she did sometimes. But as you know, I'll say anything for a quiet life.

So, you'll be back. You'll be needing an explanation. What sort of 'why' will bring you back is another matter. Curiosity has shaded into indignation of late, not just about me, but about the whole sorry mess of what we do to the world and one another. I wonder whether I'll show you this, whether in the circumstances it would serve any purpose. Is it possible to convey what it was like to be alive in that time when so many of us failed ourselves? Can idealism accommodate the simple truth that good people do bad things without necessarily becoming bad people? What message will you read in this? Writers never know how their words will be read. Writing is only realized in the reading and the reader is the final arbiter of what has been said. There may be no point to this at all. But I will persevere. For the present, it's all I've got.

It's all I've got? I catch a whiff of something other in those words, not just self-pity, but the suggestion of a hidden agenda. Maybe this screed is addressed to me as much as you. Perhaps that's the point. I am trying to understand it all myself, excavating what has been tamped down too long, a private obsession locked away in the bottom drawer of my desk. Another life lesson from your dad: what we think we are doing is rarely what we are doing. Just as our most cherished beliefs about ourselves are often the most mistaken, the projects we set ourselves almost invariably conceal some hidden purpose of which we are unaware.

POSTCARD FROM THE PAST #5.

In the days before Hitler's arrival, I had been kept busy planning the cultural excursions and visiting the designated galleries to calculate what could be seen in the allotted time. I mentioned Houston Stewart Chamberlain earlier. He was an Anglo-German author whose nitwitted "theories" inspired many of National Socialism's more deranged beliefs. How anyone could have placed any confidence in him is beyond me. You only had to look at a photo of the man. He looked like a chicken that has had a cold forefinger unexpectedly inserted up its rectum. I never managed more than half a page of his noxious fantasies, but if he ever got something right, it was that jibe about Rome being the capital of chaos.

The last days of April were a positive festival of pandemonium. I particularly pitied the museum directors. For years, they'd been begging for funds to carry out essential repairs, funds that had been conspicuously absent in a country led by a man who regarded the plastic arts with the enthusiasm of someone who has just discovered a dog turd in the palm of his hand. But now that Hitler had to be impressed, the money was forthcoming, and the curators had to make good years of neglect and complete months of restoration work in a few weeks. Some galleries looked like they were being dismantled prior to removal elsewhere.

And my own state of mind was no less decomposed.

Despite my lack of political faith, I knew I really ought to do something about the men I was meant to be guiding, neither of whom was exactly on the side of the angels. Like his confidant Putzi Hanfstaengl said, Adolf only played the black keys. And if there had ever been anything angelic about Mussolini, well, he had long since left his wings in the waiting room. As a halfway-educated, halfway-liberal man who was tolerably attached to his own liberty and well-being, and even had the occasional scruple about the liberty and well-being of others, I was, in all conscience, duty bound to kill these people.

I was to accompany the dictators for much of the time, indeed, most of the time as it turned out. I knew the programme, could plot our progress within the constraints of my timetable. I was even due to sit in the same car as them on occasion. If anyone was well placed to carry out a double assassination, it was me. All it would take was a little timing, a little luck, and a little courage. The Ponte Vecchio, for instance, seemed ideally suited for dropping a bomb into an open-topped car. Excepting yours truly, the collateral damage would be limited, space restricting the crowds, while the Fascist "renovation" of the bridge's facade and the quays along the Arno was such that it would mitigate the vandalism of any violent act. As it turned out, the Gestapo had already thought about that. They had more experience of these things than I did. In any case, I had by then decided against it. Almost.

The first problem was a question of practicalities. I mean, I'm really not cut out for killing people. I can skewer them with words, but organizing the nitty-gritty of physical harm is beyond me. I could get a knife, possibly even a gun. But where do you buy explosives? And how do you cobble them together? I didn't have a clue. Could I really see myself engaged in an act of frenzied stabbing, brandishing a pistol, pressing a button to vaporize me and my immediate entourage? Can you see yourself doing that? If you can, I suggest you visit a doctor.

Opportunity is often presented to people incapable of seizing it. That's why dictators last. They employ people with no talent for conspiracy. I don't mean the Himmlers and Bormanns. They can conspire with the best of them. Only being nonentities dependent on their leader's patronage, they fail to constitute a threat. But the sideways on characters like me, who have a brief moment when we might change the course of history, invariably miss that chance. In part, it comes from a lack of conviction. We are not revolutionaries fired by a passion for reforming the world. You need fundamental convictions if you are to persuade yourself it's worth killing people. Vague misgivings are insufficient.

Something else deterred me too, a kind of fatalism that told me the coming war was inevitable, perhaps even desirable, that the conflict might just usher in a new age, not the one envisaged by the dictators, but one beyond their wretched hate-filled creeds. I didn't believe. I have never been a believer. But I knew which beliefs would have been more appealing had I been a believer. And if war was necessary, was there any point trying to prevent it? Quite apart from anything else, people who go round blowing up other people generally don't get a very good press.

Finally, there was a question of character. I've always been a spectator rather than an actor, interested in observing others rather than having an impact on them. And I was curious with that fatal curiosity of the inveterate reader. Not your sort of curiosity, not the why, but the what and the who and the how, above all the who. I wanted to watch the two self-styled "supermen" at close quarters. It wasn't for me to try and change the world. What, after all, can one man do against the forces of history? Isn't this just one of those things that's a lot bigger than you and has to be accepted as such?

You remember that daft game we used to play on holiday in Brittany when you were a kid, Chasing Back the Waves? I'd take your hand and we'd work ourselves into a frenzy, swearing we were going to do it this time, we really were, we were going to chase the waves away. And when a wave broke, we'd charge down the beach hand in hand and rush into the receding water, bellowing, "Get back waves! Get back waves!" Then the following wave would form and we would suddenly stop, ankle deep in water, hesitating a second before whirling round and fleeing, me screaming "Run away! Run away!" dragging you behind me while you giggled uncontrollably. The games adults invent for children, no matter how silly, are never just games. They are sly lessons in ways of looking at the world.

Glance back and you will see a lot of questions in the preceding paragraphs. They are worthwhile questions even for people like you who are in the privileged position of not having to come up with a practical response. For me, a mix of cowardice, incompetence, diffidence, and fatalism held me back. I could always change my mind. I nearly did. Had we known how the detention camps would metamorphose into dedicated killing machines . . . but we didn't. I can't say if that would have changed anything. All I can say is that I slept poorly in the days before Hitler's visit, plagued by questions, persuaded of my own uselessness, that nothing would happen, but half waiting for some external stimulus that would make something happen.

POSTCARD FROM THE PAST #6.

"Don't tell me, Mr. Expert," he says. For a man reputed to have a frigate-sized chip on his shoulder about "experts," Hitler's manner is affable. "I have made a particular study of this."

"I'm sure you have," I say. "Please, tell us all about it."

"A most particular study," he repeats, a tic turning the corners of his lips upward. If I am to be subjected to the hypnotic eyes, now's the moment. We met a few minutes ago. Hitler, Mussolini, and me. Well, it's not as intimate as that. There are a dozen others besides, among them bruisers like Sepp Dietrich who look like they spent their childhoods rubbing the scales off butterflies' wings. We are in the Pantheon, which is fitting for two supermen. Alas, impertinence has already got the better of me. *Please, tell us all about it.* It sounds sarcastic, even to me. I should be transfixed. *The eyes: bright blue, bordering on violet, a penetrating glint, like a sliver of silver that slices through you . . .* no, not really. A deal of what is taken for charisma comes from people saying a person is "charismatic." If you expect the eyes to possess you, they probably will. And if they don't, you'll say they did to share in the drama of having been close to charisma. But that is not my purpose here. And it is not what I saw.

I have made a particular study. He has, too. He reels off statistics, rubbing his index finger across his moustache, watching to see how his recital is received. Dates, details, above all dimensions. The fact that the Pantheon has the world's oldest and largest concrete dome is the most important consideration. Size and durability count. Mussolini closes his eyes and flexes his neck, pleased to possess this symbol of imperial authority. When Hitler concludes his performance, I incline my head and mime applause, careful to avoid any hint of insincerity.

"Our Führer is a very great artist," this whispered into my ear by Rudolf Hess. He bears an uncanny resemblance to a badger. I can imagine him digging holes in embankments and eating earthworms. The line about Hitler being a great artist is one I am to hear again in the coming days. *Ein grosser Künstler.* Several members of the delegation make the assertion. It is not an opinion. They are conveying a fact that has to be repeated in case I don't cotton on first time round. Talent, like charisma, is often a question of repetition.

"Our Duce is an artist, too," I say. "*Claudia Particella, l'Amante del Cardinale: Grande Romanzo dei Tempi del Cardinale Emanuel Madruzzo.*" As it happens, I never got past the first ten pages of his novel. The title alone sapped a good deal of my resolve and the book was soon slipping from my fingers. A lot of books slipped from my fingers in those days, not because I was particularly ham-fisted, but because letting go was the most charitable thing to do. Chamberlain's *Die Grundlagen des neunzehnten Jahrhunderts*, Hitler's *Mein Kampf*, Mussolini's *L'Amante del Cardinale* were all eminently droppable. Dorothy Parker said *The Cardinal's Mistress* was not a novel to be tossed aside lightly—it should be thrown with great force.

The Constipated Prick shakes back the cuffs of his jacket, pouting in a moue of dissent. Knitting his eyebrows, he holds up one hand. The gesture is pitifully stagy, but it works. Everyone waits, even The Flatulent Windbag. At length, the Duce speaks, every syllable weighted with significance, the clauses broken by idiosyncratic pauses.

"In youth," he says, "writing is like . . . intellectual calisthenics. We ponder the manifoldness of life . . . even if the world . . . rejects our writings as unrealistic or . . . untimely. At eighteen, we are . . . phrase slaves. The phrases, they are like the pretty women with whom we . . . fall in love. At forty, the facts of life must be faced. *The Cardinal's Mistress* was . . . fustian . . . a feuilleton . . . mere political propaganda. And yet . . . it is true to say . . . I am not a statesman . . ." There is a longer pause here, as if a top-notch epigram is in the making: "I am more like . . . a mad poet!"

I do not beg to differ. It would be rude.

The guests are stunned. They understand the words. Mussolini spoke in passable German. But the idea that he should admit to madness flummoxes them. Madness must be a sensitive subject in a movement like theirs.

Hitler visits a lunatic asylum. The patients give the Hitler salute. As he passes down the line he comes across a man who isn't saluting.

"Why aren't you saluting like the others?" Hitler barks.

"Mein Führer, I'm the nurse," comes the answer. "I'm not crazy!"

Max Amann, the party's business manager and publisher, looks particularly flustered. Publishers tend to take fright at mention of mad poets. But Mussolini means what he says. He really admires men like Baudelaire and Rimbaud, would love to possess the luminous madness of a romantic, to be living life on the edge, weaving magic with words.

"Yet you are destined to be a great statesman," says Hitler. "A towering historical figure, uniting your people, and building a new and vigorous nation on the ruins of Italy. You, my friend, are the poet of politics."

Mussolini sketches a bow. Acolytes murmur appreciation, both of the Duce's towering historical figuredom and the Führer's astute recognition of the fact.

"The poet is a prophet as well," says Mussolini, "a mirror of the . . . shadow we cast upon impending time. But the shape of things to come is . . . forever shifting. Thinkers, poets, we are like . . . storm petrels. We feel a tempest brewing, but know not from which . . . quarter the wind will blow or . . . what changes it will bring about. A statesman needs . . . imagination. Without imagination, without . . . poetry, no one can achieve anything."

By this point, I am more or less paralyzed by horror. If they intend carrying on like this for the next five days, I'll be slitting my wrists and the wrists of anyone else in the vicinity who doesn't look like they'll be up to the task themselves.

"So," I say, a little desperately, "we have a painter, and we have a poet. And I believe you, Herr Goebbels, had ambitions to be a playwright and a novelist?"

This is injudicious in the extreme. Goebbels scowls at me. He does not care to be reminded of frustrated ambition. That's another novel that slipped from my fingers, *Michael: Ein deutsches Schicksal in Tagebuchblättern*. Though in that instance, it might have been worth persevering. Apparently, the protagonist dies in a mining accident. I like a happy ending.

"I put my ambitions to the service of a greater good than mere scribbling," says Goebbels. "And what about you, Herr Colgan? What are your ambitions?"

"Oh, I've always felt ambition is the mark of a vulgar mind," I say.

"You will not succeed if you do not want to succeed," says Goebbels. "Our Führer has shown that everything is a matter of will. And look what he has achieved. He has not accomplished so much by having a vulgar mind."

Realizing I am on dangerous ground, I steer the conversation away from myself by citing the classical concept of *otium,* leisure time spent thinking, writing, speaking, as opposed to an active engagement in public life, which is the proper field of ambition. I end, a little lamely, lamenting the fact that in English *otium* has declined to the negative concept of negotiation or a synonym for redundancy in otiose.

There is a brief but painful silence when I finish and I am pathetically grateful when Hitler fills it with another phrase with which I am to become familiar in the coming days.

"You see, gentlemen," *Sehen sie, meine Herren.* "The English language cannot articulate concepts that go beyond what is tangible. It is because German has this capacity that ours is the nation of thinkers. And as our expert says, time spent thinking, writing, speaking . . . above all speaking, is of the greatest value. It is the spoken word that changes history."

Sehen sie, meine Herren. Whenever a comment interested him, Hitler would employ this phrase, then elaborate on what had been said, deforming it to fit his own ideas, as if the world must inevitably accommodate itself to the pattern he preordained for it. Later, when his early successes were over and he lurched from one setback to another, I almost pitied him. The distress to a mentality like that when the world fails to adhere to the blueprint one proposes for it must be terrible. It makes things a lot easier if you start out persuaded of your own inconsequentiality. That was one of the issues between your mother and me. She could never get her head round the gleeful futility of Chasing Back the Waves.

In this case, *Sehen-sie-meine-Herren* is a statement of faith, speech being the supreme value for a man who talked his way to the top. Hitler was no thinker. Basically, he had three ideas: "the-fit-shit-upon-the-unfit," "go-East-young-German," and "a-big-Jew-did-it-then-ran-away." But like many people of limited intellect, he was dearly attached to the ideas he did have, cleaving to them with a passion that leant them an unusual potency.

As he expatiates on the topic of the magical transformations conjured by the spoken word, I fall back a few steps to recuperate from my imprudence and observe my subjects at one remove. The Constipated Prick glances furtively at his guest, like someone who has spotted a celebrity in a restaurant. There's something wrong about Mussolini. The marionette walk, the stilted speech, the mad eyes randomly placed in the wide face. He's like a badly drawn cartoon. It is as if he is mimicking himself and can't quite carry off this Being Mussolini business. He is absurd, yet he cuts a tragic figure, the bully whose inadequacy is exposed and who is forever after scrabbling to keep up with the kid who keeps proving more powerful than he is, the kid with the gob and the gab and the ruthless streak that he lacks.

He's still gabbing now, both ends. *Hey up, Rover!* Max Amann's perturbation at The Constipated Prick's confession of madness has been replaced by a look that suggests he is trying to pretend something highly invasive and unpleasant isn't really happening at all. Probably wants to put a cork in it. He is, after all, the only man known to have curbed The Flatulent Windbag's verbosity, persuading him that *Viereinhalb Jahre (des Kampfes) gegen Lüge, Dummheit und Feigheit* wasn't a very snappy title and that *Four and a Half Years (of Struggle) Against Lies, Stupidity and Cowardice* might usefully be whittled down to *Mein Kampf.* There is a definite tendency in totalitarian literature toward titles that cannot fit on the spine of a book.

Something, perhaps our presence in the Pantheon, has got Hitler onto the pernicious influence of Christianity. Mussolini tosses his head, listens in silence. There's nothing else to do. It's impossible to converse with Hitler. You ask a question and inspire a speech. I wouldn't mind betting that was what happened at his trial after the beer hall putsch. The judge asked him to confirm his name and that was it, he was off, talking for the next twenty-four days.

"Christianity is a foul disease," he says, "the first faith to murder its opponents in the name of love. The law of life states that God helps him who helps himself. Yet Christianity denies this fundamental rule. Taken to its logical end, it implies the nurturing of failure. And Bolshevism is Christianity's bastard child, engineering on a material level what Christianity achieves on the metaphysical level. Both were devised by

Jews to confound society, you know. Paul used the Galilean to defeat the Roman Empire, which the Jews hated because it was appropriating their most sacred possession, the treasure they had hoarded in their temples. He undermined Rome by advancing the principle of equality before a single God and appointing himself God's representative. The Galilean sought something quite different. He wasn't a Jew, you know. They wouldn't have let the Romans judge one of their own. No, he was the son of a prostitute and a Roman soldier, and he was leading a popular rebellion against Jewry. He wanted to free his country from Jewish oppression. He opposed Jewish capitalism and materialism. That's why he was eliminated, you see. Paul perverted Christianity, which was really a declaration of war on the golden calf and Jewish egoism. He took that idea and used it to turn the slaves against the elite. And Communism is just the same. The Jews don't change, you know. They always stir up the plebs against the ruling classes. They foment discontent and turn peoples of the same blood against one another. Thus, any doctrine that is anti-Communist or anti-Christian must, ipso facto, be anti-Jewish as well."

Don't worry, I won't do that often. But unless subjected to a facsimile of it, you cannot conceive how that man overwhelmed one with words. I don't mean his public discourses. They were more subtle, tapping into emotions latent in his listeners' hearts. But his private monologues were a tidal wave of repetition and circular reasoning. At best, one could switch off and let it wash over you. But try to follow it and you were swamped. Of course, illogicality is the dictator's principal tool. The more meaningless the phrase, the better it works. Mussolini knew that with his gnomic dictums. *"You must obey because you must."* Let people apply their critical faculties and the game would be up. Nevertheless, even by the standards of dictatorship, Hitler set the bar pretty high. Sometimes his farts were more rational than his rhetoric.

He has two bright spots on his cheeks. At first, I think he is flushed with the pleasure of listening to himself, but the colour is synthetic. He is wearing rouge to brighten his complexion. The cosmetic accentuates his curious androgyny. His walk is ladylike, dainty steps, punctuated by a peculiar sideways movement.

Sepp Dietrich and Robert Ley step in front of me. Ley is a notorious drunk and so corrupt that even his fellow Nazis find him unsavoury. He seems sober today, but it's hard to imagine the man who is responsible for the Strength Through Joy movement indulging in anything more gymnastic than sniffing the cash register. His most remarkable characteristic is his resemblance to a red mullet. There's something piscine about Himmler, too, but in his case it's the vacant look of a dead pollock. Ribbentrop, meanwhile, doesn't even aspire to that level of vitality. His eyes are as cold as the crushed ice on the counter, his lips as generous as a leg trap. Another reason for pitying Ciano. As his counterpart, he has to deal with this man.

The Gestapo are about to shoot some Jews when the commanding officer walks up to one of them and says, "You look almost Aryan. I'll give you a chance. I have a glass eye, but it's not easy to tell. If you can guess which eye it is, I'll let you go."

Immediately, the Jew answers, "The left one!"

"How did you know?" asks the Gestapo commander.

"It looks so human."

I am looking at Sepp Dietrich's bottom when . . . no, that didn't come out right. They're a bunch of arses, but one can see other aspects of the anatomy. It's just that I've noticed a pistol bulge below the tail of Dietrich's jacket. I'm looking at Sepp Dietrich's gun when I become aware that someone is in turn watching me, one of the few warm-eyed members of the party, Joseph Goebbels. He has a reputation for being a man who likes nobody and whom nobody likes, not even his friends. In retrospect, he reminds me of a diminutive version of Jonathan Brewster in *Arsenic and Old Lace*. Except he knows how to smile. He can also laugh. And make it look natural. He's not laughing now, though. He's watching me and I'm worried he can see scorn in my features. I try to compose my face into a mask of attentiveness. Just in time, too. The Flatulent Windbag is speaking to me. I have a momentary panic. What was he saying?

"That is the problem with today's architects, is it not, Mr. Expert? Their vision is short term. They do not build for eternity. One must always build in granite."

"Quite so," I say, grateful for the man's compulsive need to repeat himself. I don't doubt he has said this several times already. The trick is to catch the gist then tune out for the duration.

"It's because the architects know they won't be remembered." It is a measure of Hitler's loquacity that we are taken aback to discover that Mussolini is capable of speech. He looks surprised himself, as if the utterance sneaked out of its own accord. Having managed to get a word in edgeways, he hastens to secure the advantage. "It is the patrons who are remembered: the Pantheon of Agrippa, Caesar's Forum, the Augustan Forum, Trajan's Forum, the Diocletian baths, the baths of Caracalla . . ."

"Mussolini's Forum," I add, immediately regretting it. As if clay tennis courts and Fascist iconography bear comparison with the *fora* of antiquity. All those statues of self-absorbed ponces with big tits and stranglers' hands and jockstraps that look like bagfuls of fruit.

I'm not counting with The Constipated Prick's vanity, though. He nods approvingly, perhaps forgetting that Debbio and Moretti are still alive and very much associated with the stadium they designed. They can count themselves lucky it's not Hitler who is asserting the inconsequence of architects. If it were, he would probably have them eliminated to prove his point. He is not one to let an anomaly get in his way.

Actually, that's not fair. I'm not underestimating his ruthlessness when it comes to remodelling the world to match his expectations. But unlike Goebbels, the failed writer become book burner, Hitler's bitterness as an architect manqué is directed less at practising architects, more at the profession's gatekeepers, the academics who wouldn't let him study architecture. As long as they do work he fancies he would be doing himself, Hitler loves architects.

"Mnesicles and the Propylaea," he says, "Phidias and the Parthenon."

A look of panic crosses Mussolini's face. I don't think he knows who Mnesicles and Phidias are. He can do emperors, but architects don't count. He glances at me, a fleeting glance, but Hitler spots it.

"What do you say, Mr. Expert?"

Oh, my God! I've only been with these people twenty minutes and I'm being asked to settle a dispute that cannot be settled without causing offence. I've already got Goebbels on my case. The little sod is glowing with pleasure at my discomfort. I can't afford to alienate a dictator, too.

"Mnesicles and Phidias," prompts Hitler.

"Our Führer is a very great artist." This from Julius Streicher, Hitler's principal hate-merchant and a man so low he leaves a slick trail behind him. I'd like to slap him, only I don't think he's doing this to goad me. He's too stupid for that. It's possible that Hess's remark has just penetrated the soupy matter that passes for a brain in the Streicher skull and he is repeating it as a choice bon mot, much as the medieval blood libel struck him as an innovative idea that had to be broadcast by his newspaper. Such stupidity inspires me. Beside these dimwits, anything I say is going to sound brilliant.

"The Führer is referring to classical Greece," I say, offering them my most dazzling smile, hoping my dentistry might blind them. "In Greece there was a cult of personality that celebrated talented artists, which is why we remember the architects there. However, Il Duce was talking about imperial Rome where the individual was subservient, indeed eclipsed by the majesty of empire. I think you will find that is the source of the misunderstanding."

I am not sure I have ever uttered such twaddle in my entire life, and I can assure you, my dear, as a television pundit, twaddle has been bread and butter to me for many years. Yet this perfect imbecility appears to satisfy both parties. It occurs to me that I might actually enjoy myself in the course of the coming days.

"That's our saviour," murmurs Hitler, apparently without irony. "The man who knows everything." *Das ist unser Retter, der alles weiss!*

Only Goebbels watches me with any suspicion. I doubt he knows enough to know in what precise detail I am talking bollocks, but he recognizes bollocks when he hears it. He, after all, talks bollocks for a living, and is shrewd enough to know it, knows, too, that, to be effective, bollocks must at least sound plausible. *Sehen sie, meine Herren!*

POSTCARD FROM THE PAST #7.

En route to the Palazzo Venezia for refreshments. The leaders sit opposite me, waving at the crowds. Beside me is Hitler's photographer, Heinrich Hoffman, a beefy, balding man, famed for his devotion to beer, ribaldry, and the Führer. Pennants displaying swastikas and fasces hang from pediments and parapets. The balconies are ribboned with banners declaring *"Mussolini is always right!"* *"We will fight for peace!"* *"Believe! Obey! Fight!"* I am feeling out of sorts, dismayed by the sight of the cheering crowds. Surely Italians are too nice, too humane to believe the hateful creed behind those flags they are waving? Italians are not good at hate. They can jeer and sneer, but hate? Or am I slipping into a prejudice antithetical to but no less reductive and wrongheaded than the German conviction that all Italians are cowards?

"The audacity!" says Hitler, as if reading my mind and denying the stereotype. "The skill, see how they turn." He's watching the wobbly motorcycle escort. "Personally, I prefer the motorcar. Never drive myself, but I've always been keen on cars. Göring used to drive on the wrong side of the road, you know, blowing his horn. Like most drivers, he has a mystical faith in himself. We would try to run over Communists in the streets. What fun we had!" At first, it is hard to understand to whom these observations are addressed. Hitler has turned aside, is waving at the crowds. Mussolini is doing the same on the other side of the car, glancing back at his guest. Then Hitler says: "It's a relief to be in a car. Your king had me riding in a ridiculous carnival carriage that lurched along in a lamentable fashion."

"There is hope," says Mussolini, "that in another . . . half century the court will discover the . . . internal combustion engine."

Hitler laughs, then inspects his fingernails, which are close bitten.

"That court," he says, "all those toadies and perverts. Doddery old men and dried-up nanny goats. And you, my friend, obliged to give them precedence. It's not right, you know. They are obsolete, Duce, obsolete, I tell you. We are the new men." He sits back, lifts his knees so that his feet don't touch the floor, like a child on an adult's chair, raises his hands, forefingers and thumbs pressed together, and speaks in a high-pitched, prissy voice: *"How many nails, Chancellor, does one find in the German infantry boot?"* Hoffman snorts. Hitler looks from Mussolini to me, wide-eyed with innocence. "What was I to say?" he says in his normal voice, opening his arms to elicit our sympathy. "I don't know how many nails there are in the German infantry boot. I have German infantry boot makers for that." The voice changes again: *"The Italian infantry boot, Herr Hitler, has no less than seventy-four nails. I insist upon it."* Hoffman is laughing out loud now and even Mussolini looks amused. Hitler focuses on me, unwilling to let slip a single member of his audience. *"I stake my crown upon it, Herr Chancellor. Fifty-two in the sole, fifty-two mind, and twenty-two in the heel. It is the foundation of our empire."*

He is mimicking Victor Emmanuel. I've only seen the king once, but from the newsreels, I can tell that he's got him spot on, the pinched lips, the bantam-like precision of the gestures. My face must reveal dawning comprehension and amusement. Hitler beams at me, glad to have got me on side with a funny story.

Not to be outdone in geniality, Mussolini leans toward his guest and says: "The advice his father gave him was, *Remember: to be a king, all you need to know is how to sign your name, read a newspaper, and mount a horse.*"

Hoffman nearly falls off his seat and Hitler slaps his thigh before settling back, waving again. "The monarchy is doomed," he says. "Nowadays people need a strong leader and that is obviously you. The court is composed of cretins, but they still keep the best men from the highest posts. And this is what paralyses your efforts. You must settle this question, you know."

Mussolini slumps back against the bench muttering: "*Aragoste.*"

Seeing his guests' puzzlement, I translate: "Lobsters. I believe it is what the Fascists call the king's courtiers, for their red livery."

"Lobsters?" asks Hoffman. "Or do you mean shrimps?"

Hitler laughs, but Mussolini seems put out. He glares at me with an intensity that is too studied to take seriously, like something he has read about in a self-help book.

"What a joy this man is," says Hitler, indicating Hoffman. "You should see him with Amann and Goebbels. They can't stop laughing. And when Dietrich joins them, it's total mayhem. Sepp's a bit slow, you see. By the time the others are onto the third joke, he's just getting the first one, and he starts laughing, a huge laugh that goes on and on."

"It's not my fault if the king is no bigger than a bottle," says Mussolini.

Hitler shifts in his seat, leaning to the left. It is a distressing move. Before long my suspicions are confirmed and I wish I was in an open carriage with the king.

Hitler: *My dog, he has no nose.*
Göring: *Mein Führer, how does he smell?*
Hitler: *Terrible!*

That was another one of his favourites. He was a great man for a laugh.

Sehen sie, meine Herren.

CETOLOGY #1. DEFINING OUR FIELD OF STUDY.

You *must settle this question.* Worrying counsel coming from Hitler. Whenever he called something a "question" it implied quantities of ordure being heaped upon other people. He was full of "questions": the Jewish question, the gypsy question, the Christian question, the Bolshevik question, the Czech question, the Polish question, the Ukrainian question . . . there was scarcely a European population that didn't pose a question as far as Hitler was concerned.

The Austrian question had just been resolved by staging a show in which a gang of youths went swaggering off to war as if they were tackling some mighty empire rather than a tiny nation with enough native Nazis to ensure there was no actual fighting. No matter. They'd done it, they'd played war, and they'd won. They felt like big, tough men, and all thanks to The Flatulent Windbag. That's something else you may find hard to understand, but a good deal of Hitler's popularity was due to his very bellicosity. Plenty of people welcomed war as an escape from the drudgery of dull little lives in dreary little suburbs.

You must settle this question. One of the few things to be said in Mussolini's favour is that when push came to shove he wasn't very good at settling questions. It was the king who would get rid of him rather than the other way round. I'm not saying he was a lovely man. In many ways, I despised Mussolini more than I did Hitler. But when one is among the Fascists . . .

By the by, I should point out, my dear, that when you call me a Fascist, you don't know what you're talking about. Your generation uses "Fascist" as a handy term of abuse for anyone you deem vaguely hidebound, regardless of political beliefs. It is an understandable mistake. Ideologues like Evola and Rosenberg did their best to define Fascist dogma, but their best wasn't very good and never could be, because they were applying reason to the irrational. Theory is not the strong point of antirationalist movements. Nobody paid much attention to them, least of all the leaders they wanted to impress. But there was a kind of creed behind it all, one premised on cynicism and contempt.

The basic belief was that men are moved by grievance, greed, fear, and envy. The politician's job is to use these selfish instincts to get power and stay in power. Hitler says as much in *Mein Kampf*. He was never very devious, not like that anyway. Power was the end, not the means, ideas a vehicle to be ditched if necessary, dangerous if they became an end in themselves. "The doctrine of Fascism," said Mussolini, "is action!" This is a very liberating principle. If you write down articles of faith, other people can interpret them and point out inconsistencies in your behaviour. Keep it simple, though, *might-is-right, somebody-else-is-to-blame, your-barn-is-my-barn-because-I've-got-A-BIG-COW*, and you can do anything you like.

The other thing you need to be a Fascist is enough ego to sustain the illusion that reality must conform to the agenda you determine for it. When you look at it like that, my dear, I suspect you will find as many Fascists among your young friends as among the ranks of old farts like myself. Maybe more. People like me are too disappointed in ourselves to be Fascists.

I was saying, Mussolini wasn't a very good dictator. He had the moves. Can't fault him there. If you wanted the posturing, gesticulating imbecilities, he was your man. But he always seemed to be faking it, like a little boy shouting "Me, too!" I mean, being sent into internal exile might have been a bore, but at least it didn't involve men in macs taking you down into basements. He could be nasty, but not quite nasty enough. And when he was nasty, like in his imperial ventures, he wasn't competent enough to pull it off. He read too much, as well. Never a good idea for the cultivation of a totalitarian mindset. As a young teacher, the kids called him *Il Tiranno*, but his classes were a riot because he had no authority. And yet . . .

> *You're the top!*
> *You're the Great Houdini!*
> *You're the top!*
> *You are Mussolini!*

Cole Porter in "Anything Goes." He changed the lyric later. But it was more than a facile rhyme. Mussolini was the epitome of perfection as well as a buffoon. Churchill, Freud, Shaw, Roosevelt, even Gandhi for God's sake, they all had nice things to say about him. Nothing is as simple and clear as we would wish. You should remember that, my dear. It's too easy to blame from the comfort of youth and historical distance. Your generation specializes in it. I sometimes regret moving to France. Set against a backdrop of Calvin, Jacobinism, and *j'accuse*, the indignant moralizing of a people compromised by collaboration, hollering condemnation to hush an uneasy conscience, has influenced your education. Things are more ambiguous than you think. You should look to one old fart your generation admires, Alberto Moravia, who was in conflict with the Fascists from the late twenties until the regime collapsed in 1943. He recently said: "Mussolini was not a bad man. We Italians understand what Mussolini was. His worst fault was his abysmal ignorance of foreign affairs." Sometimes it seemed even the anti-Fascists weren't really anti-Mussolini. He simply didn't inspire the same fear and hate as Hitler did.

Which begs again the question of what we could have foreseen concerning the crimes of the principal villain of the piece. I've told you to imagine a time when what we know happened had yet to happen. And there's good reason for that. This was a period of major changes, changes way beyond the vision of most people. My parents were born into a world where individuals mattered, a world in which torture was illegal so long as you didn't have the misfortune to have a dark skin and live in a warm country cursed with abundant raw materials, a world in which it was understood that armies went off to fight each other in some conveniently located spot where they wouldn't do too much damage. Somewhere like Belgium, for instance. You, by contrast, were born into a world of homogenized men, a world where torture is institutionalized, where war is waged between populations, not armies, where premeditated extermination is the norm. That change happened during my lifetime. I didn't appreciate it at the time. But there were those who did, among them both demons and angels.

I mentioned that Hitler didn't hide the nature of his beliefs. He was also candid about his objectives: the reversal of Versailles, the "reunification" of Germany, the expansion eastward, even what was to become of the Jews was intimated in *Mein Kampf*. I'm sure you haven't read it. You wouldn't want to sully yourself with something so sordid. You'd be right in a way. But it's instructive nonetheless. Everything is there one way or another. Take this, for example, about World War I: "If at the beginning of, or during, the war 12,000 or 15,000 of these Jewish corrupters of the people had been plunged into an asphyxiating gas . . . the sacrifice of millions of soldiers would not have been in vain." Hey ho. "No human being," he said, "has declared what he wanted more often than I have." It's self-pitying, like so much that he said. Hitler often sounded like a blues lament, *Nobody knows the trouble I know* and so forth. But that particular plaint is justified. Time and again, he did tell everyone what he was going to do. The reason his opponents were always so surprised was that they hadn't been listening.

And the angels? Well, we pretend the Nazi regime was an unprecedented event none of us could have predicted. Except some did. The journalists on the *Munich Post* spent a decade warning what would happen if Hitler came to power, portraying a regime that would be craven, corrupt, criminal, and murderous. They even spoke of a "final solution" for Germany's Jews. And in 1936, Friedrich Reck-Malleczewen noted the parallels with the sixteenth-century Anabaptist rebellion in Münster, a regime led by a charismatic prophet protected by thugs, a regime moved by greed, lewdness, sadism, and a lust for power, a regime founded on hysteria, terrorism, and vice, a regime that divorced the city from the civilized world, a regime that burned books, murdered opponents, and employed a propaganda chief who limped!

Marx said that history repeats itself, first time as tragedy, second time as farce. It's not true. History repeats itself, but the tragedy and farce are contiguous at all times and in most things. It's just a question of what you choose to accentuate.

POSTCARD FROM THE PAST #8.

"Did you know, the Duce and I were both employed in the building trade in Germany at the same time? It was fate, really, a sign. Two men, two nations, two movements. Of course, he led the way. I mean, the Brownshirts couldn't have happened without the Blackshirts. It's a fact. The success of the march on Rome, gave us the impetus we needed."

He's still talking. I don't know how he does it, but I wish he wouldn't. I feel weak at the knees. And this is still the first day, the first morning. He's not leaving till Monday! Worse, he has taken a fancy to me. As we head into the Palazzo Venezia for our refreshments, he buttonholes me (he damn nearly has the lapel off my tatty tunic) to make sure I'm at his side to hear what he has to say. And he has a lot to say. And he is going to say it. And it's never, ever, ever going to end. I'm beginning to think I'd better kill him after all. This may seem frivolous, but I'm trying to conjure the past, and as far as I was concerned right then, The Flatulent Windbag's principal crime against humanity was that he was boring me seven sorts of rigid. With trembling fingers, I reach for my fags, then think better of it, but he hasn't missed my gesture and interprets it correctly.

"You will be spending a lot of time with me in the next few days, young man."

?

"You can learn from my example."

??!!!

"You know, I experienced terrible poverty in my youth. For months, I lived on milk and dry bread. Never had a hot meal. Yet still I smoked forty cigarettes a day! Thirty kreutzer spent on tobacco every single day. Well it struck me that five kreutzer would buy a bit of butter for my bread. So I threw my cigarettes in the river and I have never smoked again. It is a matter of will with me, you know. When I decide not to do something, I don't do it. Ever. It's as simple as that. And I am persuaded that, had I continued to smoke, I could not have endured the constant strain of my political career. Perhaps Germany owes my leadership to this minor detail."

Give the man tobacco! I reach again for my fags, but he releases me and moves on, glancing from side to side appreciatively. There is much to appreciate. The halls are lined with pictures by Veronese, Mainardi, and Raphael, and cabinets containing majolicas, icons, gold bowls, goblets, and Murano glassware. Thumbs tucked into his belt, Hitler leans forward to inspect the paintings. Those he likes elicit a grunt of approval, an observation or question, followed by the inevitable "*Sehen sie, meine Herren.*" Mussolini is at the far end of the first hall, waiting with ill-disguised impatience.

"And to think, if Bolshevism had come here, if the Duce had not prevented it, all this would have been destroyed." It is a phrase he will repeat in the coming days, a refrain like *Sehen sie, meine Herren.* I forget which picture inspired the accolade, but I remember Mussolini hurrying back to enjoy the compliment. "It would have been a tragedy for Italy," continues Hitler. "There is no doubt that you, Duce, are the heir of the great men of the past, successor to the universal empire of the Caesars."

Mussolini is ecstatic, not quite lying on his back with his legs in the air to have his tummy stroked, but very, very pleased.

"The virtues of classical Rome . . . the achievements of the Romans of old . . . are never far from my thoughts," he says. "It is a . . . legacy that I . . . try to turn to good account. History is a great school for rulers. Above all, I love . . . Caesar. He was unique in that he conjoined a . . . warrior's will with the . . . genius of the sage. He was a philosopher who saw everything—forgive my learned references—*sub specie aeternitatis*. It is true that he had a . . . passion for fame, but . . . ambition did not cut him off from . . . the love of his subjects."

I am beginning to think I am going to have my work cut out for me if I want to take the piss out of these two. How can anyone compete with such pompous, sententious nonsense? But I'm underestimating myself. Not my pomposity and sententiousness. I know I can make a strong showing in those fields. But my capacity for taking the piss.

"Do you really believe a dictator can be loved?"

It is out before I know it, but the moment it's out, I wish it wasn't. I mean, I might as well start calling them The Constipated Prick and The Flatulent Windbag to their faces and have done with it. Something of my alarm must show because Hitler is smirking. Of all the possible reactions, amusement is the one I least expected. But he finds my discomfort funny. Mussolini's humour, meanwhile, is as constricted as his bowel.

"But, of course," he says. "Provided people . . . also fear him. The crowd loves the strong men. The crowd, she is . . . like a woman." Thankfully, he does not elaborate on this sentiment. From a notoriously priapic individual, it is a troubling statement: "But the daily practice of politics can sterilize the imagination. One must stay fertile . . . stay in touch . . . with the human side of affairs . . . with real, living, breathing people."

A gentle clearing of the throat and Goebbels materializes himself between the two dictators. Despite his club foot, he has a knack for moving stealthily.

"I have been told," he says, "that when you left the Socialist Party, Duce, you shouted, in response to their noisy abuse, 'You hate me because you still love me!' Is that correct?"

The Constipated Prick inclines his head, accepting authorship.

"Paradox is a valuable tool," he says. "It confuses opponents, making them . . . wonder whether what you say is perhaps true, and while they are working it out . . . you can go ahead and do what needs doing. But love and hate are . . . close kin. Only the genuinely passionate man can understand hate. Your own Bismarck once said, *I didn't get a wink of sleep all night. I was hating all the time!* And Dante's resentment was such that he would not forgive his enemies . . . even in hell!"

There *is* a surreptitious sense of humour lurking behind that uptight facade, after all. I can't imagine him telling a funny story, but somebody who appreciates paradox is not immune to humour. Mind you, I don't suppose he would have appreciated the joke your mother was preparing for them. It was a few days before I got it myself.

CETOLOGY #2. METHODOLOGY.

Hitler and his chauffeur are driving through the country-side. They're passing in front of a farmhouse when they run over a cockerel. Hitler gets out, knocks on the door, tells the farmer's wife what happened. "Look, I'm really sorry," he says, "but we just didn't see him. Anyway, I want to make good the damage. I want to replace your cock." The farmer's wife looks at him a bit funny, then says: "All right, if you really want to. The hens are round the back."

No, not one of Hitler's. He had a selective sense of humour. Didn't do self-deprecation, didn't get that at all. I made a quip one day, something about my being trivial without having attained the more desirable attribute of frivolity, and he looked at me like I was a lunatic. I guess he was so attached to the self that even in others self-deprecation offended him. To my mind, it has always seemed a mark of moral elegance.

Hitler and his chauffeur are driving through the countryside. They're in the middle of nowhere when there's a loud bang. Turns out they've run over a pig. Hitler sends his chauffeur to find the pig's owner and explain what happened. The man's gone ten, fifteen, thirty minutes. Eventually comes back an hour later, blind drunk, staggering about with a basket stuffed with sausages and cheeses and hams and bottles of schnapps.

"My God, what happened?" says Hitler.

"I don't know, I don't understand it at all," says his chauffeur. *"I just said 'Heil Hitler, the pig is dead,' and they started pouring drinks and giving me all these presents."*

There are people unknown to history who warrant statues, street names, stamps, and commemorative plaques, unconventional heroes, but heroes nonetheless. Traubert Petter was a fairground showman from Paderborn who had an act with performing chimps. Taught them to give the Nazi salute when they saw a uniform. The Nazis thought this was brilliant till they realized the chimps were also saluting the postman. Then it dawned on them that a monkey was being made of someone and it wasn't necessarily the chimpanzees. They passed a law, the Nazis, I mean, not the monkeys, though the monkeys might have displayed more sagacity in the matter. Any chimp caught saluting was to be executed. And they sent Traubert to the Russian front. He had the last laugh, though. He survived.

Hitler and Göring are standing on top of a radio tower. Hitler says he wants to do something to cheer people up. "I know," says Göring, eager to help, "why don't you jump?"

In 1941, the British Ministry of Information spliced together footage of Hitler saluting goose-stepping soldiers, then dubbed "The Lambeth Walk" from "Me and My Girl" on top, so that it looked like they were mincing about in a musical. *Schicklegruber Doing the Lambeth Walk, Assisted by the Gestapo Hep Cats* was cheap propaganda and not exactly an overwhelming rib tickler, but when Goebbels saw the footage he was so furious that he stormed out of the screening room kicking over chairs and screaming obscenities. Now that is funny.

> Hitler has only got one ball,
> Göring has two but very small,
> Himmler is somewhat sim'lar,
> But poor Goebbels has no balls at all.

We'll talk about that later if you're not too squeamish.

I know these jokes aren't very funny. But along with slurs, scurrilous rumours, and scatological jibes, they are all we've got. Like all egoists, Hitler and Mussolini hated people laughing at them. Hence we are duty-bound to laugh. There is nothing as potent as mockery and nothing more humanizing than self-mockery. If certain people don't have the grace to do it themselves, we are compelled to help them out. And laughter makes less mess than tears.

I'm not just being glib. I mean it. Life is messy enough as it is and lamenting the mess only leads to resentment, bitterness, and rancour, which in turn create more mess. But laughter makes life lighter and brighter, neutralizing bile and reducing discord. It is an altogether tidier method of proceeding, especially for a species whose members are prone to persuading themselves that they are the injured party in every transaction.

Hitler lets rip with an enormous fart in public. It's so loud that everyone turns round. Hoping to blame it on Himmler, Hitler says, "Himmler, stop it!"

"Certainly, Mein Führer," says Himmler. "Which way did it go?"

There are two tools for coping with tyrants: demonization and derision. We can't admit they are like us. So we play their game, reducing people to caricatures, making them super monstrous or super ridiculous. Mussolini helps when it comes to derision. He wasn't an idiot, but he did a very good impersonation of one. Hitler is trickier. You have to strip away the carapace of metaphysical evil that has accrued around his person. But if you can manage it, what you are left with is a little man who farted a lot. And when you've got that, you have something human, something that can be encompassed.

Hitler, Göring, and Goebbels are at sea. There's a storm and their boat sinks. Who is saved? Germany.

Chaplin regretted making *The Great Dictator.* He said that, had he known about the death camps at the time, he wouldn't have made it. I know, but persist. Laughter is a device for disarming evil. We have a duty to derision. It's not lighthearted. But like everything in life, you make do with what you've got.

Hitler tells Eva Braun they're going to do a sixty-nine.

"What's that?" she says.

"Don't worry," he says. "I'll show you."

They're just getting into position when Hitler farts, a really villainous fart, and Eva wriggles away. Hitler reassures her, says he knows what he's doing, and they assume the position again, but the same thing happens. And again, and again. The fifth time the blast is so violent that it knocks Eva out of bed.

"Oh, no, Dolfie, no," she wails. "I really can't take another sixty-four of them!"

POSTCARD FROM THE PAST #9.

"You will travel with us," says Hitler.

?

"Yes, he will travel with us, will he not, Duce?"

??

"I want him with me all the time."

!!!

"The man who knows everything."

???!!!

The joke's on me now. In the next few days, I gather that The Flatulent Windbag has taken a shine to me. Why? Because I'm the type he takes shines to. Physically I resemble my mother. I don't mean I've got breasts and look good in a long dress. But I'm tall, blue-eyed, and blond. I am a candidate for that new race he has in mind, the international ruling class to be recruited from appropriate stock in each country and, somewhat arbitrarily, dubbed "Aryan." I suspect he is also amused by my habit of unwittingly asking impertinent questions then squirming with embarrassment. I think he likes people who squirm.

"You will travel on my personal train."

??????!!!!!

I wish I'd been living in Italy a little longer, had gone native, turned short and dark. A hooked nose wouldn't have gone amiss, either. And a red beard to be on the safe side. But the black shirt, no matter how shabby, is not enough to make me look like a Calabrian peasant, and my features bear no resemblance to one of Degas's scheming Jews, so I am stuck with Hitler for the duration. In fact, the shabby shirt may have been a contributory factor. Inspired by the sight of an immensely tall porter wearing a silver-laced uniform, Hitler is waxing lyrical on the subject of men in coloured shirts. Judging by what he is saying, the shabbiness of the shirt is inversely proportionate to the quality of the wearer.

"A fine fellow," he murmurs. "You know, Duce, in the early days, I had some really remarkable specimens in my Brownshirts. Children in many ways. Close to nature if you know what I mean. But their hearts were in the right place and they were totally devoted. Followed me everywhere. Couldn't use them in peacetime, of course. But in times of turmoil such jolly rogues are invaluable. They wouldn't let the country be sold out to defeatist scum. They'd learned to fight in the war, you know, could size up a battleground at a glance. I knew I could build a party with chaps like that. What sacrifices they made! All day working at their jobs and at night out fighting for the Party. A bourgeois in a stiff collar would have bitched up everything. So I always recruited the most dishevelled lads."

"The bourgeois," says Mussolini, "are as soft as . . ." The pause is longer than usual, as if he is contemplating a vast array of possible similes. In fact, his German has let him down. He turns toward me with a wave of his hand ". . . *pantofolaie!*" He nods and I supply the translation: *ladies in slippers.* He's not finished yet, though. I suspect he is beginning to understand that once he has the floor, he had better keep speaking. "They do not appreciate that the . . . result of a battle is secondary. Struggle is . . . its own reward, even if one is defeated. This is the core of . . . Fascist philosophy. I was once asked to expound . . . Fascism in a single sentence. I wrote . . . Life . . . must not be taken easily. Pain is the only creative factor."

Two sentences actually, but I curb my tongue. Hitler, who looked uneasy at the notion that winning might not matter, cheers up when he hears about laborious life and creative pain.

"All life is paid for with blood," he murmurs. "It is the law of nature. All creatures devour one another, you see. If we failed to respect this law, we would be eaten ourselves, the prey of wild animals. It is imperative that we impose our will on inferior species. Any man who denies this principle should renounce life altogether, for it shows he is not fit for the struggle."

We are past the liveried porter now. I glance back at him. He really is enormous. God knows where Mussolini found him, but I wager he has been trundled out expressly to show the Germans that there are some really big Italians about, too.

"The bourgeois don't understand this," says Hitler. "They say we are barbarians. But we are proud to be barbarians, we want to be barbarians. It is an honourable title."

At which point, his face lights up and he gazes at me rapturously. This is appalling. I am a vulgar man, but I don't care to be the archetype of a barbarian.

"*Schöne Frauen!*" he says. To my immense relief, I realize he is looking over my shoulder. "Such beautiful women in Rome," he continues, clicking his tongue against his palate. "I saw it earlier, from the car. Such elegance. Such grace. Italian women have this poise because they are used to carrying heavy weights on their heads."

Where he got this idea from, I do not know, but he clearly loves clichéd images of Italy (I wouldn't be all that surprised if he asked Mussolini to rustle up an ice cream), and has perhaps seen pictures of peasant women from somewhere like Lucania. But in 1938, the only object most women in Rome carry on their heads is a tilt hat, which probably doesn't have much impact on their posture.

Not that the girl who has excited his attention needs any accessories to set off her beauty. Turning to follow his gaze, I curse myself for losing my touch if it takes a dictator to draw my attention to a beauty like this. She is behind the refreshments table and she is dazzlingly pretty. There is something familiar about her, but I can't place where I might have seen her before.

"You may find this hard to credit," says Hitler, leaning toward me, "but when I was your age, I was a bit of a loner. Really, I managed very well on my own. I've changed though, you know. Nowadays I need company. And I like nothing better than taking tea with a pretty girl. It makes me bright and cheerful. After an hour listening to a girl's silly chatter, I am totally revived and can return to work refreshed."

For a moment, I cannot bring myself to move. It's not the confession that stops me short, nor the disquieting thought of Hitler becoming any more bright and cheerful. It's his breath. I am overwhelmed by a foul stench, something beyond halitosis, some visceral corruption that wouldn't be out of place at the bottom of a compost heap.

I never thought I'd have cause to say this, but to my very great delight, Goebbels walks into the room. I seize the opportunity. Jumping back smartly, I snap my arm up, and cry "Heil Hitler!" It's embarrassing, but it gets me out of breath range. The others are caught unawares. There's no call to be issuing the Heil-Hitlers right now. But there's something Pavlovian about this. Some of them are probably salivating. Goebbels is the first to respond and then they're all at it, fingers high like proud parents measuring the growth of preternaturally tall children. I get a few suspicious glances, but I have a feeling that no matter how often I do this, they will respond. During dinner? At the opera? In a urinal? Again, I am seized by a sense of potential. There is fun to be had in the most improbable situations.

The moment's confusion over, we turn toward the table. The girl's eyes are bright with humour. I am acutely conscious of what I have just done in front of her, but there's complicity in her look. Or so I hope. I'm sure I've seen her before, but still can't say where. There's no time to speculate, though. She's bending over the table, offering a plate piled high with sweetmeats, cakes, and biscuits. Everything is sugared, glazed, candied, crystallized, caramelized. The plate is not all she's offering, either, not in a waitress's outfit cut like that. Behind the confectionary, her breasts do what breasts tend to do when a woman in a lacy décolleté top bends forward. In front of the confectionary, assorted Fascists, Nazis, and one misplaced Irishman do what men tend to do when a woman in a lacy décolleté top bends forward.

"And who made these, my dear?" asks Hitler, beaming at her. I think he's talking about the cakes. Otherwise, the answer is God. Swallowing hard, I translate.

"I did," she says. "I made them specially for the Führer." She wasn't lying.

I feel something at my back. Glancing over my shoulder, I see Mussolini. It's hard to tell from this angle, but I have the impression that his nostrils are flaring. I don't dare look too closely, though. I'm not terribly up on the etiquette in these situations, but I'm fairly sure you're not supposed to stare up the nose of a *duce*, especially not a *duce* in rut.

"And what are these?" says Hitler, selecting a *marron glacé*.

"It is Reichsmarschall Göring's favourite confection," says Goebbels, watching me with an air I do not find wholly comforting. "He buys several kilos every time he visits Italy. At night, he puts a dozen beside his bed, opens the windows wide, and leaves the box at the far end of the room so the cold air will deter him from overindulging. But once he has eaten his ration, he lies there in a torment, unable to sleep, yearning for just one more. Eventually, he jumps out of bed, scuttles down the room, grabs the box, gobbles them all, then scurries back to bed!"

There's mirth at this, not much from Hitler, but plenty from the Reichsmarschall's other colleagues. Then a quiet voice intervenes. It is Himmler: "And how do you know all this, Herr Goebbels?" The voice is soft, but the delivery is sibilant with malice.

There is a brief pause before Goebbels says, "I had him under surveillance."

Hitler pops the chestnut in his mouth. Somebody else has done his homework, I mean somebody apart from Goebbels. The Flatulent Windbag eats prodigious amounts of cake and chocolate. He loves anything sweet and sticky. This goes for sentiment, too. And apparently his sweet tooth is partly responsible for a certain digestive disorder.

POSTCARD FROM THE PAST #10.

"The girl comes, too."

?

"As well as the man who knows everything, the pretty girl with the cakes."

??

This time it's not me, it's Mussolini who is puzzled by Hitler's insistence that "the girl" accompany us. I'm quicker on the uptake. I've placed her. She was that fleeting vision at the station. I can understand why he wants her company. Forget the cakes. She's the sort of stunning Mediterranean beauty that lured me out of Ireland. Damn the climate. I wanted another sort of warmth.

Mussolini feigns puzzlement a moment longer. I think he's faking it, at least. He is The Phallus in Chief, after all. He can spot a pretty girl when he sees one. And he has yet to comprehend the nature of Hitler's relationship with pretty girls, so hesitates to put this prime example of Italian womankind in the path of anyone other than himself. But then he remembers the need to impress his guest. If Hitler expresses a fondness for *signorine*, he must have his *signorine*. A nod of the head to his *majordomo* and it is done, The Girl is added to the party along with The Man Who Knows Everything. At least she is not there under false pretences. Well, she is, as it happens. But she also genuinely fulfils her designated role. A Beautiful Girl and a dab hand with cakes, too.

I'm not sure how you're going to feel about this, my dear, but it was Hitler who brought your mother and me together. Given the gulf in personality dividing your parents, I would guess only extreme circumstances and an extreme intermediary could have achieved such an improbable union. It didn't last long and now she's gone for good, but I must be one of the few people left alive who owes the Führer a debt of gratitude.

POSTCARD FROM THE PAST #11.

The stamp that conveys the message. If you were to set a price, fifty *centesimi* would be about right for a couple of tin-pot dictators. I've kept this stamp for three decades. It was part of a commemorative series issued after Hitler's departure. You will note that it is attached to these pages with a paper clip. I never could bring myself to lick the back of their heads. I have my standards. But I couldn't just chuck the thing away. Even unlicked, it stuck with me, like the story I have to tell, the story and all it has entailed.

That clipping you found with its damning caption was only one part of my collection, one item in the memorabilia of remorse. If you've got this far, you will have gathered that my interest in all this goes well beyond the curiosity that initially moved me, beyond the simple necessity to address a daughter's angry words, too. It was there before. I never threw anything away. I kept the clipping, I kept the stamp. I've still got that black uniform boxed away in the cellar, the cardboard shoes, too. One of the shoes has got tooth marks in the toe. And I have the copy of *Winnetou* that Hitler pressed upon me and an empty sachet of Sorbitol I retrieved from your mother, and the diaries I wrote up every night. Above all, though, I've got the guilt. It has been there inside me all these years, nagging away. You could say that Hitler and Mussolini have dominated my life and not just because they were instrumental in my meeting your mother.

What I have never been able to get away from is the thought that, had I acted differently, ten, twenty, thirty million people might have lived a little longer. I don't want to aggrandise myself. You can't ascribe everything to the existence of one man. Maybe war was inevitable even without Hitler. But the fact remains that there was a moment when inaction on my part permitted the continuation of an entire chain of events. It's not the what-did-you-do-in-the-war-daddy that is so terrible. Prompted by your mother, I did all right in the end. But what-did-you-not-do-in-the-war-daddy, that one has haunted me for the last three decades, has had me reading monographs, diaries, a whole host of secondary and primary sources. My secret life has been a lot more serious and a lot less gay than the face projected to the world.

CETOLOGY #3. ETYMOLOGY & GENEALOGY.

Mussolini, from "mussolina," the diminutive of "mussola," after Mosul in Iraq, where muslin was first made. This is not to say that our man derived from a small piece of cheesecloth. Rather, at some point someone in his family sold muslin. Who or when, I do not know, but it was of little consequence to The Constipated Prick, who said the only ancestor that interested him was a man who killed his unfaithful wife, then fled, leaving two *scudi* on her bosom to pay for her burial. "This is the nature of the people of the Romagna. All our folk songs deal with love tragedies." *I am a mad poet.*

By the nineteenth century, the Mussolinis were small-scale landowners and the Duce's grandfather was a lieutenant in the National Guard. Mussolini *père* was a blacksmith and committed Socialist whose sexual promiscuity and preference for the political podium over the anvil proved an effective path to penury, despite the efforts of Mussolini *mère*, a schoolmistress and devout Catholic whose thrift kept the family afloat. Baptized Benito after Juárez, the republican leader who threw the French out of Mexico, Amilcare after Cipriani, the anarchist and nationalist who fought alongside Garibaldi, and Andrea after the Costa who founded the *Partito Socialista Italiano*, the young Mussolini inherited more than a handful of revolutionary names from his father, for both Alessandro and Benito were turbulent, surly, and quarrelsome characters, qualities exacerbated in the son by bitterness over their poverty.

"My mother earned fifty lire a month," he told the German writer Emil Ludwig. "My father sometimes more, sometimes less. We lived in a two-room slum. There was rarely any meat on the table. At school, the children were fed in three grades. I was in the lowest rank, among the poorest. The fact that there were ants in the bread given to us poor children no longer bothers me, but that we were graded at all still rankles. Such insufferable humiliation is what turned me into a revolutionist.

"My father was a passionate Socialist and went to prison for his beliefs. When he died, thousands of his comrades attended the funeral. All this provided a clear model for my ambitions. Had I had a different sort of father, I should have become a different sort of man. But my character was formed by my childhood. As soon as I was old enough to hold the bellows, I was put to work. Watching the hammer in the forge one learns to love the raw material that a man must fashion in accordance with his will."

So, in sum, poor lad of *petit bourgeois* stock fallen on hard times, a classification that wouldn't have pleased him, but which recommends itself on two counts: first, it's true; second, it wouldn't have pleased him. Mussolini claimed the fact that he had been born "among the common people" put the trump cards in his hand. But in etymology and genealogy, as in so much else, The Constipated Prick was trumped by The Flatulent Windbag.

Hitler, interchangeable with Hiedler, Hietler, Huttler, and Hutler. Means smallholder. Adolf, from "Athalwolf" or Noble-Wolf. You can see already that Hitler had the edge on Mussolini. "Smallholder" isn't up to much as a tyrant's surname, but in terms of totalitarianism "noble wolf" is a lot more potent and pithy than the "Blessed Manly Brother of the God Melqart," which is a loose translation of Benito Amilcare Andrea. Too many words betray insecurity. But it's in the genealogy that The Flatulent Windbag wins hands down. This is actually quite funny if you're in the right frame of mind.

Hitlers can be traced back to the seventeenth century, but we'll begin with our man's grandparents, and the brothers Johann Georg Heidler, an itinerant miller, and Johann Nepomuk Heidler, a prosperous farmer. In 1837, Maria Anna Schicklgruber, the unmarried, forty-two-year-old daughter of peasant farmers, gave birth to Alois, who would become The Flatulent Windbag's father. In 1842, Johann Georg, who had been lodging with the Schicklgrubers, married Maria, thus becoming Alois's stepfather, and making Johann Nepomuk Alois's step-uncle. Whether Johann Georg had passed through the Schicklgruber household and the Schicklgruber daughter five years earlier, nobody knows. There's some doubt about it, though, because Johann Georg didn't recognize the sprog and Alois was dumped on brother Johann Nepomuk. Alois went down in the baptismal register as being illegitimate, and kept the Schicklgruber name for four decades, hence the sneering title of that British Ministry of Information film.

When Alois did change his name in 1876, Johann Nepomuk was one of the witnesses attesting to the deceased Johann Georg's paternity, which was later validated by the Nazis, but there was speculation that the real father might have been Johann Nepomuk, who couldn't acknowledge the child because he was already married. In the 1920s, stories started circulating alleging that Maria had got pregnant in a Jewish household where she was working as a cook, but there's nothing to substantiate these rumours, which were probably just a perverse amalgam of anti-Nazi and anti-Semitic propaganda. So, Johann Georg or Johann Nepomuk are the most likely candidates for being the father of Alois.

By all accounts, Alois was a nasty piece of work, a sleeve-stroker when sleeves needed stroking, devious enough to change his name when a legacy was in the offing, and a hypocrite who knew how to present a respectable face to the world while dissembling the fact that he was a selfish brute and domestic tyrant, lording it over his family, bullying his wives, beating the children, and riding roughshod over anyone weaker than himself. I saw a photo of him in a news-paper after the war. The face was mulish, the eyes flat and obtuse, the head like a battering ram and about as forgiving. It was the sort of face that, on a frontier guard like Alois, or any petty official with a modicum of power over you, makes you want to sit down and hang your head in your hands. Compared to Alois, his son's features positively sparkled with bonhomie.

Maria dies in 1847, Johann Georg in 1857, Alois comes of age in his uncle's household, where he has been brought up alongside Johann Nepomuk's children. Alois leaves home and marries Anna Glasl-Hörer, a wealthy older woman with the wherewithal to advance his career as a customs officer. Anna gets sick and becomes an invalid. Alois gets randy and becomes a serial adulterer. The couple separate, Alois sets up house with Fanni Matzelsberger, a woman half his age who works as a serving girl at the inn where the Schicklgrubers have been living. Anna dies, Alois marries Fanni. Fanni gives birth to two children, Fanni sickens and becomes an invalid.

Lumbered with another burdensome female, Alois hires an even younger woman as housemaid and helpmeet. She's called Klara Pölzl. She is said to be hardworking, modest, pious, sweet natured, and affectionate. She is also fertile and sufficiently flexible in terms of her moral spectrum to accommodate within the confines of her piety some very idiosyncratic domestic arrangements. Alois can rely upon her. Indeed, he knows her well. A little too well. Klara's mother was Johanna Heidler, daughter of Johann Nepomuk and a girl who had been like an elder sister to Alois when he lived with his uncle's family.

Thus, depending upon who his father is, Alois and Klara are either uncle and niece or first cousins, at least in law now that he has changed his name, likely in blood, too. Which makes for a slightly delicate situation when Fanni dies and Alois gets Klara pregnant. Papal dispensation is sought citing "bilateral affinity in the third degree touching the second," papal dispensation is granted, the happy couple are wed, and five months later Klara gives birth to Gustav, who is duly followed by Ida, Otto, and eventually Adolf.

Odd? Not nearly so odd as the fact that throughout their married life Klara called her husband "uncle." I'm not making this up. The Flatulent Windbag spent his childhood in a household where a thuggish, tyrannical father was bedding the little lad's Mummy, who called Daddy "uncle" and, even if Daddy wasn't Uncle, Daddy was Mummy's first cousin and like a brother to Mummy's mummy, which made Dolfie . . . well, it made Dolfie a very confused little boy indeed. What's more, Dolfie is a sickly child and, having lost Gustav, Ida, and Otto to diphtheria and cot death, Mummy is a most doting Mummy, doing her very best to compensate for Uncle-Daddy's brutality, pampering her son and pandering to his every whim.

"Had I had a different sort of father, I should have become a different sort of man."

Sehen sie, meine Herren! Ein grosser Künstler.

HE WAS RIGHT, of course. We can't escape our parents. We carry them around inside ourselves, a nest of Russian dolls cobbled together from the shortcomings, quirks, and qualities of those who made us, some bits bigger, some bits smaller. Same goes for children. You're stuck fast inside us and you're there for the duration. The disappointments, disputes, distances, and squabbles don't dislodge love. That's another reason you'll come back with your questions. Love is elastic and will stretch to accommodate many things, drawing us back to the fold willy-nilly. It is one of the great virtues of family life. You're landed with people you might not choose to be with otherwise and you've got to get along with them regardless. This is a very useful lesson in living, because all those fantasies of perfect harmony peddled by films, books, and manifestos are just that, fantasies, so it's as well to get your head round the idea early on that you've got to deal with other people as they are, because they're always going to be there, and they'll never quite be the people you'd imagined they might be at the off. Anything less isn't fair on them and it isn't fair on yourself either.

Understanding is another matter. We never really understand our loved ones. When the loved one turns out to be pals with a couple of despots, the incomprehensibility may well prove insurmountable. I appreciate that. All I can say is that, like laughter, love and forgiveness make less mess. I know. Half the world tried hate and censure when I was young and it didn't work at all.

So I hope and I write, relying upon that native empathy you displayed as a child and which has only recently been weighed down with righteousness. Yet I still question my capacity to explain. Even with all the words in the world there is always something unknowable about what moves other people to do the things they do. And, in my darkest moments, I wonder whether explaining is actually desirable, let alone possible. Often as not, when we try to explain we just dig ourselves a deeper hole, and when you're in a hole the wisest thing to do is to stop digging. But that won't be good enough for you, I know. You'll be back, in what mood, I cannot say, but you'll be back and I'd better be ready, because the whys will be whizzing past my ears like the crockery did when I riled your Mum. At the very least, I'll need some nimble footwork and a knack for ducking at the right moment.

It will be quite like old times!

POSTCARD FROM THE PAST #12.

We're on a dais watching Italy's finest march past the podium. I'll spare you the details. They would only make you despise men who are doing what your generation decrees every liberated individual should do.

You object, my dear? You need to get out more, use your imagination. The fact that these are marching men in uniform does not mean they are any less autonomous than you and your freethinking friends. I have heard you advising English speakers you deem too uptight to "just relax and go with the flow." It is a fashionable phrase. Yet going with the flow is what people have been doing since time immemorial. It is very rare indeed for anyone to go against the flow. The flow of your generation involves lots of sex with different partners, dancing to crude but potent music that emphasizes rhythm over harmony and melody, and the ingestion of large quantities of drugs that tend to elevate feelings of benevolence towards one's fellow creatures. The flow in Europe between the wars was less benign, but no less seductive. The marching men are going with the flow as surely as your flower-power companions are going with the flow by rebelling against old farts like myself. You are fortunate to have been dealt such a beguiling hand. Not everyone is given the gifts of peace and prosperity. Indeed, the fact that so many men were prepared to go marching in my generation is probably why yours is free to play around with sexual mores and hallucinatory substances. Not only was autocracy defeated, but every libertarian movement throughout history has been preceded by a period of repression. It's your children I feel sorry for. How will they rebel when they come of age? The only revolution open to them will be back into a more orthodox conformity. The poor little tykes will be obliged to become bank managers and accountants.

Italy's finest continue parading. They are plentiful and impeccably attired. This last point does not elude The Flatulent Windbag. Jigging up and down just in front of me, he admires the soldiers' uniforms. He is particularly taken with the piping on the trouser seams. *Ah, the elegant Italians! Such innate grace!* To his right, The Constipated Prick begins jigging, too. Hitler congratulates his host on the spectacle. *Such fine fellows! Such precision! Such style!* It's altogether too much for Mussolini.

"The French and English," he says, "are . . . finished as military powers. Italy is their superior . . . even at sea. We can sink the . . . British navy in . . . fifteen minutes!" Hang on, have I misheard? We are talking clothes, aren't we? How's he going to sink the British navy? Torpedo them with his tarboosh? "But it was predictable. France has been ruined by . . . alcohol, syphilis and journalism." The Flatulent Windbag chuckles, egging his host on, but The Constipated Prick needs no egging. The discovery that he heads the greatest military power in the world is enough. "As for England, a country where . . . there are hospitals and cemeteries for animals, and parrots . . . get legacies. It is pure decadence. There are four million more women than men. Four million . . . sexually frustrated women dreaming up as many problems to titillate their senses. Since they cannot hold a man, they must . . . hug all humanity! Do you know where the Anglo-Saxon countries are heading? Matriarchy!"

Hitler roars with laughter. He loved his Mummy, but the idea of a matriarchy is side-splittingly absurd. Behind us, the Italians who understand German, the Nazis who can follow Mussolini's German, and I suspect several Italians and

Germans who haven't got a clue what's going on but don't care to be left out of the general merriment, all laugh dutifully.

The soldiers are still marching past. Perhaps the British should send over some frustrated Englishwomen to sort them out. Bugger the brolly. Get the women in, get the trousers off, and get hugging. That would be a parade to remember.

"Then they will be, as you say, all at sea." As I say? I didn't say anything. Who's he talking to? I am startled out of my reverie. The last words were addressed to me in English. Hitler looks worried. The shift to a language he does not understand and consequently to a conversation he cannot commandeer must be distressing. Perhaps that was the purpose of Mussolini's aside. I don't imagine he was solicitous of my participation and kindly wished to draw me into the group. I am just a tool. I have the impression that he is uncomfortable with all this hilarity, as if he had not intended making a joke and fears it might detract from his dignity.

"Forgive my learned references," he says, reverting to German to explain the idiom. Another group of soldiers are taking their turn on the tarmac. Mussolini breathes deeply and says, "The Italian is a good soldier. He is resilient and energetic."

Given the Germans' well-known doubts about the Italian military, I can appreciate why he breathed deeply. This is a breathtaking statement, albeit true. Contrary to popular belief, Italians are not cowards and the country has a long tradition of insanely brave soldiers badly led and poorly supplied, a tradition the Duce is maintaining with the utmost rigor.

I can't see Hitler's face. He's watching the parade again, but his back appears to have stiffened. Glancing over my shoulder, I see Goebbels smirking at me. The Constipated Prick must sense the general inward smirking of the German delegation, for his next words are delivered in a manner that, even by his exacting standards, is particularly pompous.

"To make a people great," he says, "one must send them into battle. It is the best school for man. The stark reality of war stamps the . . . mark of nobility on those who have the . . . courage to fight. Only in bloody effort do the elementary . . . values of man reveal themselves in the full . . . light of the sun."

At this juncture Hitler gives voice again. His words are so softly spoken that for a moment I wonder whether they are his. Nobody outside his immediate vicinity can have heard. Even I, only two or three steps behind, wonder if I caught it correctly.

"Every generation," he says, "requires its own war. And I shall take care that this generation gets its war."

Mussolini is very still.

"The Italian people," he says, "are ready to face every challenge."

"And if not?"

Damn! Why do I do this? What possessed me? Actually, I know what possessed me. I've just realized that Mussolini is taken in by his own propaganda. I remember when he invaded Abyssinia, he promised his people a land so fecund that you just had to fling a handful of seed at the ground and the crops would sort themselves out. I'd never been to the Horn of Africa, but I had a fair idea its agricultural sector didn't work like that. Yet I suspect Mussolini had persuaded himself that that was precisely how it would work. Miracle said, miracle done. I say Italy is mightier than the established powers, ergo Italy *is* mightier than the established powers. At that stage, I don't think Hitler was seduced by his own propaganda. Later he would convince himself that he was the greatest military genius of all time, that the endless defeats had nothing to do with him, but were the work of his feckless generals. It was a neat reversal of the "November criminals" of 1918, the politicians who had purportedly betrayed the army by suing for peace. Once he was the main politician, the traitors were perforce elsewhere. He hadn't reached that point in 1938, but in Italy the black shirt had already worked its black magic. Mussolini believed in himself or made-believe that he believed in himself. Self-belief is generally thought a positive quality, but it's a precursor to solipsism. There's nothing wrong with solipsism as long as you keep it to yourself. But you don't want it seeping into politics. Seeing The Constipated Prick's capacity for speaking credulity into being, it had hit me that Italy was buggered. It was shock that made me open my mouth so injudiciously. *And if not*, indeed.

The dark little eyes turn to stare at me. Oh, my God! If he gets together with Goebbels. The Flatulent Windbag snickers, confirming that "the man who knows everything" is really the court jester. Meanwhile, the ducal chin is up, the chest out, and the back of the head is slipping off his shoulders as The Constipated Prick peers down at me. I'm not sure how he does this. I'm taller than him, but he's definitely looking down at me.

"If not . . ." he says, at length, ". . . I shall resign as an Italian."

He's not joking. He doesn't do jokes.

"Can you do that?"

"I can do anything . . . I am Il Duce."

The parade continues. Mussolini turns to seek confirmation of his martial competence in the nicely tailored trousers. The Flatulent Windbag bends forwards. *Hey up, Rover!* I step back. He shouldn't have eaten all that cake, no matter how décolleté the girl's outfit was.

CETOLOGY #4. TRICKS OF THE TRADE.

I don't suppose it's information that's very much in demand down at the careers advisory service, but it's worth asking, how do you become a Fascist dictator?

The basic procedure for acceding to office is fairly straightforward:

1. Lose a war—or if you can't unequivocally lose a war, contrive to lose the peace.
2. Feel hard done by.
3. Gather a group of misfits and ex-soldiers who know how to hurt people, regret the dwindling opportunities for doing so, and who miss the camaraderie of the army now that they are in civvies and proving to be rather inadequate people.
4. Wait for political, economic, and social upheaval to threaten chaos. If it doesn't, give it a nudge. At the very least, tell everyone that's what is happening.
5. Raise the spectre of a malevolent and scheming enemy intent on exploiting the chaos. So long as you are consistent in blaming everything on them, no matter how improbable it may be, who the enemy is doesn't really matter. Monotheistic faiths and alternative economic systems have proved popular of late, but historically the autocrat's favourite bugaboos have been other people's despots, other nations, other linguistic groups, other versions of

one's own religion, other coloured skins . . . well, you get the picture, anything identifiably "other."

6. Persuade vulnerable parts of the population that you are the solution.
7. Beat up anybody who begs to differ.
8. Ensure existing authorities think they can use you because you're too dim and vulgar to cope with their sophisticated cleverness, then use them because they are too clever and sophisticated by half.
9. Wait for the authorities to offer you power.
10. Orchestrate a little window dressing like a march on the capital (to suggest you seized power rather than got given it) or burning down parliament (to justify seizing any power you didn't get given).

Bingo! Dolfie's your dictator, Bennie's your boss. That basic ten-point plan is what can be deduced from the rise to power of both Hitler and Mussolini. It also helps to be associated with somebody older than you who has his own Fascistic tendencies and who can act as a role model or mask of respectability.

Mussolini had D'Annunzio, man of letters, ladies' man, man of war, self-proclaimed Superman (self-proclaimed archangel come to that—anything big and flashy he was ready to self-proclaim it), and potential rival until he conveniently "fell out of a window." I must confess, having sat through one of D'Annunzio's plays, 200 minutes (I counted every one of them) of rhetorical affectation and uninhibited pomposity, I was quite glad to hear that he had fallen out of a window. Had I been around at the time, I might have volunteered to push him myself.

For his part, Hitler had Ludendorff, quartermaster general and joint leader of the German armed forces from 1916 who, when it became clear that the war was lost, got himself a false beard and glasses and buggered off to Sweden, then blamed the civil authorities for his failure, and taught

Hitler the invaluable lesson that anybody keen on the sacrificial shedding of blood should be prudent about shedding their own.

Anything else that's required? Well, judging by the life stories of our principals, a doting mother and a difficult relationship with your dad help. Also you should emigrate to avoid military service, but then enlist in order to experience points one and two of the ten-point plan. You mustn't mind making a fuss, either. You can achieve a lot if you remember that most people will go to great lengths to avoid a scene. But behind the browbeating bluster, it's good to be insecure about yourself, so insecure that you need to employ everyone around you, and I mean everyone, like the entire nation, preferably the world if you can stretch to it, to bolster your sense of identity. It never does to have a dictator who feels good about himself.

Once in power, repeat points two to seven except change number four to read, *Persuade people that, in your absence, political, economic, and social upheaval will lead to chaos.* Also, keep talking, taking care to identify with your audience and tell them what they want to hear. Hitler only started to lose popularity when he stopped addressing the nation.

Concerning public appearances overall, only undertake activities at which you can excel. Hitler said: "Famous men look foolish when they participate in fields other than their own. Asked to go swimming, Bismarck said: *I think I can swim, but from me people would expect something of which I am not capable. So I'd rather not!* The Duce should heed this advice." He was right. Mussolini set great store by displaying his physical vitality. All that bare-chested threshing of wheat and thrashing about in the sea. Most unfortunate. One newsreel even showed him wrestling with a lion cub, a lion cub that, I am reliably informed, had had all its teeth pulled beforehand. By contrast, Hitler, who clearly fell well short of his own physical ideal, about five and a half inches short, was careful to avoid such antics and to play to his strengths in public, to wit crapping on and on and on.

Another tip from the top. After retiring from public life, D'Annunzio continued to pester Il Duce with advice and pleas for "donations" for his foundation, which were in truth little more than thinly disguised bribes. Asked about this, Mussolini said: "There are two ways of dealing with a rotten tooth. Either you extract the tooth or you fill it with gold. With D'Annunzio, I have chosen the latter treatment." It's a technique that typifies totalitarian regimes. Doling out the dosh to an old poet was small beer beside what went on elsewhere. Turning a blind eye to the venality of his subordinates gave The Constipated Prick another tool for controlling them. As for The Flatulent Windbag, he didn't care what his people did in their fiefdoms, so long as they left him free to do the gabbing and strategic thinking.

So that's it really. You keep on crapping on, try not to look like too much of a silly arse, and make judicious use of corruption. Oh, I nearly forgot. Make sure—and this is absolutely vital—make sure that there's always somebody else to blame when things go wrong. The Constipated Prick tended to blame the immaturity of the Italian people for his own failings; The Flatulent Windbag blamed anybody at hand, bunging in the Jews each time for good measure. And, of course, beat up anybody who begs to differ. That's always the default position in the dictator's handbook. When in doubt, beat somebody up.

One final handy hint: don't pay too much attention to reality, notably any reality conveyed by someone who understands financial or military affairs. This tactic won't help you maintain power, in fact it will be the cause of your downfall, but at least you'll enjoy yourself in the meantime. Simple, really.

Damn. I'm doing what I promised myself I wouldn't. I'm getting bitter and angry about these idiots who did such damage then and who continue to do so now, providing the clincher in my lovely daughter's contempt for her old man. But you carry this stuff around inside you (I mean me, not you) and you think it's under control, that the nightmare is behind you, then it comes pouring out again, all the guilt and misery accumulated through living. This is another thing that is not peculiar to my generation. Admittedly, we managed to make it all a bit sharper, a bit more piquant, a bit more humiliating in the eyes of our offspring, but something very similar will have happened to you by the time you are my age.

This is not cynicism or pessimism. For all the darkness with which we infect it, the world is a very lovely place, and living is nearly always better than unliving. The Flatulent Windbag knew this. In his *Table Talk*, he describes man as "the most dangerous microbe imaginable," but goes on to say how good life is. Here it is. "Nobody should deem life not worth living. The world possesses infinite riches for those who know how to enjoy their senses. Beauty always asserts its primacy. Our duty is to teach others to see what is lovely and wonderful in life, not to become prematurely ill-tempered and spiteful."

But it comes to us all one way or another. You'll learn this in time. No matter how successful the living, bits of you get chipped away, scarred, and warped by all the mistakes you make over the years, all the little compromises and then . . . well, it's like the graffito I saw last time I was in England: *Life is like being a pubic hair on a toilet seat. Sooner or later, you get pissed off.* In the meantime, there is much that is bright and shiny and well-designed and serves its purpose admirably. *Sehen sie, meine Herren.*

POSTCARD FROM THE PAST #13.

On the train to Naples. Hitler, Mussolini, me, and My Waitress. The propaganda department claims Mussolini is so popular that he needs no special protection. That's why his train is preceded by a suicide locomotive, why he wears bullet-proof corsets, why the Via Nomentana is sealed off when he leaves for work, and why the only other tenants tolerated near his town house are 200 Carabinieri and a troupe of monkeys— write your own punch line. Yet my inclusion as a guide suggests totalitarianism is not as totalitarian as it would like to think. As for your mother's job at the Palazzo Venezia, I know she could be very persuasive, but even the most cursory vetting ought to have had her on the first train into internal exile. Her particular form of resistance had not yet graduated to homicidal intent, but it wasn't far off.

She has just served drinks, a glass of milk for Mussolini, chamomile tea for Hitler, and a *caffé corretto* for me. It's too early in the morning for alcohol, but I feel I'm going to need this. I'm dying for a fag, too. Why I have been invited onto this special train still puzzles me. Her role is clear enough, being both decorative and functional. I am neither and even my designated task is limited without the prop of a painting or some artifact from the plastic arts.

When she served us, The Flatulent Windbag was all smiles and avuncular compliments. Given what we know about his family, "avuncular compliments" are not necessarily reassuring, but his manner was innocuous enough. The Constipated

Prick was something else: chin up, jaw out, chest inflated, eyes bulging, head swelling to dangerous dimensions. I could picture his inflamed pate going very red then bursting, which led me to wonder how anyone could have been so naive as to use "ejaculate" for "speak suddenly" (we loved those passages in books when we were kids, leafing through old novels for moments when the hero "ejaculated," generally in the most inappropriate company), which in turn reminded me of that line in *Martin Chuzzlewit* when the lovely young lady brushes her fingers across the church organist's keyboard: "She touched his organ, and from that bright epoch, even it, the old companion of his happiest hours, incapable as he had thought of elevation, began a new and deified existence."

Then My Waitress winked at me and I nearly fell off my chair.

By the time I'd recovered, she had gone and I was alone with the despots.

"I have a present for you, Duce," says Hitler. "A personal present," he adds, placing a book on the table. Given his fondness for the sound of his own voice, I imagine it must be a copy of *Mein Kampf*. But my supposition proves wrong.

Mussolini leans forward, lays his forearms on the table, and picks up the book. He looks startled, a characteristic accident of morphology, the tiny pupils lending his eyes a lunatic incredulity. He leans back, straightens his arms. He has no idea what the book is, can't see the title or read the author's name. Yet even here, perhaps especially here in front of the upstart whose starstruck request for a signed photograph he refused ten years ago but who is now looking a little less upstart and a little more up-and-started-and-streets-ahead-of-everyone-else, his vanity prevents The Constipated Prick putting on his glasses.

"I was thirteen," says Hitler, a bit breathlessly. I'm a bit breathless myself. He's just farted and I have the feeling the smell is worse than yesterday. "My chum Fritz Seidl saw me reading *The Last of the Mohicans* and told me Fenimore

Cooper wasn't nearly as good as May. *The Ride Through The Desert* was the first one I read. I was totally transported by it. I had to get all his other novels then, much to the detriment of my school grades." He chuckles at this memory. Mussolini nods, but clearly hasn't a clue what he is on about. "They opened my eyes to the world. I discovered geography through him, you know. And his characters! Old Shatterhand *is* the triumph of the will, you see. It's all in there. At night, I would read him by candlelight or with a magnifying glass under the moonlight. There are three universal works. Apart from the Bible, *Robinson Crusoe* and *Don Quixote* are the two most popular books in the world."

"I read *Don Quixote* when I was in prison," ejaculates The Constipated Prick. "I found it . . . extraordinarily amusing."

"Yes, yes," says The Flatulent Windbag. "Now, Defoe's book, you see, tells the history of mankind through one man's story. *Don Quixote*, meanwhile, is a brilliant satire on an extinct society. One Christmas, I was given an edition illustrated by Gustave Doré in a style of total genius. The third universal work is *Uncle Tom's Cabin*. I could also mention *Gulliver's Travels*. Each of these books contains a great basic idea. In our literature, we have nothing of the kind, but May's work does reach a fairly high level."

With which, he stops abruptly, looking expectantly at his host. The Duce does not move, but there is something unusual in his expression, something childlike, tinged with hurt. He is either deeply stirred, or doesn't know what to say, or has already had one glass of milk too many today and the faecal impaction is proving painful.

"In my youth I was very fond of . . . Schiller's *William Tell*," he says. "I tried writing dramatic works myself . . . but never finished them. I wrote to develop my . . . ideas. Sketching the plot was more important than . . . getting the plays produced. *The Unlit Lamp* was a . . . social drama after Zola, describing the fate of . . . a penniless blind child. In *The Struggle of the Motors*, an industrial secret was . . .

stolen and, through this motif, I explored the struggle of . . . labour against capital."

Hitler scrutinizes his host, like a bird watching a worm. Reminiscences about juvenilia are not what he wants. There is a slightly embarrassing silence. To bridge the awkward moment, I tell Mussolini about Karl May. You won't have heard of him, my dear. Hardly anybody has outside Germany. Yet he is the most popular German writer ever. Sold more than one hundred million books, I believe.

Born into a family of poor weavers, May trained to be a teacher, but his career was cut short due to an unfortunate propensity for pocketing other people's money. Jailed for fraud, he became a trustee of the prison library, where he learned that living inside your head was a very good way of dodging a disagreeable reality. Freed and fortified with a taste for fantasy, he became a hack writer, churning out colportage novels and stories for the periodicals. After several years of penury, fame came with the publication of his *Collected Travel Accounts*, above all the Winnetou stories, recounting the adventures of Old Shatterhand, a German frontiersman and blood brother to the eponymous Indian chief.

Mistaking the *Travel Accounts* for reportage rather than fiction, readers wrote to the author as if he were Old Shatterhand, a misunderstanding that May did nothing to discourage. On the contrary, he started dressing up as Old Shatterhand and took to the lecture circuit, where a rather precarious hand-to-mouth existence was magicked into an altogether more commodious adventure.

May had never been to the places in his books. The descriptions came from maps and travelogues. But with his newfound wealth he did visit the countries he had written about. And, confronted with the rude intrusion of reality into his dream world, he promptly had a nervous breakdown. In fact, never a man to do things by halves, he had two of them.

So that's Karl May for you, a fantasist writing about places he had never been and experiences he had never known, a fantasist who promoted himself by playing the part of his fictional hero, a fantasist whose make-believe was so vivid that he mistook his fancies for reality and went barmy when reality failed to cooperate; to wit, someone who believed his own lies: *I am not a little man of no significance trapped in a world beyond my mastery. I am the master who can imagine into being the world I want.* And he was Hitler's favourite author.

There was more to it than that, though. May wrote about the American frontier, about westward expansion. Remember, "I discovered geography through him." What was westward expansion all about? It was about land, living space, *Lebensraum*. The options for westward expansion were limited in Germany. But eastward there was rich land full of raw materials, rolling prairies and great plains just waiting to become the breadbasket of the Third Reich, all of it occupied by a bunch of backward, undeserving Slavs who didn't know what to do with the potential wealth below their feet. You can see how May's books might have appealed to Hitler.

Klaus Mann got very hot and bothered about May, blaming him for everything Hitler became. That's unfair. May was also the favourite author of millions of other Germans, most of whom did not spend their waking hours obsessing about world domination, among them Albert Einstein, who enjoys a different reputation among the ranks of "Germans who have had an impact on the twentieth century." Moreover, as a result of his sobering discovery that reality did not accord with his dream world, May had sufficient strength of character to pull himself together without medical assistance. He then set himself the modest task of saving mankind by preaching pacifism and writing convolute allegories about the nature of being.

Of course, that's not the version of May's works I gave Mussolini. Instead, I spoke about the portrayal of a simple life close to nature and the nobility of the novels' principal characters, describing Old Shatterhand's martial and moral qualities, the fist that can smash a man's jaw with one punch, the fidelity, the fighting skill, the compassion, the courage, the goodness menaced by scheming enemies, above all the determination to overcome insuperable odds. I'm not sure The Constipated Prick was listening (he looked pained again), but The Flatulent Windbag was positively purring.

"I had never heard of him," says Mussolini. "To practise my . . . German I used to read . . . Klopstock . . . *Der Messias.*"

"Good God!" I am genuinely shaken by this. Groping your way into a foreign language with the works of a poet who considered classical epics unacceptably pithy . . . it doesn't bear thinking about. "Nobody reads Klopstock! Not after the first few lines, at least."

"No. It was the most . . . tedious work I ever happened upon." Even the memory seems to grieve him, causing him to grimace. "Otherwise, in German I read Goethe, Heine, Platen, but never . . . May. You will excuse me."

He is not apologising for the puzzling lacuna in his literary culture. He rises to leave, rises rather abruptly, too. He's got a gripey tummy. The way he stands is a little too stiff, a little too much at an incline to indicate a comfortable gut, and he forgets the book on the table when he goes. He has more pressing concerns than popular westerns. Once his host has gone, The Flatulent Windbag lets off a quiet one. *Hey up, Rover!*

"It is a riddle to me that anyone can be ignorant of Karl May," he says.

I'd been hoping to keep my mouth shut, but he does not elaborate, and is clearly waiting for The Man Who Knows Everything to explain. I suggest his choice of words is revealing, that *rätsel* (a riddle, puzzle or mystery) is the key. Westerns are not in fashion. May's books are better suited to a period of industrialization and urbanization when people feel they are losing contact with the natural world. In these uncertain times, however, the reading public prefers the murder mystery because they want a wise detective to come and put things right, solving all their problems by proposing a simple solution that will restore order to a chaotic world.

"This is what I keep telling the Duce," says Hitler.

"It is?" I find it troubling that these banalities about the popularity of Agatha Christie, Dorothy Sayers, and Ngaio Marsh should endorse the fraternal counsel shared by tyrants.

"You must always be consistent in identifying the culprit," he continues. "You cannot have more than one murderer, more than one villain. This is as true in politics as it is in mystery novels. The art of leadership consists in focusing the attention of the people on a single enemy. One must make different foes appear to belong to one category."

"Oh, that's not what I meant," I say, and I'm actually laughing, poor nincompoop that I am. Take note, my dear. There is no stage of life at which you do not look back ten years later without cringing at your own imbecility. This is worth remembering when one is tempted to be categorical. "That's not what I meant," I say. "In any case, you *can* have more than one murderer, as it happens. In *Murder On The Orient Express* for example . . ."

But that's as far as I get. An extraordinary change has come over my genial companion. Without any warning, he is up on his feet and he is shouting. I am so shocked that the actual words don't register, but it has something to do with my not knowing what I mean because this was what I had to mean because this was what he had written and so it had to be what was true. Only much later did I realize that the phrase about the art of leadership was a quote from *Mein Kampf*, a book he seemed to know by heart, which can't have been good for his sanity.

You know this, you've seen the caricatures. Only it's no caricature. It's him and he means it. Like all clichés, the lampoon images of The Constipated Prick and The Flatulent Windbag are premised on observable truth. Mussolini *is* a pompous prick, Hitler *is* a raving maniac. That's not all they are. But enough of what they are for them to go down in history under those guises.

That simple negation, that blithe and, in retrospect, idiotic assertion that *that's not what I meant*, and his whole torso is trembling and his cheeks are flushed and his forehead is fissured with distended veins, and he's striding up and down waving his arms about, spewing staccato phrases, spittle flying, pitch rising, short little legs stamping up and down in frustration at the waywardness of a world that refuses to accommodate itself to the patterns he requires. And he's shouting in my face, brandishing his fist, his fetid breath flecked with saliva while I cower under the onslaught, not because I'm scared as yet, there's not time for that, but because I am overwhelmed by the swiftness and excess of the change, which is so farcical that it should be funny, but it's not, not even for me in my quest for less mess.

And then, just as suddenly and unexpectedly as it began, he stops. He straightens the tunic of his jacket, smoothes the lick of hair, bites each of his nails in turn as if checking they're all still there, and sits down. The change is so abrupt that I cannot say whether the rage was real or staged. It seemed real, but the rapidity of the shift between states suggests anger is a tool to be turned on when necessary. He brushes a speck of imaginary dust from the book on the table and glances toward the end of the carriage. An aide is at the door. He doesn't seem surprised. As soon as he sees I am not harming his Führer, he withdraws.

This is not meant to happen. This is not what Hitler does to unimportant people like me. He treats us with decorum. It's people in power, the privileged who have had advantages he never knew, the dignitaries and diplomats and aristocrats and generals who stand in his way, these are the ones subjected to his famous rages. With people like me, he is polite and kind. Amend that. Just so long as we do not contradict him. Do not discuss, do not disagree. Say yes and furnish evidence to support his assertions: *Sehen sie, meine Herren.*

He smiles at me, almost twinkling. I do my best to twinkle back.

"You intellectuals," he says. "Your understanding of the real world is inversely proportionate to your learning. You know everything, but cannot see what is important." He speaks softly; his voice has lost its habitual rasping quality. "Focus is everything. Reading, for example, has a different meaning for me than you. People like you read all the time. You know a lot, but don't understand what is useful. Reading is not an end in itself, you see, but a means to an end. One has to identify what is useful and worth remembering, and discard everything that does not accord with one's needs. That's the secret. The art of reading consists in remembering the essentials and forgetting nonessentials. Otherwise you end up with a mishmash of chaotic notions."

It's not my way of reading. To my mind, this is a vicious way of reading, eliminating all those risks of contagion one looks for in a book, the glorious business of contaminating oneself with other people's thoughts and other lives and other values. He reads to confirm his prejudices. He's probably like that with people, too, extracting what is required and discarding the rest. Yet people are not disposable. Well, they are. If nothing else, Hitler taught us that. But we've got to pretend otherwise. Anything less would be intolerable.

The Ride Through The Desert still lies on the table where Mussolini left it, suggesting something else: that once Hitler forms an opinion, it never changes. At thirteen, he decided May was The Great German Author and he has stuck with that assessment ever since. Such immutable convictions make life simpler. No matter how often you twist the chamber, the kaleidoscope will show the same pattern. If you've got half a mind to see the world like that, you're home and dry. Half a mind is all you need. But like language, a mind that does not change is dead.

I thought all this, but I didn't like to say. You don't want to upset people.

Discretion is duly rewarded. From a drawer in a davenport beside the table, he produces a copy of *Winnetou*, which he gives me with an air of great melancholy. It's downstairs in the cellar if you want to see it.

POSTCARD FROM THE PAST #14.

We're on the platform at Naples train station and I'm glad of it. I need the fresh air. Hitler's meteorism got worse as the journey progressed (something to do with the Italian food, I imagine) and, by the time we arrived, the atmosphere in his stateroom was unspeakable. We're on the platform and the crowds are pressing against the barriers waving their Nazi flags. I consider lighting a cigarette, but think better of it when the Führer bends over. A solemn tot wearing a polka-dot red dress has slipped between the policemen to stand in front of the despots, right arm raised in the Roman salute. It should be heartbreaking, yet it's as heartwarming as the picture of any pretty child pretending to be an adult.

Hitler crouches, so they are face to face. He touches her cheek. He's good with children. Ruled by tantrums and raw egoism, he retains a bridge back into the world of unfathomable frustrations and the clamouring need to assert oneself. Corsets notwithstanding, Mussolini squats, chucks the child under the chin. He gets up quite quickly afterwards, but he's still smiling. Somehow, though, the smile is less convincing than his companion's. He is a father and grandfather, a fond parent if the propaganda is to be believed. It's not all lion cubs. Newsreels show him playing with children, too—though whether their teeth have been pulled or not, I wouldn't know. But the middle-aged bachelor, the man who hosts tea parties for the village children at Berchtesgaden, doling out the cream cakes like he's fattening them up for the oven, is more direct, more open, more natural. The mask Mussolini has constructed for himself gets between him and his emotions. Maybe this is a good thing.

It remains a puzzle to me that I felt more contempt for Mussolini than I did for Hitler. Everybody says Mussolini wasn't so bad. And it's true, he wasn't. We can ascribe something in the order of a million deaths to his policies. If you care to play at accountancy, which is the way these things work nowadays, by the standards of the twentieth century, a million dead is a poor showing. Once again, rubbish dictator. Couldn't even kill people properly. But that wasn't why I despised him. I think it was because he embodied the worst sort of vulgarity, the life-negating type. Hitler was more supple, perhaps because the more naturally devious of the two.

He rises, turns to speak to his host as the tot is ushered back to proud parents. It's hard to tell, but I'm willing to bet there's a tear in his eye. Take note. Doubtless, you are repulsed by the image of these men dallying with a child, but they are men not monsters, and the monstrous things they are to do have barely begun in 1938. You probably picture them in black and white, codified by celluloid into a past that is a little unreal. But they lived in a world that was not monochrome, a world as colourful and quick as yours, with all the same variations of warmth and light and fluidity. Mussolini seems to be making a conscious effort to control himself, too. Control is a key word for these people. They want to control everything. But when you try to control things, you end up killing them. That's what's happening to their emotions. Mussolini once described Hitler as a *sentimentalone*, a big old softie. It sounds bizarre, perverse, but it reflects a bizarre and perverse truth, that even the most brutal men need to nurture an illusion of feeling, and illusions are more theatrical than reality.

At the entrance to the station, a large crowd awaits the dictators. The Führer raises his arm to salute them. *"Sta controllando se fuori piove!"* comes a cry from behind us, a woman's voice. *He's checking to see if it's raining outside.* I turn to look. The security men from OVRA are bristling with indignation, but they are too slow to catch sight of the culprit. I have an eye for these things, though. A slender figure in a dark dress with a white collar below curly brown hair disappears behind the crowd on the platform. My Waitress!

POSTCARD FROM THE PAST #15.

Nowadays when I find myself in places where there's nothing much to do but watch people, I feel a tremendous compassion for the crowds that cross my path. Their foibles, frustrations, and deficiencies are so touchingly transparent. Sounds daft, I know, but the older you get, the more important empathy becomes. Love looms larger, too. All the superfluities are pared away. In 1938 though, I was less tolerant of other people's shortcomings, not least of a failure to be presentably turned out. This had nothing to do with snobbery. I knew that a peasant can look as elegant as a peer. It's not the cut of the cloth or the cost of the fabric, but the way you wear things. If you want clothes to be more than a supplementary skin, you need to look like you at least meant to put them on. Anything less is a mandate for derision. In this respect, as in so many others, Hitler and Mussolini did not bring out the best in me.

If this were a proper report of the Naples trip, I'd detail the hullabaloo, like the naval manoeuvres designed to demonstrate Italy's mastery of the Mediterranean. I told you about the synchronized submarines, but that was only the most celebrated moment. There were also dummy torpedoes (never was an adjective more pertinently employed), fake attacks on the dignitaries' boat (an honest foreshadowing of Italy's preparedness for war), and an obsolete battleship was bombed (doubtless to the distress of the navy bods, who must have been uncomfortably familiar with the terminology of obsolescence). As for the cannon salvoes (I'm talking about the big guns here, though our guest's guts were definitely deteriorating and he put up a good show given that he was all on his own against the entire Italian navy), there were so many damned guns blasting away that it was like a microwave war, six years of conflict crammed into a single afternoon.

What else? Oh, yes, I should have mentioned it before, but at the station there was a bloody great band huffing and puffing and sawing away at a medley of Fascist anthems (you can imagine what a magnificent musical extravaganza that was), and then there was the mindless braying of the Neapolitan crowds, who I imagine were competing to outshout the Romans, and there was even a pod of priests fluttering their fat little paws from the windows of a church. We also had to endure a Fascist "demonstration" in the Piazza del Plebiscito. I never did work out what they were demonstrating, but it could have been toasters for all I cared.

Anyway, you get the idea. I wasn't exactly gruntled by my day in Naples. Everyone else appeared to enjoy themselves though. I even saw Heydrich smile, which was pretty scary. He was the one the Czechs had the good taste to assassinate in 1942, a man . . . no, an entity so lacking in natural warmth that he resembled liquid helium poured into a uniform. Even Hitler, who knew a thing or two about indifference to human suffering, was sufficiently impressed to observe that Heydrich had an iron heart. Seeing this sliver of ice on legs smile was enough to give a grown man a fit of the screaming abdads. It's not something I want to dwell on. In fact, none of the conventional history is something I want to dwell on. Instead, my postcard shows Hitler coming out of the San Carlo opera house, where we've been watching a very indifferent production of *Aida*, in which the not hugely talented soprano nearly got brained by the crumbling set, an accident that some uncharitable observers qualified as entirely justifiable criticism on the part of the scenery.

I'm already outside, having sloped off for a couple of gaspers before returning to that smoke-free, fart-filled carriage.

As a result, I see him at one remove. He's walking a bit funny, almost mincing, his legs crossing over one another, toes pointing outward, like he's on a tightrope. At first I find it puzzling, but then it crosses my mind that he's trying to do something that he really shouldn't be trying to do. He's trying to be elegant. This is most ill-advised.

Remember, short legs, big hips, narrow shoulders, large torso, concave chest. Nobody's perfect and nobody with any sense minds the imperfections of others. But imperfection does entail a degree of discretion. You don't swan about drawing attention to your defects. They declare themselves readily enough.

Hitler knows this. In the *Table Talk*, he says: "*Is there anything more preposterous than a Berliner in leather shorts? A Scotsman can wear his national dress in the best society, but anyone wearing a Tyrol costume in Berlin looks like he's at the carnival. It was with great reluctance that I stopped wearing leather shorts. Throughout my youth, I never wore anything else. But as a political leader, I had to change clothes several times a day to fit the psychology of my visitors. The Prussians wouldn't take me seriously in shorts.*" Painful though it is to contemplate, Hitler loved lederhosen. But he knew that nobody, ever, anywhere, no matter how politically nimble and no matter how gullible the population, ever won power wearing leather shorts. It's one of those things that has never happened and never will happen. There is some justice in life. You can't govern in lederhosen. Especially not with knees like that. It's not done. So he renounced them.

And yet, here he is, sashaying along in a manner meant to convey a kind of gazelle-like grace. He's not carrying on like this because he wants to impress My Waitress. She has wisely buggered off, sparing herself the sight of what has actually prompted him to come over all soft-shoe and willowy, namely the fatal fact that he has allowed himself to be dressed up by some wardrobe flunkey (who should be given a prize or sent to the camps forthwith according to your political views) in . . . wait for it . . . white tie and tails!

I've never seen anything like it and I've been about a bit, seen a few things, not all of them pleasant. But the sight of Hitler trussed up in tails and top hat, nothing can prepare you for a spectacle like that. The impact is so very far from Fred Astaire that contrasting the two would be like comparing a medieval jousting lance with a plastic swizzle stick. The basic concept is the same, but there all resemblance ends. There's something about the way he wears the suit that makes him look like precisely what he is, a self-made man, only in all the wrong ways, cobbled together in a garden shed while more responsible parties had their backs turned. I don't know how he does it. The outfit is probably tailor-made, but there's something about that body that would drive your average draper to batter himself to death with his pin cushion sooner than unfurl his tape measure.

It may be trivial to ridicule a dictator's sartorial deficiencies, but given the enormity of what these people represent, we have a right, even a duty, to assert a little triviality. Trivial is a good word. It comes from the Latin for common or vulgar, but like many words it is a metaphor, its source being *trivium*, a point where three roads meet. The truly trivial is a place of congress where travellers who make no pretence at being anything other than run-of-the-mill gather to exchange information about their experiences, detailing the dangers and delights, the pleasures and pains that await us in the ordinary course of our ordinary voyage through life.

In 1938, being ordinary required a degree of courage. I realize that such bravery may seem exiguous beside the daring displayed during the years that ensued, but it is no less valid. Remember, this was the era of the *Übermensch*, a Nietzschean term filched by the reactionary-revolutionaries of the early twentieth century. They debased what was actually quite a complex idea, stripping it down to a rudimentary my-bollocks-are-bigger-than-yours ethos, defined for Hitler by race and survival of the fittest, and for Mussolini by . . . well, by bollocks really. *Übermensch* can be translated as Overman, Above-Human, Superhuman, or simply Superman, which is my preferred option, as it conjures images of dicey characters in phone booths whipping their underpants on over their trousers.

If Hitler and Mussolini were *Übermenschen*, there was no way I wanted to be anything other than a member of the *untermenschen*, that is an under-man or a subman, in other words ORDINARY. Being ordinary was an act of resistance in itself, a way of maintaining distance and preserving a speck of self-respect. I grant you, it's not the sort of resistance to have a daughter declaring, "Ooh, what a big brave daddy you were," but it does lend a little dignity and set one aside from the desperately striving dickheads whose self-proclaimed superiority let them dispense with conventions like kindness, caring, and not killing other people.

But even being an *untermensch* wouldn't have excused wearing an outfit like that with such surpassing graceless-ness. What did explain if not excuse it was the fact that the wearer was the most *über* of *übermenschen,* because if there was one thing Hitler and Mussolini had in common it was their capacity for picking inappropriate clothing. You'd have thought The Arse's Uniform, the *fez,* and lederhosen would have been enough to be going on with, but these were ambitious men, reluctant to be outdone in any domain. For the Bierkeller Putsch, Hitler wore a tailcoat so ill fitting that even his admirers recalled how ludicrous he looked. As for what he did to a mackintosh, a raincoat just seemed to pine away the moment it was draped over his shoulders. Mussolini meanwhile was a past master at this stuff, attending his own simulated coup in morning coat, white spats, and a bowler hat, recklessly having himself photographed on a sled wear-ing nothing but a peaked cap, sweatpants, and lace-up boots, and ordering a white dress uniform, which was not a good idea for a bloke who was nothing if not short in the body and broad about the midriff. He also wasn't above donning a Tyrolean Alpine hat, like Pinocchio, which one would like to think he wore in a spirit of playful irony, but I suspect not. Anybody capable of wearing a Tyrolean Alpine hat is beyond irony. When it comes to the history of fashion, the part played by the Tyrol is not a glorious one.

So, if you want a definition of the *über übermenschen,* they were blokes who dressed like bloody idiots. That's not all they were. But it's a useful starting point. *Vestis virum facit* was Erasmus's adage, the source of "clothes maketh the man," in which case Hitler and Mussolini were a couple of clowns. Why didn't we laugh then? Well, some of us did. But not loud enough, not long enough, not hard enough, and by the time others realized they ought to be laughing loud, long and hard, it was too late and precious few people were inclined to laugh at all. Even if more of us had been laughing, it probably wouldn't have made a difference.

Fascism was mass theatre and, like all theatre back then, the performances were stylized, over the top, and hammy. They look and sound ridiculous today. They did then, too. But they were performances done in the idiom required by contemporary audiences. And the act was deliberately provocative. Doing their silly walks, putting on the funny voices, the Fascists were daring us malcontents to laugh. You've seen the newsreels, you've heard the roars. Who could laugh loud enough to drown out 100,000 voices bawling *Duce! Duce!?* Who could out-chuckle a half-million strong chant of *Sieg Heil!?* Try disrupting a bunch of children at a *Punch and Judy* show and see how far you get. That's about the level of it, that's what those balcony speeches were like, only without the sand and ice cream.

So the message on this postcard is simple. No matter how preposterous they looked, The Flatulent Windbag and The Constipated Prick were peddling a product people wanted and it seemed that nothing could distract from that. Not even the trichology.

CETOLOGY #5. TRICHOLOGY.

Meteorism, monorchism, trichology . . . there are a lot of obscure words here, a fault for which I have two excuses. First, no study can take itself seriously until it develops a vocabulary that is impenetrable to the uninitiated. A visit to any good library will confirm this. No branch of any academic discipline has ever been sufficiently secure in itself to forgo gobbledygook. The more opaque the lexis, the more highly esteemed the field. Nowadays the dialects of some disciplines are so rarefied that even their practitioners no longer understand what they are saying. Attend a vernissage and you'll soon see what I mean. It's painful to watch aficionados of modern art talking trade. Sometimes I fear they are about to swallow their own heads. Hitlussolinics or Mutlerism or whatever it is we are doing here is not excepted from The General Theory of Inscrutable Terminology.

Gratuitous incomprehensibility is not, however, the sole reason for using obscure words. Obscure words also describe obscure corners of human being. Admittedly, any idea that cannot be expressed in words a five-year-old child would understand is probably a heap of steaming horse manure. But that does not mean the words a five-year-old child does not understand are redundant. For one thing, they take up less space.

Trichology is a branch of dermatological science dedicated to the systematic study and analysis of hair, hair loss, hair disorders, and the health of the scalp for academic, medical, cosmetic, and forensic purposes (you see what I mean about less space). In this instance the matter has more to do with hairstyling than hair health, but there are sufficient follicular and moral disorders involved to excuse the conceit. What, we must ask ourselves, is in a haircut?

Well, with Mussolini, obviously not a lot. Hair patterns are normally inherited from the mother. I mean through the maternal line. No man, no matter how proudly hirsute, would want his mum's chest lagged with a copious pelt of fur. But judging by photos, The Constipated Prick's alopecia was passed onto him by his father, Alessandro. Tellingly, the principal cause of hair loss is an excess of testosterone, a hormone that is basically all about bollocks. You can see where this is leading, can't you?

In 1903, when he was in Switzerland evading conscription, Mussolini was arrested for advocating a strike. In the mugshots, he has a decent head of hair with a perky quiff perched above the brow. But by 1917, when a change of heart found him fighting in the Italian army, the forehead is already a little high. Come the March on Rome in 1922, his hair has slipped down the back of his head and it's clearly not going to be climbing back on top again.

Being half bald can't have been easy for a man who dismissed lakes as a stupid compromise between rivers and the ocean. Nonetheless, he tolerated the situation for another decade until what was left of his hair turned white, at which point he took drastic action. He kidnapped a barber. Actually, I don't know if sequestration was involved first time round, but thereafter he didn't want to risk having the same man brandishing a razor about his head every morning, so he had barbers picked up at random and brought in to shave the ducal bristles. He still didn't leave anything to chance, though. The hairdresser was watched by an armed guard, while Mussolini kept a cocked pistol in his lap under his bib.

This was a very Fascist solution. Not the gun under the apron, though that was Fascist, too, but the idea of shaving the entire head to conceal incipient baldness and make one-self look more virile. That is the totalitarian way, when in doubt wipe everything out. It was the technique employed in Italy's colonial ventures. They displayed none of the subtlety of the British who contrived to have inconvenient foreigners starve themselves to death, neither did they opt for that cunning French technique of "educating" people into submission, or even the Belgian system of dismembering dark people who didn't work hard enough. No, the Italians just went barging in and murdered everybody, then claimed that those who happened to have survived had been liberated. A clean sweep and a clear scalp, that was the Fascist way.

In the case of The Flatulent Windbag, alopecia might have been desirable, not least because he was described by the racial hygienist, Max Von Gruber, as having "the head of an inferior, crossbred type." Even his own evangelists reckoned Hitler's head wasn't up to scratch, so baring all might have spoiled his appeal and made living in Europe in the coming years more pleasant and less perilous for a good many people. Sadly, the follicles were in fine fettle, dissembling the inferiority, and furnishing our man with that famous forelock and the dab of philtrum felt.

It's odd how neutral things can be tainted with negative meaning. A Sanskrit symbol for peace is inverted into an emblem of hate, a bundle of rods becomes the catch-all curse of "Fascist," the thousand-year career of the name Adolf is terminated in a decade, and the toothbrush moustache is turned into the personification of evil. The forelock remains relatively unsullied. Any number of dashing young men will have something similar flopping across the forehead. But the moustache! It's the most potent patch of facial hair known to man, an ideographic gift to graffiti artists and mischievous children. And it was invented by the Americans.

The nineteenth century was the golden age of the moustache. You had your Handlebar and the Pencil, plus the Walrus, the Imperial, the Stromboli, the Horseshoe, the

Fantastico, and that ultimate symbol of finger-twirling villainy, the Kaiser—that's the one with the fiddly bits at the ends as opposed to the more voluminous *Kaiserbart*, which was an Imperial with knobs on it. But by the end of the nineteenth century, the United States couldn't be doing with all these fancy Old World lip furnishings. Great Americans like General Burnside, Mark Twain, Wyatt Earp, Edgar Allen Poe, and Teddy Roosevelt had all boasted distinctive whisker arrangements. Now, though, the nation needed something that would reflect the simplicity and standardization being promoted by assembly-line America. So they invented the toothbrush moustache, which was neat, economical, and very low maintenance. It was the Tin Lizzie of moustaches. Anyone could have one, any colour you liked, as long as it was black. And like everything else that came off the assembly line, they exported it. There was a tussle in Germany between the toothbrush and the *Kaiserbart*, but when the toothbrush was taken up by a debonair young infantry officer who became a national idol in the course of a transcontinental motor race, its future seemed assured. Then Hitler came along.

Initially, Hitler did not favour the newfangled fashion from overseas. He didn't opt for the full *Kaiserbart* like his dad, but pictures from the First World War show something remarkably Kaiser-ish with distinct pointy bits. However, pointy bits were a liability on the Western Front. Hitler was told to clip his moustache tips because they breached the seal on his gas mask—and if anyone was in need of a gas mask, this was the man. Would that his superior officers had favoured something more flamboyant! I'm not just being flippant. There's a theory that Hitler's war experiences were so harrowing that he went off his head (a reasonable, even laudable response in the circumstances), after which a man who had shown no leadership qualities whatsoever, and who had not been notably anti-Semitic, was transformed into the charismatic chief of a homicidal movement targeting Jews. Big whiskers might have saved lives.

As for the political impact, would Hitler's public appearances have been less compelling if he had kept his tips or taken to the podium with a bare upper lip? Probably not. But I wouldn't mind betting the moustache was a shrewd diplomatic move. I remember when it was "a Charlie Chaplin moustache." I remember how silly it looked when pictures of Hitler first appeared in the international press. But I believe he knew that looking silly now would make others look silly later. Time and again, the people negotiating with Hitler underestimated him. He was a little clown, like the Little Tramp. What if Chamberlain, Dollfuss, Schuschnigg, Beneš, and Daladier were unable to shake off the suspicion that they were dealing with a comic turn, that any moment now the pratfall would come and their preposterous opponent would be hit round the back of the head by a plank? These things happen sometimes.

POSTCARD FROM THE PAST #16.

The *Mostra Augustea della Romanità* at the *Palazzo delle Esposizioni*. Law, leisure, religion, industry, education, decorative arts, fashion, furniture, numismatics, mores, maritime and military technology . . . no facet of Roman civilization has been overlooked. I am beginning to suspect that this exhibition tells us rather more about ancient Rome than I care to know. I'm tempted to make a jest about the jakes when we round a corner and come to the hygiene section.

"And to think, if Bolshevism had triumphed," murmurs the Führer. I don't believe he is referring specifically to the classical plumbing. For all his flatulence, he is not fixated on the toilet facilities. Rather, the observation is ritual, an allusion to the manifold glories of antiquity that the Bolsheviks would, presumably out of sheer philistinism, have vandalized had The Constipated Prick not done his constipated prick stuff back in the twenties.

There is a whole gang of us today, so I am saved from the personal attentions of the principals and only overhear this remark because the group happens to have clustered together beside a diagram depicting the system of sewers feeding the *Cloaca Maxima*. I say "saved" though it's possible that proximity to Windy and Dicky might not be such a bad thing, given that in their stead I have got stuck between Alfred Rosenberg and Karl Brandt, in whose company the term *Cloaca Maxima* takes on an altogether more personal significance.

I mentioned them earlier. Rosenberg was the sorry piece of work who considered himself the intellectual among the Nazis, which may not seem like a great boast, but did inspire him to pen several works outlining the ideological foundations of the movement, works of such stupefying boredom that even the most devout Nazis were compelled to skip to the end to find out what happened. What happened was that Rosenberg got hanged at Nuremberg (largely, I suspect, because his prosecutors had been obliged to labour through his oeuvre) and a very good thing, too. So did Karl Brandt and that was an even more desirable outcome. He was Hitler's personal physician, not the needle-wielding charlatan, but the True Believer who listened to the creed with the close attention of the HMV dog peering into its gramophone trumpet, except without the critical faculty displayed by the dog.

"It will, of course, be damnably difficult." Mussolini is not, inspired by the diagram, offering an opinion on his next bowel movement, but responding to something his guest has said. I didn't catch what, but it seems to concern a confederation of European states uniting the continent as it had been in the days of the Roman Empire. "In America, it is . . . much easier. They have only one language and their shared history is . . . short. But in Europe, each nation has its own . . . character, its own tongue, its own . . . culture. And in each nation, a proportion of these features is totally . . . original, which . . . generates resistance to any sort of fusion."

"It is a Herculean task," says Hitler, "but once we establish the proper conditions of racial purity, where one is born will be of no importance. You'll see. It will be like all this," he declares, gesturing at the *Cloaca Maxima*. "What boldness! What grandeur! These men were giants. Imperial history must be our model. It is the greatest epic of all time. Sadly, the imperial history of Germany has been neglected by our great writers. The best Schiller could do was celebrate a Swiss crossbowman. As for the English, they had Shakespeare, but the history of his nation furnished him with nothing but idiots and lunatics to serve as heroes."

Mention of the English seems to irritate Mussolini. He snorts, then shakes back the cuffs of his jacket, as if they are chafing his wrists. Sensitive to the change of mood, Hitler makes some disparaging comments about the English, noting that pride is the only thing at which they excel and that is premised solely on the possession of India. Mussolini is mollified. He even smiles when Hitler goes on to observe that, in England, culture is the privilege of good society and that the English love music—but their love is not returned.

"Music," says Mussolini, "is stimulating if . . . taken sparingly, but too much induces . . . nervous fatigue. It is a toxic drug that is beneficial in small doses and . . . deadly in large ones."

"Then we must send our orchestras to England," says Hitler, "with strict instructions to play *Der Ring der Nibelungen* in its entirety."

He's on fine form today and his quip about the tin-eared English inspires his companions. You won't find what follows funny, my dear. One of the few things your mother and I agreed on was that your education should be scrupulously internationalist. But back in the thirties, casual talk of stereotypes was commonplace. Mussolini starts it with one of his customary boasts.

"Blindfolded, I could . . . identify the music of Germany, Italy, France, or Russia. The language of music is . . . universal but its expression is national. Thus the music of Slovenia is barbarous and . . . derivative. They have stolen it from other people and, being lumbering . . . bumpkins, destroyed it."

I forget who spoke next, but before long assorted sycophants were jockeying for position, chipping in with snide comments about other nations. As I recall, the Poles were said to be stupid, idle, and vain, the Swiss were dismissed as hotel-keepers, the Russians derided as anarchists who reckoned vodka the mainstay of civilization, the Hungarians were vilified as poseurs, the Dutch were contaminated by Malay blood, and the Scandinavians were deemed so far beyond the pale that they were simply vermin.

The only quote I noted concerns the Ukrainians: "Best not teach them to read," said Hitler. "They won't want us taunting them with learning. We'll give them coloured beads and bright scarves, all the gewgaws colonial peoples like." This was greeted with considerable hilarity by all except Mussolini and Ciano, who seemed alarmed by the implication that the Ukrainians might soon be a colonial people administered by Germans rather than Russians.

You will find this banter hard to understand, but it's worth making the effort, for it was through such reductive typecasting that people who were not incapable of compassion persuaded themselves there was a kind of hierarchy to humanity that justified eliminating some of the lower rungs on the ladder. Even those of us who were not contaminated by deranged ideologies were touched by the sad fantasy of Social Darwinism that declared survival of the fittest was the law of *all* things, not merely species, but nations and races, too. This was a banality at the beginning of the twentieth century. The fundamentalism with which the Nazis applied the idea was not. But the basic notion infected everyone and everything.

We move on, Hitler expatiating on the kinship of Italy and Germany, their respective languages forged by rebels (I presume he means Dante and Luther), the nations unified by one man despite dynastic interests and the opposition of the pope. He also had a bizarre idea that . . . well, I didn't really understand it and consequently remember it almost word for word.

"The Romans loathed crossing the Alps," he says. "But the Germanic peoples were very keen on crossing them—in the other direction, of course. We needed a warm climate to cultivate our qualities, you see. In the south, we found an environment that favoured our spiritual development. In the north, it took centuries to generate the conditions required for civilized life."

What he means by this I have no idea. It's something else they don't tell you in history books. But if I were an Italian, I would find this a most worrying theory. I am not though and I don't have the leisure to ponder the matter because Rosenberg is watching me.

"You have a problem with the Ukrainians?" he says.

"Not as far as I know, no," I say. "Should I?"

"There was a nasty look on your face when our Führer spoke about the Ukrainians."

"That's just my smile," I say. Rosenberg offers me one of his own, a wintry little job that I would imagine he learned from a book and practised in front of the mirror. It seems to cause him some distress. It certainly causes me some distress. His eyes don't participate in the smile, scrutinizing me in a way that suggests he might just be subtle enough to note the mockery. But I'm in one of my moods and fail to control myself. "Wasn't the first Frau Göring Swedish?" I ask, knowing full well that she was.

Rosenberg hesitates. It is well known that he and Göring hate each other, representing as they do the two poles of National Socialism—on the one hand the arid, pseudorational veneer of intellectualism and mythologizing; on the other, the brutal corruption and sybaritic self-indulgence. But clan loyalty holds for the present.

"Organically speaking," says Rosenberg, "the Swedish people are not totally incompatible with the Nordic blood-soul. It is true that, in the particular circumstances in which we find ourselves at this point in history, the natural mystical vitalism connecting individuals to their collective racial identity has been vitiated, but we can say with some confidence that the corruption is not totally beyond correction."

What he means by this, I do not know, but I know I do not want to know, that this is the sort of linguistic quagmire that can reduce the most coherent thought to unintelligibility, and I very much doubt this was a coherent thought in the first place. Mumbo jumbo notwithstanding, I am not inclined to let my mark get away so easily. If he has the temerity to smile at me, he must pay the price, and in this instance, I know the currency in which he must pay. I don't know where I learned this, but it's the sort of trifling fact that tends to stick in my mind.

"I believe you and Reichsminister Göring share a birthday?" Not just the day of the month, but the year, too, the twelfth of January 1893. This is almost too good to be true. Maybe there is a God after all. My guess that the synchronicity is one Rosenberg must find appalling proves sound. He gives a little jerk, as if I have just tweaked his todger.

"There is an inevitability to our movement," says Brandt, insensible to my mischief making. "The coincidence of birthdays is nothing beside the parallels of national destiny. As our Führer clearly indicated, the peoples of Germany and Italy are united by a common history. We have both fought wars of unification, been cheated of our rights, and now our twin revolutions are boldly marching toward a shared goal. The papers talk of the Alpine frontier, but that is a distraction. The people on either side of the Alps are as one. The real frontier is that which divides the Germanic from the Slav world."

I don't know about the movement, but there is something inevitable about Brandt. He speaks with the assurance of the invincible bore. Rosenberg is used to this. He is visibly tuning out, twiddling internal dials in the hope of picking up a signal from some obscure blood-religion frequency or whatever still small voice it is he cares to listen to inside his head. Brandt is oblivious, chuntering on about frontiers.

As well as being Hitler's personal doctor, Brandt is one of the regime's principal eugenicists, a man of purely scientific bent, doing things to helpless people because he can and is curious to see what happens when he does. He is also the man who calculated how much money could be saved by getting rid of "unnecessary" mouths belonging to "defective" human beings (quarter of a million marks a day if you're interested, or to be precise, and he was nothing if not precise, 245,955.50) then set about making the necessary savings. He really is a repellent creature. My only comfort is that, as a member of the inner circle, Brandt must be obliged to spend a large part of his life being bored rigid by his boss recounting the same sorry opinions and inane anecdotes over and again. The sad thing is, he probably feels privileged to be subjected to this drivel, which I suspect he is currently quoting at me.

"It is our duty to place that frontier where we see fit. If anyone asks by what right we expand our living space, we reply that it is inherent in our national consciousness. Success justifies everything. It is intolerable that a superior people should subsist on inadequate terrain, while ignorant masses who do nothing for civilization occupy the richest land in the world. We wrestle a field from the sea and struggle to drain marshes, yet in the Ukraine vast tracts of fertile soil lie waiting for us."

You'll be horrified, but you need to know this. I'm not pretending such sentiments were the currency of every conversation, but they were the substance of a certain type of discourse. Nationalism validated by the sham ethics of Social Darwinism informed our thinking then. I'd like to say we were all with Arletty and her immortal riposte to the bigots who had her imprisoned for her affair with a Luftwaffe officer (you remember, "*Mon coeur est Français, mais mon cul est international*"), I'd like to say we all understood that nationalism is nearly always expressed by hating somebody else's country rather than loving one's own, that we saw it for the shallow, callow sentiment that it is, that we knew nationalism is counter to nation, a vapid doctrine that, like all empty vessels, sounds loud, a slimy cocoon nurturing corruption and decay and a sclerotic morality . . . I'd like to say all that, but it wouldn't be true. My generation cleaved to nation, like we cleaved to class and dogma and the specious ideals of imperialism. While great artists responded to the spiritual malaise of modern times by painting a dismantled human form, the ungreat and uncreative sought to cram everything into convenient little boxes that would hold things together. For the Nazis and the Fascists, flag waving was a pathway to legitimacy. For the rest of us, it was a way of simplifying and rendering comprehensible what could not otherwise be readily encompassed.

I appreciate that in telling you this I am straying from my purpose. These confessions can only condemn me in your eyes. But if you are to understand how so many of us allowed ourselves to be compromised, this is part of what you need to know. Nationalism was one of the comforting lies we told ourselves. The other lie, the really big one, was equally routine. Despite what people claim, we were all anti-Semites back then. I'm not saying we were complicit in pogroms and what have you. But the casual stuff of "yids" and "them" and no-thank-you-no-matter-how-much-you-want-to-integrate-you'll-never-be-quite-one-of-us, that was everywhere.

My only defence here is that, despite my selfish frivolity, I was dimly aware that other people were still people, no matter how "other" they might seem. Moreover, as a willing, even wilfully footloose expatriate, my grasp on the guff about nation was tenuous in the extreme. It certainly wouldn't have occurred to me that the mere fact of my having fetched up in Italy implied some ineluctable destiny compelling me to lay claim to the place. And I fancied that the peoples of the east might be a bit miffed if the peoples of the west came trundling across the border toting bags full of "superior inherent national consciousness," whatever the hell that was.

"And the Ukrainians?" I say. Brandt looks a little startled. I think he had forgotten I was there. For all his volubility, he's a tight-lipped little turd, hair plastered down so flat it looks like Groucho Marx's moustache. Put him on stage in a burlesque and he'd have people howling with laughter, only he wouldn't know why they were laughing. "What about the Ukrainians?"

"Redskins," he says. It takes me a moment to understand the implications of this, but then I realize it is shorthand for Hitler's "joke" about coloured beads. "We have a duty to place the frontier where we want. The humus of the land they occupy is often metres deep."

"I like that word," I say.

"What word? Frontier?"

"No, not frontier." Having crossed a few in my time, not always licitly, frontier is definitely not a word I favour. "Humus. In Latin languages, the words for humanity and humility have the same origin as humus. It's as if coming out of the soil, being humble, is what being human is all about. Of course, that doesn't work in German, does it?"

Brandt looks at me like I might be an unnecessary mouth in need of rationalization. Most gratifying. First Rosenberg, now Brandt. A good morning's work. Not that it makes any difference. I can piss about all I like, but The Big Lie is still there, and it won't go away.

CETOLOGY #6. *SCATOLOGISSIMO.*

This is the really offensive chapter, but if you are to understand your heritage, my dear, you must understand the prejudices that surrounded your ne'er-do-well father when he embarked on the most e'er-do-well act of his ne'er-do-well life.

A story did the rounds awhile back, probably apocryphal, but too good to ignore. French foreign minister attending the dedication ceremony of a Holocaust memorial. Notices that Britain doesn't figure in the statistics listing how many Jews were murdered from each nation. Points out the anomaly. There's an embarrassed shuffling of feet. At length, one of his aides says: "Um, Britain wasn't actually occupied during the war, minister."

"I know that," says the minister, testily. "But what did they *do* with their Jews?"

He was widely ridiculed, but the assumption behind the question was valid. If necessary, the British probably would have *done* something with their Jews, like everyone else did, because anti-Semitism was everywhere and still is, like all the other latent *anti-isms* that are intent on worming their way into being. They don't go away. They just go out of focus for a while. And this particular *anti-ism* was very clearly defined back then.

I'm not talking about bully boys kicking in heads. Physical violence is nearly always marginal until sanctioned by the state. But the assumption of otherness was widespread, no matter that countless Jews did all they could to gainsay it, enlisting in the army, dying in the trenches, buying worthless war bonds, promoting patriotic causes, joining nascent Fascist movements. Like most *anti-isms*, anti-Semitism was dissembled and imperfect. But the resentment was always there, like a demon lurking in the cellar, waiting for someone to open the door and invite it upstairs into the living room. It was just a question of turning a dull dislike into a lively hate.

Hate is important in a totalitarian system. Despotic ideologies are "hateful" not simply because they invite hatred, but because they are filled with hate like a fuel tank is filled with petrol. And nobody hated like Hitler hated. He hated really well. For the record, apart from the Jews, which we all know about, Hitler hated the Slavs, the Negroes, the French, the Poles, the Russians, the Czechs, the Ukrainians, the English (at least after they started criticizing what Germans were doing with "their" Jews), the masses, the elite, the workers, the bosses, the sick, the disabled, the vulgar, the refined, republicanism, liberalism, socialism, capitalism, communism, democracy, aristocracy, Christianity, bankers, big business, trade unions, speculators, monopolists, reformers, conservatives, schoolmasters, civil servants, economists, lawyers, judges, journalists, diplomats, bourgeois conventions, patrician conventions, monarchs, courts, polite society, protocol, pity, smoking, drinking, hunting, meat eating, formal dinners, etiquette, intellectuals, equality . . .

He hated like nobody else hated, hated everything that wasn't himself, all the vices and all the virtues, all the classes and all the categories, all the habits and all the customs. Come to that, it's possible he hated himself, too, that self-hate was the covert wellspring of all his other hates. This is not to say that he didn't like anything. He liked pretty women, so long as they were a bit dim. He liked dogs. He liked fine carpets. He liked Wagner. He liked shopping. He liked giving presents. He liked late nights and later mornings. He liked talking. He really liked talking. He liked a good picnic, too. But there's only so far you can go in politics on the strength of a good picnic, whereas hate can overcome all sorts of obstacles. It's just a question of feeding the machine. Hitler possessed huge reserves of resentment upon which he could draw whenever the motive rage was flagging, and the chief assets in his portfolio of antipathy were the Jews.

The Jews were remarkably versatile, for they were behind everything else he hated, from modernism to humanitarianism, materialism to mysticism, capitalism to communism, compassion to cruelty.

The Jews always disrupt nature's order, he said, *turning the weak against the strong, the inferior against the superior, the stupid against the intelligent. Communism and Christianity are both Jewish tricks, you know. Saul becomes Saint Paul, you see, and Mardochai becomes Karl Marx; it's all the same, there's no difference. But they understand nothing of spiritual matters. The Jews worm their way into religious life with a religion that is really just a racial doctrine. And as for their artistic efforts . . . total affectation. They have no feeling, no sensibility, cannot produce a painter or a musician or a thinker. They are at once the most-wicked creatures and the most stupid. If we Aryans didn't keep them clean, they'd be so filthy they couldn't open their eyes. They are nothing, less than nothing* (which, one would have supposed, made their conspiracy all the more impressive since they were working against such insurmountable handicaps).

God helps him who helps himself! That's the law of life. Everyone knows it, everybody understands, nobody needs to learn it. But the glib little Jew plays at philosophy and gets paid to teach you what is totally obvious, smothering you with meaningless words. Look at what he says and you'll see it's all wind (I shall leave a space here;

feel free to fill it with whatever expletive or symbol of stupe-
faction you favour . . . .

. . . .). *He uses words to confound his superiors, dreaming up obscure ideas knowing that the more incomprehen-
sible they are, the more perplexed his victims will be, and
the more time they will waste trying to unravel some intel-
ligible meaning. Thus distracted by what does not exist,
they do not see what does.*

*Was there ever any dirty, deceitful plot that did not
involve at least one scheming Jew? Take the knife to a
social abscess and you'll always find a filthy little Jew
behind it, like a maggot in a putrefying body. The Jew
lies in ambush, spying on the poor young girl he wants to
seduce to adulterate her blood. I have a nightmare vision,
hundreds of thousands of innocent girls being defiled by
disgusting black-haired crooked-legged Jewish bastards.*

Everything Hitler feared, everything he hated, possibly
everything he desired was blamed on The Jew, a protean
figure who was everywhere at every moment and responsible
for everything, who was behind the abuses practised by all
religions, all economic and political systems, and who could
be held to account for pornography, prostitution, venereal
disease (did I mention VD? Hitler was very upset by the pox,
hated it with a passion that suggested intimate acquaintance),
Protestant meekness, Catholic arrogance, snobbish aristocrats, uppity workers, and all one's own personal failings and
failures . . . you can see how useful this was. You didn't need
to think at all.

Only Hitler did think and he believed. He could discard
most beliefs when they became inconvenient, but Social Darwinism and the menace of Jewish Degeneracy were sacred
creeds, despite contradicting one another: if Jews really were
so decadent presumably they would have disappeared of their
own accord without the Nazis giving them a helping hand. It
sounds absurd and it is, but ludicrous prejudices have a knack

for realizing themselves. Look at your own generation, my dear, and you will see a less malign but equally absurd selection. It is in the nature of human being to conjure prejudice. Every prejudice is absurd. But that doesn't mean they are not dangerous. Combined with an unsubtle mind, any prejudice can do damage. Combined with an unsubtle mind, prejudice can aspire to a potency that reason rarely achieves.

Can Hitler's racism be explained in a way that helps portray him as a banal little man? Probably not. The standard explanation is that he was unhinged by his experiences in the trenches and disappointment at Germany's defeat. Unable to accept the fact that the Kaiser had buggered up the governing while the generals had buggered up the fighting and that, in any case, no European country could defeat the economy of the United States, and still less able to tolerate the idea that he was fighting on the losing side, Hitler needed somebody to blame, and who better than a bunch of people who had "all" the money and ran "all" the newspapers and produced "all" the intellectuals who were preaching pacifism and revolution. Obvious when you thought about it. Like I say, you didn't really need to think at all.

Better still, this was a call to action. If, in the struggle for survival, the Judeo-Christian-Bolshevik-Capitalist-Hand-Wringing-Cripple-Commie-Bastards were about to win, the *Übermenschen* had to pull their fingers out fast. Race had to replace class and nation as the moving force of politics and the superior race was to be the Aryan caste, a super race beyond national designations that was everything the Jews were not.

Despite his protestations to the contrary, Mussolini cut a shabby figure when it came to bigotry. He may have coined the term "totalitarian," he may have pioneered the movement's principles and stagecraft, he may have been full of bollocks, but he just didn't cut the mustard as a dictator. There was no doubting his racism. Only it was paltry compared to Hitler's. In lieu of an active all-consuming loathing, Mussolini offered the nation cynicism, misanthropy, and misogyny, which are useful traits for a tyrant, but too generic and lack the motive power of a properly targeted hate. And, like Hitler said, he didn't have the raw materials to work with.

Italians are nice, easygoing people. We all know that. Nice, easygoing people given to pinching bottoms and palming backhanders. Nice, easygoing people who invented Fascism, beat each other to a pulp, invaded their neighbours, and gassed black people who got in their way. When it came to racism though, apart from the customary assumption that Europeans were the architects of civilization, they preferred to keep it in the family, expending the scorn normally reserved for foreigners on one another, the north looking down on the south, the cities on the countryside, the educated on the uneducated, the landowners on the peasants, and so forth. Any Jews who got in the way were welcome to join in, but they weren't a notable target of themselves. Besides, getting agitated about race wouldn't have been wise for members of the "Mediterranean" group, which in the hierarchy of these things ran a poor third to the "Alpine" and "Nordic" races in the rest of Europe.

In this, Mussolini was typical of his class and generation. That's why he favoured *confino* as a punishment for opponents. Like most Italians, he reckoned sending a Milanese intellectual to live among Calabrian peasants was a truly cruel act of retribution from which neither party would ever quite recover. As for the Jews, they'd been in Italy a long time and had provided him with a lover and patron, his second in duels, his first biographer, the first Fascist MPs, the founder of the Fascist newspaper, the founder of the Fascist women's movement, and at least one general. Mussolini dismissed anti-Semitism as delirious "anti-Scientific drivel" and "arrant nonsense," "the German vice" upon which Italians looked with "majestic pity." That was in 1934, though.

One thing you've got to say for Mussolini. For all his boasts about unshakeable convictions, his beliefs were nothing if not flexible and he was capable of some spectacularly acrobatic ideological somersaults. Partly to please his passionate chum, partly because he was pissed off with Italian colonists knocking up the natives, and partly to put a bit of oomph into what he feared were flagging Fascist passions, Il Duce concluded that a bit of *anti-ism* was just the ticket.

Two months after Hitler's visit, the *Manifesto della Razza* was promulgated, depriving Jews of citizenship, government jobs, and the right to practise the professions. It also declared that, contrary to popular opinion, Italians were not a bunch of crossbred bastards, but were in fact "Nordic Aryans" whose blood hadn't been tampered with since the Lombards came piling over the Alps fifteen hundred years earlier. The Italians like a good joke and this thesis was greeted with widespread hilarity (though admittedly the Jews weren't laughing very hard, seeing as how they were seriously inconvenienced by the new laws), amusement that turned to bemusement when the nation was informed this particular *anti-ism* had been Fascist policy for two decades and anyone who thought otherwise hadn't been paying attention. Some had been paying attention, though. My Waitress for one. And she wasn't best pleased.

POSTCARD FROM THE PAST #17.

She's doing it again, bending forward, displaying her lacy bits and beyond. I'm not sure I can't see her navel. Mussolini can barely keep himself inside his trousers, Goebbels's overbite is so pronounced it looks like he's eating his chin, and Hitler is all but batting his eyelashes. She's serving slices of *crostata*, but given the angle of her torso and the cut of her blouse and the way those eyes of hers are flashing from under those eyebrows of hers, I don't believe anybody's too fussed about her pastries.

I can see her to this day, pastry jigger in one hand, spatula in the other, mischief in her heart. "My Waitress." Funny, really. I mean that I should characterize her like that. She was never exactly menial in her demeanour. The only time she did any bending and scraping was when that burglar broke into our flat in Évry. By the time your mother had finished telling him what she thought of him, he had to be peeled off the carpet. You should have seen the look of horror in his eye. I think he was half inclined to phone the police himself and ask to be arrested. Not what you would call a domestic woman. But for all our misunderstandings, she was always "My Waitress" to me. Even when she was wasting away at the end, was nothing more than a bag of bones and a will to live, she still looked as lovely as she did that first day. My Waitress was in there, hiding behind the pain, as young and seductive and vital as ever.

The act she's putting on (its blatancy is such that it must be an act) would be ludicrous were it not so compelling. Yet part of the allure is the artlessness of her coquetry, which suggests the really ludicrous ones are the gawking bystanders. Do you remember how I used to tease your Mum, calling her the Queen of Tarts? I was referring to this episode. She would laugh a lot. Only later did it occur to me that I was the butt of her laughter rather than herself.

Aside from the main delectable, there is a selection of tarts on the table. My Waitress is most particular about which ones she serves the dictators. Mussolini gets apricot, Hitler cherry. The rest of us are served at random. I get cherry.

We're in the Villa Borghese. I'll tell you about the gallery later. First things first, though. Your mother will always be first for me, despite what happened afterwards. She and you. Time will come when you'll understand this, that all the doing and being and making and becoming and believing and declaring with which we fill our lives is irrelevant beside the simple act of loving. I'm not talking about grand passions and swooning away with the back of your hand pressed to your forehead, but that certainty you have when somebody else is part of you and you know that, no matter how long you live, that bit of another being will be lodged inside you and there's bugger all you can do about it, so you'd better embrace it and be glad because the loving and the living are one and the same and anything less is a waste of time.

Do you remember how brisk and businesslike she was? It drove you crazy when you were a kid, all that peremptory well-we'd-better-sort-that-out-then, but it's part of what she was, and it's in the play of all the different things she used to be that her inimitability lay, as it does with everyone. Clichés claim there are two types of people. It's nonsense, of course. The only two types of people are those who believe there are two types of people and those who know better. But it's useful shorthand nonetheless. One dichotomy contrasts those who seek to reform their environment with those who don't. Every time we moved house, your mother would be working out ways to rearrange the living space to suit our needs. I would look at the available space and ask myself, "Now how can we fit in here?" And when the space in which I find myself proves incommodious, I don't start knocking down walls. I move on. Your mother wasn't like that. She would set about changing what was around her and getting rid of anything that wouldn't fit. That's why she got rid of me when she realized I couldn't be rearranged to the pattern she required. As a characteristic, it can be wearing to live with. But when you're caught up in the middle of history, it's rather magnificent to watch.

Back in the Villa Borghese, we're still toying with our tarts and, judging by the faces around me, a desire to do something irrevocable to the bodice of your mother's outfit. She did have that effect on men, you know. You've got it, too, that fluke of form and vitality that turns heads and hearts and makes tummies somersault. It can be a bit of a burden, I know. Blokes look at you and . . . well, you know all about that. We're all doing it all the time, no matter how discreet and cultivated we seem. Just something you've got to learn to live with, because we're all defined in part by the way other people see us.

As I recall, the only men there who didn't look like something vital inside them was about to pop were Albert Speer, who was far too smooth to betray himself like that, Guiseppe Bottai, the fawning minister of education who only had eyes for his master, and Ribbentrop, who was banging away at Ciano about an alliance.

That was the main diplomatic object of the trip. The Germans wanted a treaty that would allow them to get on with their *Lebensrauming*, but the Italians were prevaricating in the hope that the British would recognize their African empire. This is an essential part of history. Most of what passes for history is a narrative of egotistical pricks spilling blood and promoting suffering. But the drama is bound together with the boring business of deal making. Ribbentrop was a rubbish deal maker. Reckoned himself Hitler's Talleyrand, but the British were closer to the mark when they called him Ambassador Brickendrop. He was persistent though, wearing people down till they gave him what he wanted just to get rid of him.

Even Ciano's well-polished veneer of charm is fracturing under the hammering of what passes for diplomacy in Ribbentrop's repertoire. It's amusing to watch the Italian's mounting irritation, though not so diverting as the spectacle provided by the Queen of Tarts, who having served all those present is looking gooey-eyed while Mussolini expatiates on the fascinating topic of his war wounds.

"Twenty-seven operations in one month," he says. "My torment was . . . indescribable. Yet I endured them . . . without anesthetic." How we got onto this subject in the context of a plateful of pastries, I do not know, but it's clear who his intended audience is, as he is speaking in Italian and General Roatta, who speaks perfect German, is translating for Hitler. "I faced horrific pain, but I am glad that the . . . road to Fascism was daubed with my own blood. Forty fragments of mortar buried in my flesh. Pulled out one by . . . one without . . . chloroform!"

"But why?" The question was prompted by genuine curiosity. I cannot for the life of me understand why anyone would willingly experience pain. I still can't, despite his answer.

"Why?" From the warmth of his voice I gather he was waiting for this very question. Bottai glares at me, peeved to have missed an opportunity to ingratiate himself. "I wanted to keep an eye on what the surgeons were doing," says The Constipated Prick. This is intended as a joke and I'm sorry to say (sorry because your mother sees it and there will be reason enough in the coming years for her to despise me) that I laugh dutifully, after which he delivers himself of another aphorism: "It is good to trust others but . . . not to do so is much better!"

"It is through suffering that Il Duce proved his fitness for his present position," says Goebbels, still watching My Waitress. He's another one with a reputation for a roving eye and roving hands and roving organs all round. I heard he was beaten up by an actor who found the propaganda minister propagating a bit too warmly with his wife. I doubt it's true, but I can understand why the story was popular. I wouldn't mind beating him up myself. I don't even know the name of the girl yet, but I have a pathetic urge to protect her. "As our Führer says, the state needs courageous men. Only those who have proved their worth in battle should be allowed to govern. Struggle is the principle behind everything."

I control myself and refrain from asking after Goebbels's own war experiences, which I know are nonexistent, and thus as painful and problematic to him as the war experiences of Hitler and Mussolini are pleasurable and politically profitable to them.

"Indeed," says The Constipated Prick, reverting to German. "The virtue of all things can be weighed in . . . sacrifice and suffering. They . . . amplify existence. This is why I do not fear an . . . assassination attempt. By serving the nation, I . . . multiply my own life."

"One can never be totally safe from fanatics," says The Flatulent Windbag. "I always stand upright in my car during parades, you know, for as the proverb says, the world belongs to the brave." He pauses to allow for a translation, watching the girl, waiting to see her reaction. Mussolini looks more puffed up than ever. I'm sure he's going to explode one day. The two most powerful men in Europe and they're competing to impress a serving girl! I'm not sure whether this makes them more ridiculous or more admirable, but it does make them more human. "If a lunatic wants to kill me, I am no safer sitting down. Besides, nowadays, there are fewer and fewer extremists ready to risk their own lives to take mine."

Of course, I don't remember every word of this, only the trend of the talk and turns of phrase I noted in my diary.

But as I said earlier, I never did get away from what I did and did not do during those days. Trying to make sense of it over the years, I turned to books by and about the principals. Reading Hitler's *Table Talk*, I realized how much he repeated himself, returning to the same maxims and anecdotes time and again. Much of the dialogue you read here comes from other sources. But it corresponds to the things I heard. And the absurdities are verbatim.

You need to know this. The despots who have gone down in history as monsters were also little men capable of saying stupid things. They were capable of saying sensible things, too. But both the inanities and the acumen have the same impact, bringing them down to earth, making them one of us, not some abstract principle of evil of which we can divest ourselves. The scatology serves the same purpose. It helps bring them back to humanity. Only when we've got rid of the demonic clichés will you be in a position to properly judge the compromises and culpability of me and my generation. I'm only just learning to judge these things myself.

"*Möchten Sie mehr Torte?*"

Rarely can a simple offer of more tart have had a greater impact. The Constipated Prick touches his testicles, not out of amorous intention, but because he has been startled and needs to comfort himself. Goebbels jerks his head up, his eyes narrowing. Even The Flatulent Windbag stops talking. As for me, I've been spending too much time with our guest. I can feel a fart coming on and I've a nasty suspicion it's not one I'll be able to hold back.

"You speak German?" says Himmler, staring at My Waitress.

"A little," she says, eyes cast down in a way calculated to elicit every courtesy at The Flatulent Windbag's disposal. What it's liable to elicit from The Constipated Prick is something I don't care to speculate about. "I was born in Merano."

Despite my own perturbation, I take the time to scan the watching faces, and in each I see an unequivocal answer to her question. Their eyes are all bellowing: *More tart! More tart!*

At this critical juncture, Hitler and I fart simultaneously. I never thought I'd say it, but I'm glad to hear him letting rip. Nobody is going to blame a sly one on me when the master farter is standing beside me. Nobody but his loyal deputy. Hess glowers at me as only a man with eyebrows like that can. Perhaps this is why the Führer is so fond of him. Hess has a capacity for looking disapproving that would make a baby blush. Thus his boss can fart at will, because I am appalled to discover that everyone else is looking at me as well, including My Waitress, and they clearly think I'm taking my translation duties a little too literally. For an olive-skinned girl, she's gone quite pink. I think she's trying not to laugh.

"Thank you," I say, a little desperately. It's the tart I'm grateful for, not the farts. I reach for a second slice. As it transpires, this is not a wise move. *More tart! More tart!*

CETOLOGY #7. BELOW THE BELT: MACHISMO, MONORCHISM, AND PLUMBING-RELATED MATTERS.

Most men notice most things about most women's bodies most of the time. I'd like to think women do the same. But when I ask about this, I have the impression the women who do admit to sizing up the baggage a bloke is carrying himself around in don't really mean it and are just saying it on principle. It's a pity, because women won't be treated as equals until they treat men equally, too, and a few pinched bottoms and leering cries of "Go on, darling, show us your willy," would do most men no end of good. There is hope though and the new fascination for the sexual peccadilloes of politicians suggests venery is gaining the place it deserves in public life. More Christine Keelers and Mandy Rice-Davieses are what we need. From what I gather, they had a wonderfully sobering effect on the British establishment. In view of the coverage given to that scandal, I am hopeful that, in a few years time, what political leaders do with their reproductive organs will be deemed as important as their policies.

This may seem puerile, but that's not all it is. Our behaviour in bed reveals what our real values are. Sexual activity involves such a fundamental recognition of the reality of another person that the way one approaches it has far wider ramifications than might seem inherent in incorporating a rather unprepossessing scrap of flesh into one orifice or another depending upon the preferences of the parties concerned. This is particularly true in a world where women have been cast in the role of the "weaker" sex.

Personally, I consider this "weaker" sex business a fantasy of the first water. You've only got to compare tummy muscles. Women have tummy muscles designed for the retention and expulsion of an eight-pound baby, one which often as not, for entirely legitimate reasons, doesn't want to be expelled at all. Men's tummy muscles are designed for the retention (in a very provisional manner) and expulsion of several pints of fermented beverage, which, in the nature of these things, is all too eager to be expelled. The tummy of a woman is, therefore, considerably more robust than the tummy of a man. Similar comparisons can be made in terms of intellect, resolve, resilience, stamina, commitment, flexibility, fidelity, generosity, maturity, and utility. Regrettably, the happenstance of a particular type of muscle and a particular type of brain has fostered the illusion that women are the weaker sex. It is a fiction, but while this fiction persists, it is instructive to consider how men in positions of power treat women.

How to approach this? I'm feeling mischievous, so let Hitler speak for himself. Are you ready, my dear? Right, take a deep breath.

It is a well-known fact, real women want real men. In prehistoric times, you see, they were vulnerable and needed a champion to protect them. So when men fight for a woman, she waits to see who comes out on top, then gives herself to the winner, who will provide her with the most security. Once she's got him, of course, she has to defend her property. That's only natural. This is clearly the source of female jealousy. The gentlest woman in the world turns into a totally wild beast when another woman tries to take her man. Indeed, the more feminine she is, the more this instinct is developed.

Perhaps another breath? You might like to fix yourself a strong drink, too, because your pretty little head is going to need it by the time you get to the end of this.

Our enemies say we are a party of misogynists who treat women as mere playthings and machines for making children, but that's simply not true. Women are vital for good works and educating the young. But they cannot separate reason from emotion, which is fundamental in politics. An angry man is not a handsome sight, but the grotesque spectacle presented by an angry woman is profoundly shocking. Gallantry demands that we do not let them make such a deplorable exhibition of themselves. Every field involving conflict is the preserve of men. Women excel in other spheres, like organizing and decorating a house. But political matters are masculine affairs, on which women cannot have a valid opinion.

You got that drink yet? I really think it would be a good idea.

Women have a talent totally unknown to men, the capacity to kiss a friend on the cheek while stabbing her in the back. We cannot change this, they are what they are, so let us be magnanimous and tolerate their little frailties. And if they need such diversions to keep them happy, we should not deprive them of their sport. Personally, I prefer to see a woman indulging in jealous deceit rather than struggling to grasp an idea. And when they grapple with metaphysics, it's a total disaster. Man's universe is infinite compared with that of woman. He lives in the world of ideas. But the universe of woman is man. Intelligence in a woman is of no importance. My mother would have cut a poor figure in sophisticated society. She lived for her husband and children. We were her world. Yet she gave a son to Germany. A woman who loves her husband, a real woman, lives only for his sake.

How are you doing, dear? Have you hurled these papers across the room? We haven't even got onto The Constipated Prick yet, but you can probably guess what he thought. *Women exert no influence on strong men. Their role is passive. In political life, they do not count.* And so forth. You know, breeding, bringing up warriors, dabbing at the sweated brow. This wasn't just idle prejudice. He had it chapter and verse from a genuine intellectual, Otto Weininger, who topped himself at the age of twenty-three, catapulting his book *Sex and Character* into the best-seller lists, and eliciting the admiration of men as diverse as Wittgenstein and Strindberg . . . for his ideas, I mean, not because he shot himself.

Weininger dealt with "the woman problem" by isolating male and female characteristics, the first being active, productive, logical, and moral, the latter in-, un-, il- and a-. Only "masculine" women could escape the roles of lover and mother. Man, meanwhile, had to cultivate his manly bits to discover the abstract love of the God who was to be found inside himself. You can see why solipsistic despots would be attracted by this thesis. And while Mussolini might have baulked at Weininger's stipulation that "abstract love" was asexual, Hitler would have been dead chuffed by the fact that the author was a Jewish apostate who dismissed Jews as being typically feminine, that is to say without faith, soul, or morality. Woman problem solved! And the scapegoats dehumanized to boot.

Basically, Flatus and Dickhead believed all the things that have you, my dear, marching and chanting and chucking cobblestones at the CRS. By the by, a word of caution concerning your hopes for equality. Don't hold your breath or put the kettle on. Nothing's going to change in a hurry. I've seen your young men. They are superb practitioners of the art passed on by their predecessors, to wit lying about being waited upon by women. Indeed, they have improved upon the model by adding casual sex to the *carte du jour* as well as the surreal idea that any woman who doesn't want to sleep with them must perforce be frigid. I wish I'd come up with that one. The main achievement of my generation was discovering the clitoris and a fat lot of good that did us. Liberation will take time, lots of it. At best, your granddaughters will see some small measure of equality. In the meantime, before you get equality of opportunity, let alone equality of outcome, you will be given every chance to enjoy equality of bother, burden, labour, and liability. Indeed, you'll get more than your share. Second word of caution. Don't for one moment think that these patronizing ideas were the preserve of despots. We nearly all ascribed to something similar. And even those who didn't, did so not out of generosity of spirit or intellectual probity, but because it was in our interests. I certainly wouldn't have been inclined to tell your mother that she had played the tart and it was time to settle down, lie back, and begin breeding. Not without hiding behind the sofa, at least.

Which brings us to what takes place below the belt . . .

> Hitler has only got one ball,
> The other is in the Albert Hall.
> Göring has two, but very small,
> Himmler's are somewhat simmler
> But poor Goebbels has no balls at all.

A vexed question, but we must ask ourselves, how many testicles were secreted about the person of Hitler? Not a pretty prospect, but these things must be grappled with, especially when you're bringing a monster down to earth. That was what the English soldiers were doing when they sang those ditties. Humour can do this, it always has, always will. Only the other day in London, I heard a little lad telling a joke about a concentration camp. *Nazi guard orders a Jew to jump off a parachute tower without a parachute. The Jew protests that this would be fatal. Nazi pooh-poohs his concerns, saying it's just a question of mind over matter: "Ve don't mind, you don't matter."* And there was that other one, even more offensive, about how many Jews you can get in a Mini. I could understand it, though. The kids were trying to comprehend the enormity of what had happened during their parents' watch. I almost joined them.

Monorchism or monochordism is the medical term for having only one testicle due to accident or illness, or because one did not drop, in which case the condition is cryptorchidism. Cryptorchidism can result in an increased risk of malignancy, which takes on a different meaning altogether when your possible monorchid is Adolf Hitler. The thing is, it wasn't necessarily just a dirty song designed to boost morale. Rumours persist to this day. Some say that when he enlisted, Hitler's VD examination took half the time it might, others that he suffered a groin injury at the Battle of the Somme, or that the Soviet autopsy on his charred remains declared the left testicle AWOL.

I can't say if any of these claims have any validity. I got close to Hitler, but not that close. I suspect it was just a scurrilous slur. The British enjoy a smutty joke and SMERSH reckoned Stalin's old rival would be better off with one bollock less than Uncle Joe. In a sense, though, the physical truth doesn't matter, because the smear on Hitler's manhood matches what many saw as a psychological truth, to wit that something, somewhere along the line had unmanned our man.

Reck-Malleczewen made no bones about it, calling Hitler the chief eunuch, a half man marked by the stigma of sexual inadequacy, whose rage at his impotence fuelled his need to brutalize others. Putzi Hanfstaengl described his patron as a neuter, neither fish nor fowl, his boundless energy born of a sexual no-man's land that offered no outlet. And Hoffman insisted that Eva Braun (who had been his shop assistant and perfectly matched the Führer's prescriptions for an unblemished vacuity in womankind) was no more than a platonic companion who owed her privileged position not to her sexual charms but to the fact that she had tried to commit suicide in 1932 when the party could ill afford the scandal.

It's plausible. Hitler's women friends did tend to end in the shambles. Of those associated romantically with him, the first didn't notice the lovelorn boy mooning after her and thus survived the experience. Thereafter though, Geli Raubal killed herself with his revolver, Renate Müller "fell out of a hospital window" when the Gestapo brought her a bunch of grapes,

Maria Reiter tried and failed to kill herself, Unity Mitford did likewise, dying eight years later from the resulting complications, and Eva Braun . . . well, we know what happened to her. Dalliance with the Führer was dangerous. But that did not discourage his admirers.

Throughout his career, Hitler cultivated a solitary image, claiming Germany was his bride and that he was wed to the nation's cause in a way that left no room for nuptials. This was not strictly true, but true enough, and Goebbels preferred to keep it that way, believing the single Führer had more propaganda value than one with a *Frau Führer* tagging along behind. He was probably right. Women adored Hitler. There are stories of his admirers prostrating themselves before him, proclaiming their infatuation in impassioned proposals of marriage, ripping off their bras (no, dear, for all the wrong reasons), eating the gravel he walked on, and expressing an urgent desire to kiss him on the bottom. It was enough to make any normal man extremely cross indeed. Like Klingsor, Hitler was a magician whose powers stemmed, in part at least, from self-emasculation.

Whatever his mystique though, there was always something off beam about the way Hitler related to others. You only need to look at his artistic endeavours. Despite a rudimentary talent as a draughtsman, he couldn't draw people. When they do appear in his pictures, they are dwarfed by the buildings and are a bit skew-whiff. He rarely did portraits. I saw one once, a drawing of Geli Raubal's naked torso, hands behind her head (he couldn't do hands; opposable thumb, all too human). The breasts were all right, competently sketched, but the rest of her was all wrong. Her shoulders were lopsided, like she had a hump, which she didn't, the arms were out of kilter, the neck looked like it had been cut from a lamppost, and she appeared to be trying to twist her own head off. Perhaps she was. But we'll come to Geli in a moment.

Given that the man was an Italian stallion modelled on an ambulatory penis, sex is the one field in which it would seem Mussolini was streets ahead of Hitler. It was only fitting that, of all the good-luck gestures he could have opted for, he felt compelled to touch his testicles to ward off the evil eye. The propaganda department played down this aspect of his personality, portraying him as a family man, propping little Romano on his hip and casting a paternal eye over the elder children on the beach.

Gossip told a different story featuring buxom "Fascist visitors" smuggled into his rooms, handy cushions lying about the floor of his office, and the open secret of his mistress Claretta Petacci, who endeared herself to the population at large by swanning about in furs dispensing charity to poor people while her family prospered from peculation and promises of patronage.

Above all, there were rumours about ravishing women, "ravishing," that is, as a transitive verb, not an adjective. Mussolini boasted about this in an early draft of his autobiography, but at the height of his power, he didn't need to boast. There was a cachet to being ravished by the Duce and his victims would do the boasting for him, describing how he had pounced on them, detailing his unfettered, primal ferocity, his frenzied pawing and mauling and biting, the frantic pumping and humping, all of it totally uninhibited and totally indifferent to his partner's pleasure, and all finished (with typical Fascist efficiency) within two minutes.

It didn't sound like a lot of fun, not for the women at least, and this was quite as galling as The Chief Eunuch's popularity. There we were, ordinary blokes like me, muddling through as best we could with a little guile, a little tenderness, and a little generosity, whereas what you needed to be successful with women was either to have your bollocks off or to carry on like a rampant caveman. Granted, being a totalitarian leader with absolute power probably helped. But one did sometimes wonder whether all that drivel about real men didn't have something to it. It was all very well for us to sit there being superior, saying these macho types used women to bolster a shaky sense of their own masculinity. We were just a bunch of jealous losers mumbling into our beer. Meanwhile, Mussolini could state that "Orgasm is good for you: it sharpens your thoughts, widens your horizons, and makes your brain vivid and brilliant." By which token, he was a towering figure of staggering genius, which was more or less what the propaganda department was telling us anyway.

What we didn't know was that maintaining his vivid and brilliant brain came at a cost, one comparable to that of a flirtation with The Flatulent Windbag. We didn't know that when Mussolini was strung up by the ankles in the Piazzale Loreto in 1945, among the bodies displayed alongside his would be the corpse of Claretta Petacci, skirts pinned between her knees while a big brave man lewdly poked her with a stick. We didn't know that the Duce's affair with Claretta drove his wife, Rachele, to try and kill herself. Above all, we didn't know about Ida Dalser, the woman who supported him when he was nobody, the woman he married and who gave him a son as well as all her money, the woman he abandoned to bigamously marry Rachele. When Ida protested, all documentary traces of the liaison were destroyed and she was banged up in a mental asylum, where she conveniently died of a "stroke." And when her son, Benito Albino, objected, he was also locked up in a loony bin where he, too, obliged his dear old dad by dying of "consumption."

But even here, in a field where The Constipated Prick was forever polishing his rod and carving notches in his bedpost, what The Flatulent Windbag lacked in volume he made up for in sordid detail.

The two things most people love most are sex and children. But not at the same time. First comes the sex, then the children. Put the two together and you get a hell of a mess. Tricky then when the great love of Hitler's life was a seventeen-year-old girl who was remarkably childlike and who came into his life when he was in his forties. Trickier still when the girl was the daughter of his half-sister, Angela Raubal. Tricky? Not for a man who had grown up in a household where his Mum called his Dad "Uncle." Not when Uncle-Dad was twenty-three years older than Mum, which was only five years less than the difference between Hitler and Geli.

He was infatuated by his vivacious niece and she was flattered by the attentions of her munificent "Uncle Alf." They lived together for six years, six years of a relationship that was as intense as it was ambiguous and controversial. The only points everybody agrees on are that he was devoted to her and became increasingly despotic, displaying an oppressive, possessive jealousy, and that she was flighty, flirtatious, frivolous, and increasingly restive. The rest is a mess of conjecture and conflicting reports about jealous rages, sexual perversion (urolagnia and coprophilia if you must know; there are places even I won't go), secret lovers, unwanted pregnancy, and mounting tension.

On the nineteenth of September 1931, Geli's corpse was discovered in Hitler's flat. She had been shot through the chest with Uncle Alf's Walther 6.35. The bullet had gone in above her heart and ended up down by her hip. The gun was lying beside the body. The circumstances of the body's discovery were confused, different people claiming it came about in different ways. The authorities were not informed until a cabal of high-ranking Nazis had discussed how best to deal with the situation. The police investigation was botched, the doctor's report patchy, there was no inquest, there were contradictory stories about who was where when, what wounds the girl had actually sustained, and the body was promptly buried in Austria, beyond the jurisdiction of the German police.

Accident, suicide, murder? Nobody knows, but nobody tells a very uplifting tale about the episode. Hence the blackmail potential of Eva Braun's suicide attempt a year later. A second dead damsel could have sunk the whole movement. According to the detective charged with investigating the death, Hitler was distraught. "She was the only relative I

was close to," he said. "And now this has to happen to me."
Me. Not *her*.

So, if a halfway decent-looking woman got anywhere within bedding distance of Mussolini, she was raped, and if she went to bed with Hitler, she was as good as dead. I'm not implying that their sexual antics and ethics were in any way worse than gassing black people who were impertinent enough to protest about the theft of their country, or than sitting down and plotting to get six million Jews onboard a train bound for oblivion. But these squalid details bring the perversity and brutality down to a human scale. It's not beyond comprehension.

Anything else? Oh, yes, I nearly forgot. Rachele Mussolini's mum was Anna Lombardi. After the death of her husband, Agostino Guidi, Anna became the lover of the widowed Alessandro Mussolini. So The Constipated Prick married the daughter of his dad's mistress. They liked to keep it in the family, these despots.

POSTCARD FROM THE PAST #18.

Villa Borghese. Titian's *Sacred and Profane Love*, a bride sitting on a sarcophagus beside Cupid and a naked Venus. Hitler leans forward to inspect the painting, gray-gloved hands perched on his tummy, like a couple of plump little pigeons. So far, he has displayed a distinct predilection for exposed female flesh. At the Museo delle Terme, he got quite carried away by the *Venus de Cyrene*. I probably shouldn't be telling you this, but the *Venus de Cyrene* is a truncated statue of a naked woman. No head. No arms. Just the essentials.

"I prefer the profane," he says, taking a quarter turn to look at his entourage.

Sepp Dietrich rubs the pistol bulge on his bum. Every time he sits down, he leaves an imprint on the upholstery. He really is a dim-looking thug. He dotes on his gun, fondling the barrel with an indecent devotion. Mussolini gazes at the door. Titian's Venus is too small breasted for his tastes, but she gets The Flatulent Windbag going.

"The title is a moralistic reading of the painting," he continues, surprising me with an insight that is as accurate as it is unexpected. "The artist was celebrating both earthly and heavenly love. But others saw profanity in this display of naked health. Doubtless a priest named it. Nakedness is a torment to them. They cannot see that sacred and profane love are the same. But prejudices against what is natural are dying out. Even priests understand that man can't sweat his sperms out through his brain. In the countryside, they always sleep with their servants, you know. Of course, there are accidents, but there's no harm in a woman fulfilling her biological destiny. That's what I say. Better a skivvy who has a child out of wedlock than a virtuous old maid. The old maids always go mad. Country people understand all this. It's the urban elite, the puritans and hypocrites, who make bourgeois distinctions like in the title of this painting. But it is a thing against nature. *Sehen sie, meine Herren.*"

"*Unser Führer ist ein grosser Künstler.*" Goebbels gives me a venomous glance, but neither despot appears to notice my irony. They don't hear things in what the French call the second degree. It's all first degree with dictators. Dietrich glares at the painting, rubbing his pistol ever more briskly. Haven't these people heard of Freud?

"And to think that if Bolshevism had come here . . ."

Mussolini tilts his chin, as if preparing himself for a party trick involving a pile of plates and a broom handle.

If Bolshevism had come here? If Bolshevism had come here, would artists like Renoir, Manet, Cézanne, Van Gogh, and Degas have been banned from the galleries like they have in Nazi Germany? And in Italy, would a man like Ziegler be lauded as a great artist? Actually, he probably would if The Constipated Prick was around, seeing as how Ziegler is known as the Master of Female Pubic Hair after his penchant for painting women's genitalia.

"I always feel that Titian paints without passion," I say, using the word I know Hitler employs to condemn expressionist art, *unfleissig.*

"You do not understand," says Hitler. "You should have been in Germany last year. The Degenerate Art Exhibition would have made it clear. Any so-called artist who paints a green sky and blue fields deserves to be sterilized. I will not let these frauds cheat the public. If they really see blue fields, they are deranged, and should go to an asylum. If they only pretend to see them, they are criminals, and should go to prison. I will purge the nation of them."

"I was busy at the time," I say. "But I heard about the exhibition."

Wished I'd been there, too. Ziegler was the curator. He is Hitler's favourite painter, blessed with numerous advantages, ranging from an opportune neoclassical conservatism to a fondness for "Aryan" themes. And he's called Adolf, which is bound to please. Notable artistic talent, however, is not among his gifts. He is a very second-rate artist, little better than a pornographer, but second-rate artists do sometimes see clearly, and Ziegler has an eye for a painting. When he made his selection of works by "chatterboxes, dilettantes and swindlers" that tended to "insult German feeling, destroy or confuse natural form, or simply reveal an absence of adequate manual and artistic skill," among those identified as displaying "decadence," "weakness of character," "mental disease," "racial impurity," and a propensity for "canvas smearing" were Klee, Chagall, Picasso, Kandinsky, Mondrian, Matisse, Beckmann, Corinth, Nolde, Grosz, Dix, and Kokoschka.

"You did put it on in a bit of hurry," I add, which is true. Ziegler's commission assembled the exhibition in a fortnight. "There wasn't much time for those of us elsewhere to make arrangements for a visit."

"There is never enough time!" There is real pain in this exclamation. Hitler may be an idler, but he's a man in a hurry, too. With a sweep of his arm, he encompasses the gallery. "If I was still a simple citizen, I would spend weeks here. Sometimes I wish I hadn't gone into politics at all." I can only concur, murmuring my agreement *sotto voce*. Goebbels, who has edged round behind me, gives me a sharp dig in the kidney with his forefinger, but The Flatulent Windbag is so wrapped up in his own grievances that he doesn't hear my gasp of pain. "I am an artist, not a politician," he continues. "I always wanted to be a great painter in oils, you know. When my programme for Germany is achieved, I shall take up painting and spend the rest of my life as an artist. I believe I have it in my soul to become one of the great

--- 155 ---

painters of the age and that future historians will remember me not for what I have done for my country, but for my art. I shall return to Italy and retire to a small villa and pass my time incognito in the museums and roaming around the countryside as an unknown artist."

I have the impression that he means it, that he might quit being a dictator as another man might quit smoking. There would be withdrawal symptoms, but it's a nasty dirty habit that can, potentially at least, be put aside. The Constipated Prick evidently believes he means it, too. He is aghast. He might be a mad poet, but the idea that someone should give it all up is too much for him. Or perhaps it's the thought of spending weeks in a gallery.

"If I could do whatever I liked," he says, "I should always . . . be at sea. As that is not possible, I console myself with . . . animals. Wild animals personify the . . . elemental forces of nature. And the mental life of domestic animals approximates that of man, yet they don't . . . demand anything of him. Horses, dogs, and my favourite, the . . . cat."

This is from the heart. Rumour has it that on his desk at the Palazzo Venezia he keeps a photo of his cat, not his children, still less his wife. It's a wonder that he can work at all in such a fussily decorated office as the Sala del Mappamondo, but that would not be a problem for a man who is impervious to the plastic arts. Il Duce may obsess over the written word, but when it comes to Raphael, Caravaggio, Bernini, and Bassano, he doesn't disguise his lack of interest.

He crosses some galleries without stopping. In others, he peers at a picture's label, as if checking the price. He stands in front of Domenichino's *Diana*, puffed-up and prognathic, staring at the work in a way that suggests he is inspecting a blank wall. The one time he appears interested is before Canova's *Pauline Bonaparte*, but even then I suspect his principal emotion is one of regret at the lack of orifices.

At first, the Führer seems oblivious to Mussolini's impatience. He cannot conceive of someone who is not touched by the possibilities of paint. Only as we descend the spiral staircase does it dawn on him that the Duce is keen to escape all this bloody art. Hitler stops in his tracks and expresses himself. *Hey up, Rover!* It's not mere flatulence. It's shock. And the upset is such that this is the smelliest fart he has delivered to date.

CETOLOGY #8. *EIN GROSSER KÜNSTLER.*

From an early age, Hitler was persuaded that he possessed great artistic talent. His mum thought so, too. He certainly had an "artistic" temperament. All that lounging about crapping on about how brilliant he was and how rubbish everyone else was, the bouts of torpor punctuated by spurts of activity, the aversion to routine, the petulance, moodiness, egoism, and wild swings of emotion; in all those things he was the epitome of the bourgeois's stereotypical "artist." Unfortunately, he lacked the necessary talent, training, creativity, and discipline.

Twice—to his very great astonishment—rejected by the Viennese Academy of Fine Arts, whose admissions tutors failed to find "an understanding of human anatomy" in the tyro-artist's portfolio, Hitler spent his early twenties as an indigent drifter, scoffing cakes in coffee houses when in funds, queuing at soup kitchens when not, and sleeping in doss houses while he scraped a living painting billboards, post-cards, and watercolours of famous buildings. According to the glazier who acted as his agent, most of his pictures were bought by Jewish patrons.

The pieces I've seen are amateurish, but not incompetent. He could have been a decent drafting technician. But there's something eerily inert about his more ambitious watercolours, like photos that have been painted over. As for the post-cards, they are lifeless sketches churned out to earn a few *pfennigs* to pay for the next meal. They were hawked by another vagrant, Reinhold Hanisch, until the pair fell out and Hanisch began doing his own postcards. When his ex-partner became famous and a market developed for the politician's juvenilia, Hanisch expanded his repertoire to include "Hitler originals." Whether the word forgery is apt here, I wouldn't like to say, but the scam was enough to get Hanisch sent to prison, where he died in 1937. This was a wise move. He wouldn't have wanted to be alive a year later when Austria was annexed by the Nazis, because Hanisch had also been selling juicy stories to anti-Nazi journalists, explaining how young Adolf had been a lazy, bombastic lickspittle with a lot of Jewish friends, which wasn't at all the image being promoted by Goebbels.

By the time I met him, Hitler had put all that behind him. I heard that he kept a pad of paper on his desk for sketching, that anyone presenting an architectural plan could be assured of an audience, and that he was inordinately proud of The Brown House, the refurbishment of which he had personally overseen as "proof" of his artistic abilities. But that was it as far as the practice of art went. Pronouncement on art was another matter. He was The Flatulent Windbag after all and he was always ready to pass judgment, delivering his verdicts with the irrefutable confidence of a failed practitioner. He had an opinion about everything, from disproportionate Parisian windows to the inadequacy of Shakespearean acting in England and (quite inexplicably) the futility of academies of fine art. He revered Vermeer and Cranach, but preferred Bürkel and Defregger. As for Ziegler, he reckoned the artist's *Terpsichore* ought to be hung by gold chains. Hanged, I would say. It really is posh porn, the sort of "tasteful" nude designed to obscure the fact that all the blokes are ogling the silky bits between the girl's legs.

We've had words about this, of course, warm words! But I have to admit, much of what passes for aesthetic sensuality in conventional art is simply voyeurism. A particularly invidious version of this is the voyeurism that revels in the abjection of women, taking the moral high ground the better to enjoy the view. Last month I was in Barcelona for the *Miró otro* retrospective and I was taken by a colleague to see Llimona's *El Desconsol*, a sculpture of a prone, naked woman, head bowed, face hidden by a cascade of hair. It is a moving work, but much of what it moves is moved for all the wrong reasons. I don't doubt that Hitler, a man who couldn't pass a classical nude without pausing, would have loved it.

There were plenty of classical nudes in The Great German Art Exhibition, staged at the same time as the Degenerate Art Exhibition to promote the virtues of Nazi-approved art. About 400,000 people visited the "Great Germans" at the *Große Deutsche Kunstausstellung.* Two million attended the "Degenerates" at the *Ausstellung entartete Kunst,* a million more on its tour of the provinces. Nowadays the Great Germans have disappeared into the vaults and the Degenerates are romping out of the auction rooms. History tells a good joke sometimes.

POSTCARD FROM THE PAST #19.

Musei Capitolini. Mussolini has stopped to inspect an exhibit, no small concession, seeing as how he has been telling everyone he had never visited a museum before this week, implying that it is not a mistake he intends repeating. It's sad, really. He needs to brag about his boorishness as much as he does about his erudition. He reminds me of those sorry creatures who feel compelled to tell you how unconventional they are, as if eccentricity has to be proclaimed to exist. You know, *I'm-a-wild-and-crazy-guy-me-I'll-do-anything*. Your generation is full of them. There are wild-and-crazy people, of course. Always have been, always will be. But the genuinely wild and crazy don't need to tell you about it. It's like humility or probity. Boast about it and it's immediately impaired.

Mussolini really is at his wits' end, though. Ten minutes ago, he was hissing in my ear, telling me to hurry things along before we all died. As we entered the numismatics hall, he was muttering about the number of rooms, as if the multicameral quality of the place was its main attribute. Now though he has planted himself in front of a reproduction of the Ides of March denarius coined by Caesar's assassins. Rocking back and forth on the balls of his feet, he glances from side to side to ensure everyone is listening.

"Ah . . . Brutus," he sighs, then turns to give Ciano and Bottai a commiserating smile. They laugh dutifully, if a little uneasily.

"As we walked in the gardens back there, Duce," says Hitler, "I saw your profile beside those of the Roman busts and it was clear to me that you are a true Caesar."

Comparing the contemporary despot with one who was stabbed in the back by his best mates seems a tad infelicitous. Bottai looks a little pained. But Mussolini treats the analogy with the satisfaction he accords everything related to himself. His body swells as best it can beneath the corsets. I'm not sure I don't hear a stitch giving way, though that might be a stifled parp from his guest. It must be a strain, dishing out the flattery rather than receiving it.

"The Caesars . . . are a great school for rulers," says Mussolini, repeating a line he used the other day. "Their achievements are always . . . in my thoughts. Rome is eternal, the . . . matter I have to shape unchanged. And the problem of power remains the . . . same: how to govern with the least . . . friction."

"This is a fundamental point," says Hitler, the torment of listening having proved too much. They have been together for four days. Diplomacy has its limits. Personally, I could do without fundamental points issuing from that quarter, but the situation is beyond remedying. "The nature of power is crucial," he continues, making little chopping movements with his hand. "For two millennia, the word 'Caesar' has signified supreme authority. And it is essential that the authority of state and leader remain synonymous. Power must be personified in one man: the Caesar, the Führer, the Duce. The leader and the creed are the same and everyone must do what the leader orders. Only he can know the ultimate goal."

Mussolini is contemplating the coin again. "I wonder why he did not read the list of . . . conspirators when it was handed to him?" he says. "Maybe he let himself . . . be murdered because he had reached the . . . end of his tether. During his last days, you know, even Caesar became a phrase-slave."

We have heard this before, too. I can't place it, but I remember the words. The phrase "phrase-slave" is one he favours. In fact, he is so fond of it that he repeats it then moves on before my translation opens the way for the Führer to indulge his own slavery to phrase making.

CETOLOGY #9. THE PHRASE MAKER.

Mussolini was no poet, but he was a good journalist, a wordsmith who understood that you don't have to worry about consistency and veracity if people like the sounds you make. His "diaries" turned up recently. They were fake. I knew it the moment I read "the sun today explodes in a hymn of life over the priceless expanse of the City." Mussolini was full of bollocks, but not that sort of bollocks. Describing a stifling summer on the island of Maddalena, he wrote, "Everything seemed to be nailed down under the sun." Now *that* was authentic, "nailed down," not the guff about a hymn of life.

It was with such phrases that he wrote his way to power and it was only when the gap between his words and the world became too wide that his popularity waned. And he was popular. Fascism was the regime in Italy for more than two decades, long enough for its defects to become obvious to everyone. This, after all, was a system so sleazy that one enterprising pensioner conned hundreds of thousands of lire out of would-be clients on the strength of an entirely fictitious friendship with Rachele Mussolini. It's quite something when a swindle is based on its victims' faith in bribery. But it was the party functionaries who were blamed. Most people believed the corruption, nepotism, stupidity, and ineptitude were aberrations the Duce would put right if only he knew about them.

Mussolini started his literary career as a polemicist penning diatribes attacking a catalogue of targets varied enough to elicit the admiration of Hitler himself, ranging from Free-masons to Catholics, landlords to nationalists, militarists to neo-Malthusians, big bosses to the petite bourgeoisie. At the inn where his father and Anna Lombardi installed themselves, he amused himself by writing plays, novels, and short stories while wooing Rachele—apparently his first choice had been the elder daughter, Augusta, but she preferred a man with better prospects and married a gravedigger instead.

The real creative writing came later, though, when Mussolini returned to journalism and used the medium to manipulate the world into a more pleasing shape, one in which he took centre stage as war hero, voice of the people, and supremely competent supreme leader, capable of excellence in every field. There was real artistry in this. Plenty of Italian politicians had their newspaper, it was pretty much obligatory, but none had the impact of *Il Popolo d'Italia*. Granted, his work wasn't always very subtle. He dismissed Prime Minister Nitti as Turdface and said Socialists were just masturbating waiting for the millennium. But his words had the desired effect, transforming him from a querulous nonentity into a Nietzschean Superman.

He carried on this creative activity throughout his life, from the *Diario di Guerra,* which gives the impression that he won the First World War single-handedly, through *Parlo con Bruno,* a piece of pious propaganda eulogizing his dead son (a pilot who had contrived to fly into a house) and conveying a relationship of imperishable intimacy that had in fact never existed. He pulled off similar sleights of hand in book after book, article after article. His collected works run to thirty-five volumes, which is enough to make anybody dizzy. You can understand why Italy was bedazzled. The nation was overwhelmed with verbiage.

As for the words of others, I never know what to make of Mussolini's pretence to have read everything. In one sense, he had, because when he came to power he was an absolute demon with a red pen, obsessing over censorship and insisting that his office be the final arbiter of what got consent, what got bowdlerized, and what got binned. He was good at it, too, fussily revising, suggesting subtle changes, and arranging things so that he could pretend the press was free. In many ways, he was less the mad poet and more the demented bureaucrat. It was the same with the imposition of internal exile on enemies and malcontents. Nearly every case of *confino* (and there were 13,000 of them) passed across his desk, often more than once. The Führer had a horror of administrative detail, but the Duce was sufficiently uptight to want to pore over the fine print. Little wonder he was rubbish at strategic thinking. He was doing all the clerical work.

Mussolini was infected by fakery, writing himself up and editing others down, and even his reading was contaminated by deceit. He once told a journalist he had never read Benedetto Croce, then changed his mind, saying he had been making a rhetorical point and had, in fact, read the philosopher's complete works and was a great admirer. When Croce heard this, he noted that the one time Mussolini had told the truth, he had been obliged to backtrack.

There were also persistent rumours that this great Nietzschean spirit hadn't actually taken the trouble to read Nietzsche at all, but had been drilled in the basics by his mistress, Margherita Sarfatti, who had written lists of the main points for him to memorize. As for his public persona, the image that has gone down in history was lifted directly from D'Annunzio's Nietzschean novel *Il Fuoco,* in which the hero spends his time haranguing the masses from a balcony. That, perhaps, is the most telling point. Whenever I was in his company, I had the disconcerting impression that The Constipated Prick was performing himself, playing a role.

I despised the man, but I confess, I can feel a certain compassion for him. There's a photo of him at his desk in the Sala del Mappamondo. The hall is vast, the desk tiny, and empty. There is nothing on it but a slim folder. And the Duce is bent over the folder with a pen in his hand. He could be doodling or playing noughts-and-crosses for all I know, but the image speaks to me. He is dwarfed by his surroundings, a little man lost in a large and elaborate and overwhelming world, and he is taking refuge in the written word. I can identify with that.

POSTCARD FROM THE PAST #20.

En route to Florence where the tour will end. My Waitress is nowhere to be seen, but she's on board and I'm glad, because this is Hitler's train. I hate to think what would happen if she was travelling with Il Duce, but I can picture her staggering onto the platform at Santa Maria Novella afterwards. Better she shares her sweetmeats with The Flatulent Windbag. He's sitting on a sofa mopping his neck with a white handkerchief. His skin is pale, perspiration plasters the lock of hair across his forehead, and his eyes are dull. He smiles at me. One of his incisors is capped with a patch of spinach leaf. I have just witnessed the most extraordinary performance . . . no, not witnessed, I was part of it, subsumed by his need.

We were an hour out of Rome when he sent for me. He was standing in front of a full-length mirror inspecting himself with evident dissatisfaction. He told me the others were "too familiar" with it all, weren't "feeding" him like he needed, that he wanted "somebody fresh." Had it been Goebbels talking, I might have thrown myself out the window at this stage. There was something nocturnal about that man, something about his foxy features, warm eyes, and soft, deep voice. If he said he "wanted somebody fresh," you'd be scrabbling about for the silver bullets and cloves of garlic and what have you. But there was a sad quality to Hitler's words that was almost plaintive. He invited me to sit down, told me to listen, and then he began.

I won't attempt to reproduce his words. They scarcely matter. The content was of secondary importance. It was about the Sudetenland and the plight of the Germans living in Czechoslovakia, a "question" that would be answered in a few months time with characteristic dispatch on his part and characteristic pusillanimity on the part of everyone else. He started tentatively, feeling his way into his words, as if not knowing what to say, why he was there, what was required of him. He spoke of historical injustices and fraudulent political processes, of his own forbearance and tireless diplomatic efforts, of hypocrisy and humiliation, duplicity and affliction. And as his speech progressed, his assurance grew, his words came more readily, and he began repeating phrases, like one of your blues singers, only instead of the refrain being *Baby make love to me, love to me, love-to-me*, it was *Take justice, justice-justice-justice*. And by reiterating the same words, he seemed to hypnotize himself, the tongue teasing his mind into an elsewhere of its own devising. And he began multiplying the incidences of treachery, lamenting his thwarted efforts to find a peaceful resolution, accusing the conniving political class at the head of the so-called Czechoslovak state of abusing his goodwill, spurning his pacific overtures, but now his long-tried patience was wearing thin, and he could take no more and it was time that the legitimate concerns of a suffering people be taken into consideration. Aggrieved innocence fed umbrage which bred rage in the wake of which everything else fell into place. He spoke of persecution, and the intolerable conditions under which his countrymen laboured, of refugees and reprisals, of reigns of terror and torture, of villages burning, of bombings and shootings and massacres. It was the speech he made one way or another throughout the thirties. Perhaps that was why he couldn't afford to let it go stale, had to work at the emotion so relentlessly.

But more important than the words was their delivery. As he spoke, his slack features acquired a mercurial volatility, the putty-like flesh remodelling itself, passing rapidly through expressions of pain, dismay, incredulity, and indignation, alternating states quicker than the tongue could name them, but touching the heart each time. One moment he seemed so close to tears that I almost felt compelled to console him, the next his cheeks were mottled, his eyelids bruised with wrath, and I was touched by a sense of righteous anger quite alien to my temperament. A carnival barker became a revivalist preacher, a sentimental ham hatched a palm-thumping pugilist who gave birth to a noble visionary gazing at a brighter future glimmering on the horizon. His arms flailed, threatening to topple him over, then his elbows were tucked tightly against his ribs, wrists raised and pressed together, pleading for understanding. The hands took on a life of their own, pointing, clenching, clamping, cupping, spread wide to embrace the world. He tossed back his head, luminous with revelation, then slumped in despair, before snapping upright, pummelling the air to clear the atmosphere and claw back his beautiful vision.

It sounds absurd, it was absurd, mad even, but by God, it worked. I watched, transfixed, knowing the performance was virtually epileptic in its intemperance, knowing that what he was saying was exaggerated if not entirely factitious, yet he was speaking to something inside me, for me and of me and through me, and before long I was half inclined to invade Czechoslovakia myself. He was doing it deliberately, of course, working himself into a rage, cultivating his sense of grievance to justify what he wanted to do anyway, searching for the stimulus he required to carry him through. But it went beyond that. The words were not a way of describing reality, but a means of re-creating reality, accessing the emotion that might transform the world, the emotion inside himself and inside others, the energy on which he could feed. And through this process he achieved not only power over others, but power over himself, too, over that wellspring of hatred that dwelt within him. He was building a bridge into a fantasy world that better accorded with his prejudices. Like a dervish turning in circles or a charismatic talking in tongues or a shaman beating on a drum, he was accessing something other. He wasn't simply switching the heat on. He was capable of that, but he also had to nurture it, stoking the fire, tending the flame so that it would burn brightly when it was needed.

Most remarkable was the degree of self-awareness. Even at his most possessed, he was watching me and glancing at the mirror, not for vanity, but to see what words and what gestures were having what impact, to see what worked how and with whom. It wasn't like when he went off his head because I disagreed with him. It was more subtle, faked and bona fide at the same time, fuelled by him but fuelling him, too. That image of a bridge is perhaps the best. With words he built bridges between himself and others, built bridges into himself and into other varieties of being. It was a genuinely creative act, perhaps the only artistry of which he was capable, the reason he was the Führer on whom the others depended, because without the bridges he built, the rest of them were nonentities, nasty little nonentities, but not nasty enough to get anywhere on their own.

Why me? Why stage such a display for the benefit of a nobody? Obviously, it wasn't for me. At most, he may have wished to gauge the impact of his oratory on someone of a certain background and certain education, a type he was unlikely to encounter in his immediate circle, but with whom he might have dealings in the future. Yet why risk exposure, the ridicule if others knew how his rages were generated? In truth, there was no risk. Nobody would believe I had heard Hitler rehearsing the grievances he would exploit to invade Czechoslovakia.

Gripped by his performance, I barely noticed the fug of effluvia that filled the atmosphere, but afterwards I was persuaded he had been farting as furiously as he was shouting, as if he had to expel wind from either end to maintain equilibrium. Certainly, my eyes had misted over, and it wasn't just because of his emotive words. The farts were getting worse by the day.

He discards the sodden hanky, unglues the forelock, and runs a finger along his wilted collar. Then he becomes animated again and gets to his feet. And as if to prove his histrionic versatility, he says, "Here, look, who's this . . ." and his chin is in the air and his lower lip is pouting and his hands are at his hips and his dark little eyes are glaring down the length of his nose at a seriously disappointing world and The Flatulent Windbag has transformed himself into The Constipated Prick. A couple of movements, a couple of gestures, and the impression is perfect, he doesn't even need to speak. I can't help myself. I'm laughing.

Yes, my dear, Hitler made your daddy laugh. But we might as well get it all into the open, let you know everything, good and bad, then we'll see where we can go from there.

He sits down, picks a grape from a bowl on the table, apparently satisfied to have both moved me and made me laugh, as if that were his sole purpose in life.

"Mussolini is a great man," he says. "Unfortunately for him, he is an Italian. Even he will never make anything but Italians out of Italians. He lacks the material a leader needs to make a nation great. You can tell by the language, really. When you listen to it, Italian is a tongue that sings. But when you translate it, nothing is left, it's just empty noise. Now we Germans, by contrast, we do not talk simply for the sake of it. No, we are not in love with the sound of our own voices. When we speak, it is to say something. You do not believe me?"

I think I must be gaping at the enormity of this.

"No, it's just, I mean, yes, I believe you. But . . . I didn't know you spoke Italian."

"I don't," he says, looking at me as if my lame reply has revealed hitherto unsuspected depths of imbecility. "I don't need to. Besides, I had no aptitude for languages at school. I could have done, but the teacher was an idiot, a disgusting creature with a dirty beard and greasy collar. He hated me because I didn't learn a thing. But speaking foreign languages is no proof of intelligence. Spanish women do it and they're outstandingly stupid. And in a hundred years, German will be the language of Europe. Everyone will learn it, like you, to communicate with us. All my teachers were bullies, you know. Most of them were a bit mad, too. They had no empathy with youth. You could tell that from my school reports. I got bad marks. They just wanted to stamp on any hint of originality, stuffing our heads to turn us into erudite apes like themselves. Schooling like that is a waste of time. It only overloads the brain. But a bright youngster can always get the better of a man dulled by the grind of teaching."

Reminiscing about how bad his education was, he becomes nostalgic for his youth and starts telling me anecdotes about his school days, how he and his peers tormented the teachers, misinterpreting instructions, pretending not to understand the "Itler" of a master who could not pronounce his aitches, asking embarrassing questions in bible study, blowing kisses to nuns in the convent, inventing vices to shock the priest during confession, releasing cockchafers into the classroom, shifting benches into the gangway to form a bottleneck trapping the teacher . . . he rattles on with the same relentless insistence as the train clacking across the tracks, while I listen, appalled and fascinated, for in his confessional mood he is revealing a childhood much like any other, a boyhood of scrapes and misdemeanours and small rebellions.

I wish I had his words on tape to play to people now, particularly to you, my dear. All you hear are those demented rants at rallies, but behind them there was a banal little man, one capable of boring the world into submission as much as he bulldozed it into submission, a softly spoken man, modest in demeanour, modest in everything save his overweening egotism and the madness of his dreams. And yet, even in the banalities, he is capable of surprising one. He ends his reminiscences with an anecdote.

"You know, in my last year, I had lodgings in town. Well, after the final exam, we had a little party. It's the only time I ever got drunk. I had my certificate and was due to return home. My classmates and I got together over a quart of wine. I've forgotten what happened that night, but I woke up at dawn, lying in the road in a shocking state. Back at my lodgings, my landlady, Petronella, asked if I had my certificate. I looked through my pockets, turned them inside out, but it had totally disappeared! What was I to tell my mother? I was already thinking up an excuse: I had taken it out on the train, in front of an open window, and a gust of wind! But Petronella said I should ask the school for a copy. Well, the director kept me waiting a long time, I can tell you. It turned out that my certificate had been handed in by somebody who had found it in the road. But it was torn into four pieces and in a somewhat inglorious condition. Apparently, my head muddled by wine, I had confused the precious document with toilet paper! I won't tell you what he said to me. I'm still mortified. But I promised myself I would never get drunk again and I have kept my promise."

This leaves me speechless. Hitler is said to guard the dignity of his office obsessively, never even writing a *billet doux* to Eva Braun lest it fall into the wrong hands and compromise his authority, yet he is telling me that as an adolescent he wiped his arse with his school certificate! Either he has absolute confidence in me, or absolute contempt for me such that he knows I won't dare reveal what I have heard, or he has information concerning some precipitate and fatal malady to which I am subject unbeknownst to myself. Given who he is and the resources at his disposal, I prefer not to think about this last possibility.

"I wonder whether Petronella is still alive," he says, apparently talking to himself as if he has forgotten I am there, which, all things considered, would be the desirable denouement for this particular conversation. "We were very fond of her, you know. She looked after us in all sorts of ways. Small acts of kindness. She was always stuffing our pockets with dainties. Oh well, it's all past now. But remembering her treats makes me peckish. How about some cake?"

CETOLOGY #10. THE FORK AND THE SPOON
AND THE CURIOUS CASE OF TOTALITARIAN MORALITY.

It wasn't just cake. In fact, when it comes to what the despots ate, there were a lot of things it wasn't. Pure mischief on my part, my dear. But since you have been so insistent lately about the immorality of eating meat, I can't resist. That both The Flatulent Windbag and The Constipated Prick preferred to ruminate rather than gnaw is one of those niggling details that are difficult to disregard. It's a bit like the fact that homicidal dictators have a distressing tendency to be failed creative artists. It doesn't mean all failed creative artists want to kill everyone out of pique. But a disproportionate number do. Poets are particularly suspect. Mussolini, Stalin, and Mao were all would-be verse makers. And vegetarians are equally fishy. Two of this century's top four tyrants favoured a diet without meat. I don't know how many vegetarians there are in Europe, but I doubt it's 50 percent of the population.

Due to his ulcer, Mussolini's regimen was a milksop affair supplemented by occasional omelettes, small portions of boiled fish and pasta, a few grapes, and plenty of fresh vegetables. Like Popeye, he was particularly fond of spinach and olive oil. Come to that, he was also choleric, unmannerly, muscle-bound, and given to gurning. I don't think Popeye was especially ascetic, though, whereas the Duce was ostentatiously abstemious, boasting about his Spartan lifestyle and frugal diet, not because he was proud of his ulcer, but because habits imposed on him by infirmity happened to tally with the

Fascist doctrine that action was everything. You didn't want to sit around sucking on a bone and hypothesizing. You had to get out and get on with doing stuff. Food was a distraction.

The advantages of advocating abstinence in a country where half the population could rarely afford meat were obvious. Unfortunately, it backfired when war came and Mussolini told everyone the sluggish English couldn't possibly win because they ate five meals a day. If you were an impoverished peasant surviving on a spot of pottage and a spit of olive oil, five meals a day sounded like a very good idea indeed, no matter how lethargic it made you.

You won't remember much about Italy, my dear. You were still a toddler when we left. And despite your mother's pastries, your idea of Italian cuisine is probably all pizza and pasta. But back in the thirties, Italians valued bread above all else. There was no higher praise for a woman than saying she was "as good as bread." And the passion for bread was behind what, as far as I know, was The Constipated Prick's only stab at free verse, inspired by a campaign to make the country self-sufficient in grain. I don't have a copy to hand, but it's not the sort of thing you forget, no matter how hard you try. It went something like this:

> Italians! Love bread: heart of the home, redeemer
> of the repast, saviour of health!
> Respect bread: sweat of the brow, pride of toil,
> poem of sacrifice!
> Honour bread: glory of the field, fragrance of the
> soil, banquet of life!
> Do not squander bread: wealth of the fatherland,
> gift of God, holy reward of labour!

"I am a mad poet"? I don't know what Ezra Pound would have made of it, but I can imagine what your average peasant thought when told to venerate this splendiferous provender without being invited to eat any of the stuff. Apart from that verbal extravaganza, the nearest I saw Mussolini come to sybaritic self-indulgence was a fortnight after Hitler's visit when the Fascists staged a "Rustic Fair" in the *Circo Massimo*, with fake rustic villages and fake rustic taverns serving regional dishes while a lot of fake rustic peasants drifted about being decorative and eyeing the food they couldn't afford. Mind you, his animation that day may have had less to do with the gastronomical display and rather more to do with the rustic bosoms of the rustic wenches serving in the rustic taverns.

As for The Flatulent Windbag, it's a job to know where to start with his relationship to food. For one thing, his table manners were deplorable. He made no effort to curb his farting, he bit his fingernails, clutched his cutlery in his fists, and continued talking, leaving no one in any doubt as to the progress of his *risotto al Parmigiano*. Yet he was fussy about what went into his mouth and enjoyed putting meat eaters off their food by detailing how animals were slaughtered. Which came first, the diet or the dodgy guts, is open to question. It's said that he didn't become vegetarian until Geli's suicide, after which he could no longer countenance dead flesh. But I'd rather not consider the implications of the idea that he could conflate his niece's corpse with a couple of slices off the cold meats counter. Whatever their origin, though, his dietary habits had acquired a coherent moral and medical justification by the time I met him.

Forever predicting that the future would be vegetarian, he would cite samples of superior physical performances fuelled by diets that didn't depend on meat, from conquering Roman legionaries to piano-toting Turkish porters. According to his own account, when he ate meat he would drink a gallon of liquid during a political rally and still shed nine pounds, whereas after he became vegetarian a sip of water was enough to keep him going. Offer a child the choice between meat and fruit, he said, and they would instinctively opt for the latter. It was only natural. Meat caused caries and cancer. Even vegetarians no longer enjoyed the full nutritional value of food, because cooking spoiled the raw ingredients' natural properties. And was it not absurd that, in a country where the potato was the staple food, only 1 percent of the land was given over to its cultivation while 37 percent was dedicated to cattle, yet if only 3 percent was planted with potatoes it would be enough to feed everybody?

But it wasn't simply reason that inspired him. There was emotion, too. Hitler couldn't watch a film featuring cruelty to animals. He had to turn aside and shield his eyes until the scene was over. He often quoted Frederick the Great: "Now that I know men, I prefer dogs." And he meant it. Conservation and the protection of animals were key issues in Nazi Germany, notably under the aegis of their other great sponsor, Hermann Göring. Tracts of land were reforested and reserves were set up for endangered species; slaughterhouses, livestock transport, cooking crustaceans, shoeing horses, hunting, fishing, trapping, and animal experimentation were all regulated, while vivisection was banned outright; those who treated animals as mere chattels were condemned—and sent to concentration camps.

Hitler was a bit of a hippy really. He shared your respect for nature and contempt for man's destructive arrogance. True piety came from being in harmony with nature, which could satisfy all our metaphysical needs. Aspirations to dominion over nature were illusory, dispelled by a simple storm. This is what he said. This is what he believed. Sound familiar? Are these not the things you tell me? And are right to tell me, too, because they are true. I've said as much myself. Do you remember how exasperated Mum was by my admiration for weeds, muscling their way into the garden regardless of her efforts, cracking up the patio despite her plucking and picking and spraying? Nature does puncture our pretensions, repeatedly. It is a principle that is no less true because spoken by a prophet whose main message was something other.

In the same unorthodox spirit, Hitler hated hypocrisy in sexual mores and reviled the bureaucratic conventions of matrimony. Above all, he despised prejudices against children born out of wedlock. Nature doesn't care for such things. Nature just cares for fecundity. Make love, not war! And like you, my dear, he rebelled against the materialism that alienates us from the natural world. Even Mussolini said the materialistic concept of happiness was unattainable. Anything else? Well, I can't vouch for this, but Albert Speer claimed Hitler considered nuclear weapons immoral. Nobody knew for sure what would happen once you started splitting atoms. Nature Boy wasn't delighted by the idea that a chain reaction might reduce the world to a bright white light in somebody else's sky.

So basically these people were animal loving, CND-supporting environmentalists who accentuated the sacred dimension of life, and had an enlightened attitude to divorce, unwed mothers, and illegitimate children. Still ready to con-demn? You should be. Mussolini's antimaterialism was genu-ine, but as with frugal eating, declaring that the pursuit of material well-being was futile served a useful purpose in a country of chronic poverty and massive disparities of wealth. As for the Nazis, they may have come up with some of the right answers about man's role in the universe, but for all the wrong reasons. Removing the ethical divide between people and animals is a prudent move if you intend treating people like animals. And if the main lesson of nature is survival of the fittest and, through sheer brutality, you are proving more vital than everyone else, so be it. Like the man said, *nature spontaneously eliminates everything that has no gift for life*. Ergo, anything we eliminate has no "gift for life" and has to go.

I repeat, pure mischief on my part, pretending these des-pots were a couple of Bohemian idealists, but it's mischief with a purpose. Hitler is like a curious cloud pattern or a Rorschach blot. Reading him, we read ourselves. He was a monster? He was inhuman? Insofar as doubt is characteristic of humanity, yes, he was inhuman. Totalitarianism has no room for doubt. But more than that, he was an inhuman monster because that is what we fear we are as a species and wish to export onto someone else, because kinship with all that is "inhuman" and "monstrous" inside ourselves is unendurable. Look at the better bits, though, the bits that sound like the selves we would like to acknowledge, and you will see that the kinship is as undeniable as it is unendurable. No matter how cynically motivated they were, the shared values bind these people to us, like a couple of tin cans tied to the newlyweds' rear bumper, and no matter how fast we drive, they will keep clattering along behind us.

POSTCARD FROM THE PAST #21.

Hitler is besotted by My Waitress and the sentiment seems mutual. Summoned to his stateroom, she has come spouting perfect German (picked up, she explains, in her Alto Adige childhood), and carrying a plateful of *amaretti* and other confectionary. She palms me off with a couple of vermilion macaroons, keeping the *amaretti* for her forelocked friend. A special treat. She even has the temerity to claim she developed the recipe expressly for him, which proves to be true in a way, but irks me because I happen to know that the biscuit was invented for an eighteenth-century bishop. The Führer doesn't bat an eyelid. Well, he does, but not because he disbelieves her. He finds it normal that a new biscuit should be devised in his honour. It reminds me of the old joke about Paul von Hindenburg visiting Frankfurt. Asking the name of a particularly magnificent building, he's told that it's Saint Paul's Cathedral. "Oh, you shouldn't have," he says, modestly. "I'm only here for the afternoon."

The Führer accepts a second biscuit and flutters his eyelashes. No, that's not true. He isn't cooing and coming over all coy. Neither is she. But they are so busy exuding salvoes of charm at one another that I can imagine any cliché of seduction manifesting itself. He takes a bite of his biscuit, continues holding forth on the city of his dreams, Florence. It's conventional stuff—harmony, proportion, cradle of the Renaissance, etcetera. Nothing about Savonarola and the bonfire of the vanities.

My attention wavers as I speculate whether My Waitress suffers some form of congenital idiocy given her inexplicable preference for him over me. But then, after about six biscuits and a score of platitudes, I'm all ears because Hitler says, "but then that's the sort of man I am." If I'm here for a reason, it's because I want to know what sort of man this is. I've missed the key statement and I know that it's nearly always a bad sign when somebody feels the need to tell you, usually with great emphasis, what they ARE. Still, I listen.

"You see, I'm an optimist really," he says. "I'd find life unbearable otherwise. Pessimists complicate things for no good reason, you know. Some of them even say the world is evil, that they want to end it all. Imagine? I *like* the world. I always tell the suicidal to wait awhile, that things will improve with time. Besides, one cannot escape the world. We belong to nature and our purpose is to sustain the cycle of life on this planet. Our purpose and our pleasure! I dream of the day when every man knows that he lives only to preserve the species. We are duty-bound to promote this notion and the men who do most to serve the cause of humanity must be awarded the highest honours."

I have my doubts about his sunny disposition. He has already proved he has a sense of humour and optimists don't do humour. It's the tool of pessimists. There again, given the way this rather unprepossessing middle-aged man is look-ing at this dazzling young woman, maybe he is an optimist after all.

I sometimes wonder what the despots saw in your mother. I mean, I can guess what Mussolini saw: a body that looked good in skirts and would look better out of them. But Hitler? Apart from being pretty, she was everything he hated in a woman—intelligent, independent, pugnacious, and ungovern-able. Naturally, she dissembled all this back then, but Hitler normally had a knack for seeing through impostors. I think it was the type of her physical beauty that beguiled him, above all the eyes.

I used to call her "Spaniel eyes" because of the way the brow and eyelids sloped up toward the glabella. It's a configuration of flesh and bone that gives an impression of sympathy and warmth, suggesting a personality that is soft, sweet, and forgiving. I think that's what got to him. Which is funny really. I loved her dearly, but it would never have occurred to me to call your mother soft, sweet, and forgiving. The Queen of Tarts was tart, too, tough-minded and sharp-tongued, and I think if she had lived long enough to lose her marbles, the last thing she would have forgotten would have been the grudges. I liked that about her. Intransigence has its own charm. It implies a commitment to life that I lack.

She offers him another biscuit, smiles when he pops it between his lips, as if it is a *billet doux* conveying some intimate message intended exclusively for him. Perhaps I really ought to do something about bumping him off. This is the golden age of the railway murder mystery, after all: *Stamboul Train, Murder On The Orient Express, The Lady Vanishes*; and I am on a train with a man who will shortly earn a reputation as the greatest mass murderer of all time. If I were to just . . .

And so to Florence, where I nearly did what I ought to have done but didn't and didn't do what it would have been wise for me to do. And it was because I didn't do what it would have been wise for me to do that I won my own modest celebrity as a partisan.

POSTCARD FROM THE PAST #22.

My Waitress has gone, whisked away by the Podestà to concoct something flaky for her newfound friend. Meanwhile, The Man Who Knows Everything sits in a limousine and shams omniscience, inventing what he doesn't know in the near certainty that The Constipated Prick's vanity and The Flatulent Windbag's wonderment will prevent them questioning any assertion, no matter how far-fetched.

There's a tricky moment when Mussolini asks how deep the Arno is. I haven't the faintest idea. *One metre seventy-five!* The look he gives me suggests this is too shallow for a good Fascist river, so I tell him it's low at this time of year and that when in spate it's six metres deep. Honour is saved. He turns to wave at the crowds.

They press close to the motorcade, proximity intensifying the oppressive impact, lending the compacted bodies a charged, almost electrical presence that clearly pleases Il Duce. I suspect the adulation of the mob is vital to him, a staple without which he could not live. Perhaps it is the purpose of his political career. Like someone who is so uncertain of himself that he must shout loud to be sure of being heard, Mussolini requires the recognition of others to shore up his sense of self.

Hitler, meanwhile, is more subdued. He has repeatedly said that this will be the highlight of his trip, that Florence is the city he always wanted to visit, but now that he is here, he seems almost overwhelmed by it all. I very nearly pity him. He is grinning the gormless grin of a clumsy boy who has been given the biggest train set in the world and fears he is bound to break it. But he soon punctures my nascent compassion.

"And to think," he says, "if Bolshevism had come here, to Tuscany, all this would have been destroyed like in Spain." The fact that he and his penile chum have been instrumental in generating the destruction in Spain is irrelevant. He slaps his palm with his gloves. "I will not permit the propagation of such ideas in Germany. They must be eliminated with the utmost violence. Here the Duce has won the respect of all humanity!"

It's an odd sentiment, given that in Nazi Germany, so far as I can work out, all the Communists are dead, dying, hiding, or behind barbed wire. His agitation at this mythical menace to the Fatherland is revealing. Hitler may be human, he may be one of us, but he applies a compulsive, almost neurotic twist to that humanity. Despite lacking the womb, there is something hysterical about The Flatulent Windbag, not just in his histrionics, but in his mood swings and that neurasthenic flatulence.

We're crossing the Ponte Vecchio, the bridge that inspired my wild fantasy of bomb lobbing. Glancing up, I see faces that are clearly not the faces of starstruck Fiorentini, faces wearing the alert looks of men who expect other men to do awful things, in large measure because they have been trained to do awful things themselves. My fantasy was even wilder than I had thought.

I start telling the story, which I suspect is apocryphal, about the etymology of bankruptcy, insolvent merchants on the bridge having their stall or *banco* broken to prevent them continuing to trade so that they were *bancorotto*. Mussolini smirks, as if he also finds this picturesque legend implausible, a tale for tourists and children, but Hitler nods his head. He apparently believes he is being treated to the inside gen on the "real" Florence that other tourists don't touch upon because they are too unimportant and too stupid to get access to it.

It was a long day in Florence. I won't try and reconstruct every detail. But given its importance for me and your Mum and for that clipping that is proving so prickly a souvenir, I'll try to tell you enough so you don't think I'm hiding anything. And I'm not hiding anything, not from you, not anymore. Maybe from myself. But not from you. All those years teaching you how to read, I mean really read, reading all the things a writer communicates without meaning or even wanting to, you'll find them useful now. That's the buggeration with children. You only know you've succeeded with them when the tools you taught them are deployed against you. This goes for good stuff and bad stuff. Reading is good stuff.

POSTCARD FROM THE PAST #23.

The Palazzo Vecchio balcony. Achille Starace, the Party Secretary, is conducting the crowd, carrying on like a pantomime dame working an audience of delirious infants: *Duce! Duce! Heil Hitler!* I-can't-hear-you! *Duce! Duce! Heil Hitler!* I-still-can't-hear-you! *Duce! Duce! Heil Hitler!* And in keeping with pantomime, there is a *He's-behind-you!* moment.

I've managed to detach myself from the main party. Appearances notwithstanding, I have my standards and I'm not bloody venturing onto a balcony above a bawling mob. I'm standing inside the doorway, out of sight and hopefully out of mind.

A gang of Lesser Bigwigs bunch behind the leaders, who are cock-a-hoop, capering about, joshing one another, as chuffed as a couple of kids left in charge of a candyfloss concession. Beyond them, the Piazza della Signoria is splashed with fasces, swastikas, and the Florentine *fleur-de-lys*.

Despite the crowd's agitated waving, the flags flap listlessly. They're made of Lanital, a synthetic textile processed from an extract of skimmed milk that serves as a substitute for wool, cotton, and silk. Starace is Lanital's prime champion. He has even persuaded Dino Grandi, ambassador to Britain and a great admirer of his own dignity, to wear a suit made from forty-eight pints of the stuff. Hasn't caught on, though. Milk goes off, after all, and wet Lanital smells rancid. What's more, Lanital jumpers tend to make your tits look saggy. Not an issue at your age, my dear, but as a middle-aged man who recently discovered that when he runs downstairs his tits start wobbling, I can tell you, a droopy-boob sweater is not desirable.

Anyway, I'm standing inside the doorway when there's a breach in the line of bodies in front of me. The Lesser Bigwigs have edged outward to get a better glimpse of the grateful multitudes, thus presenting me with a clear view of the dictators' backsides. This is not pleasant. They're stamping their feet and nudging one another and flipping the tails of their coats like a couple of courting birds trying to attract a mate. But what strikes me most is that they are both close to the balcony edge.

The parapet is low, about midriff height. And there's nobody between us. I have a clear run at them. I don't need guns or bombs or any of the paraphernalia that pleases the sort of people normally given to political assassination. All I've got to do is rush them. One good shove and I could guarantee that at least one would topple over the edge. Grab and dive and I might take them both out. This could be the balcony scene to end all balcony scenes.

But I hesitate and, in that second's hesitation, I catch sight of something out of the corner of my eye. There are dozens of men milling about the room, Brobdingnagians, bodyguards, flunkeys, and so forth, but it's not them that distract me. It's more insinuating, more sinister. Tucked in the corner, off to the left, Goebbels is standing in the shadows, a hand in his jacket pocket. He's watching me. His eyes gleam in the gloom of the room, bright with their own interior light. And he's very still, just watching, waiting, warm and amused.

Then the bodies behind the dictators close and the moment has passed and Goebbels slips onto the balcony, squeezing past the Lesser Bigwigs. I'm left inside, wondering whether I have just missed the opportunity of a lifetime. As it happens, I haven't. I am to be given another chance in short measure. And that by the man who was watching me a moment ago. Goebbels and me, we're both creatures of the shadows. Perhaps that's why he will also be responsible for my presence in the lift.

POSTCARD FROM THE PAST #24.

Giardino di Boboli. I'm all at odds with myself, disturbed by Goebbels's scrutiny. I must watch my step in his presence and watch my tongue even more closely. I cast a critical eye over the gardens. Like many things in Florence, they are greatly overrated. It's similar to that business about Hitler's eyes. I swear people were hypnotized because they had been told they would be. And in Florence, most visitors are awestruck by its beauty because they have been informed beforehand that this is what they should be feeling. The Boboli Gardens are marred by too many straight lines, too much manicuring. I never understood the rectilinear obsessions of European gardeners. They seem incapable of going near something green without getting their rulers out.

Mussolini is looking dismissive, too, put out by the statuary and fountains and finicky artistic flourishes. Even the nymphaea fail to please. But he brightens up at the staging of two Italian traditions. Hitler is elated, too. The displays that excite them are reenactments of the *Palio di Siena*, the barebacked horse race that takes place in the Piazzo del Campo, and the Pisan *Gioco del Ponte*, in which two teams done up in ersatz sixteenth-century Spanish kit compete to push a cart across a bridge. The horse race is spectacular, but the game of the bridge is a surpassingly daft display of brute force. If this is an iconic national sport, the nation should be put out of its misery forthwith.

Both games have their origins in medieval festivities that were basically prearranged mass brawls. I always supposed the point of sport was to protect the well-being of society by transforming the natural propensity of young men to batter one another about the head into a diverting entertainment. But the fact that the two middle-aged men most responsible for the coming war should take such childish pleasure in the performance of mock hostilities suggests games are more about promoting than purging belligerent instincts. This is disturbing. As we are all about to find out, war is not a game.

POSTCARD FROM THE PAST #25.

The virtues of the Piazzale Michelangelo have not been exaggerated. The view across the city toward the distant mountains really is splendid. The Flatulent Windbag is fortunate in that it rained yesterday afternoon. The air is so clear that the countryside of Fiesole has been seduced into a virtually incestuous proximity with Florence and the bluish band of the Apuan Alps resembles a distant wave rolling toward the city. It's all really rather magical until the man opens his mouth.

He has been gazing at the vista for some minutes and is evidently moved by what he sees. This is what he wanted, this is why he came to Italy. Forget the foreign policy accords, the incipient conflict, the need to safeguard the southern frontier, what he really wanted was to witness this glorious Tuscan afternoon. And to do it justice, to honour the achievement of his life's ambition, to acknowledge all the artists and grand historical figures who have made Florence famous, to locate himself and all his yearnings in the context of this unique setting, he makes an indistinct noise in the back of his throat, and says:

"*Endlich. Endlich, versetehe ich Böcklin und Feuerbach!*" Böcklin and Feuerbach?! I'd be speechless if I wasn't mute already. Böcklin and Feuerbach?! That *is* what I heard? Böcklin and Feuerbach?! *Finally, finally I understand Böcklin and Feuerbach.*

Böcklin and Feuerbach were Northern European painters who fell in love with classical Italy and never got over it, men who spent their days looking so hard at the past that when they bumped into the future it left a nasty lump on the back of their heads. They were supremely proficient technically, but so out of kilter with their times that they have been reduced to footnotes in the history of art. To visit Florence, the city that produced Boticelli, Giotto, Leonardo, and Michelangelo, and think, *Right you are, Böcklin and Feuerbach,* is a bit like defining beef by a hamburger or spaghetti by the treatment meted out to it in a canning factory. As with Messrs. Wimpy and Heinz, Böcklin and Feuerbach identified a good thing, but they hardly represent its most sublime manifestation.

I'm sure you'll be casting about for your high horse by now, my dear, disgusted by my snobbish condescension, which is only as it should be. It would never do for young people to deem their parents' opinions spot on. If that were the case, both parties would be bereft of a very versatile and gratifying source of grievance. But snobbish condescension *can* be useful. I suspect it was due to snobbish condescension that I proved relatively impervious to Hitler's famous capacity to captivate.

From what I've read, the people who did not fall under his spell generally possessed either vast quantities of blue blood or vast quantities of higher education. If I can characterize the man as nothing more than an ambulant fart, it would suggest a certain superciliousness on my part, and I believe that is what saved me from the "spell." It wasn't a *sine qua non*, but if you could look down on him, it helped. On the personal level, I mean. Looking down on him on the political level was a catastrophic misjudgment that resulted in him coming to power in the first place then plunging the world into war.

Before we leave the esplanade, there is another example of how pedestrian Hitler's intellect can be. I forget what inspired the observation, but without any preamble, he points out that the decorative motifs of classical art in the Mediterranean all come from Greece. "But we don't know," he says, "where the ornamental themes of Germanic art come from. Yet they must have some source, a comparable culture that disappeared. I believe these motifs stem from the lost culture of a lost continent. They clearly reference the empire of the lands of Atlantis that sank into the ocean. *Sehen sie, meine Herren.*"

At first, I think he's joking. It's no joke though. That Atlantis is a legend sustained by little more than the invincible credulity of mankind is neither here nor there. It's the same logic as the Jewish conspiracy. The fact that you can't see it doesn't mean it's not there. On the contrary, you can't disprove something you can't see, which is tantamount to verification of its actual existence. Invisibility just shows how cunning they are.

Mussolini glances at me, aware that something doesn't quite cohere, but uncertain what. I scratch the back of my neck, determined not to speak unless spoken to. How my governess would have marvelled at my self-restraint! The Duce makes a gesture of negation with his forefinger, but before he can speak, Hitler expresses himself again.

"And to think," he says, turning toward the mountains, "if Bolshevism had . . ."

Oh, come on! Even Stalin couldn't knock down the Apennines.

POSTCARD FROM THE PAST #26.

We spend several hours in the Palazzo Pitti and the Uffizi, painting after painting enrapturing Hitler and exasperating Mussolini. Our party includes Ribbentrop, Himmler, Goebbels, Dietrich, Ciano, Bottai, and Starace. I can take a break from my duties as resident know-it-all, because we are joined by Friedrich Kriegbaum, director of the German Institute of Florentine Art, a cultivated man who flinches whenever The Flatulent Windbag speaks. Kriegbaum died five years later in the first bombardment of Florence, more or less voluntarily as I understand it, such was his despair at the turn the world had taken. For the present though, he is doing his best to enlighten the Führer. If I am wise, I will stand back and let him get on with it. Unfortunately, it is here that my tongue gets the better of my resolve to remain mum.

Hitler is particularly taken with the *Doni Madonna* and fails to hear me when I point out that the grass is green and the sky blue. A clumsy attempt at humour, but Kriegbaum can't quite suppress a snort of stifled laughter. Goebbels gives me a look so dirty that I catch a whiff of midden, though that may be The Flatulent Windbag. He is less keen on Caravaggio's *Sacrifice of Isaac*, remarking that had the angel not intervened, we would not now be faced with a worldwide conspiracy of greasy, grasping, money-grubbing, glib-lipped profiteers. Kriegbaum turns aside, quelling what appears to be a compelling urge to throw up.

Later we pause in front of Perugino's *Pietà*. It is not my favourite lamentation. Too rigid, both in its piety and painting, Christ's body balanced awkwardly on his mother's knees with none of the broken abandon one sees in more naturalistic versions. Still, it is an image of compassion, caring, and grief. The cradled body, the Madonna's faintly androgynous face, the mournful Mary Magdalene, speak of gentleness and the fragility of life. Beside such tenderness, the bored indifference of Mussolini and the callow enthusiasm of Hitler are equally repugnant.

Watching them, I realize that the art I studied in such a dilettante manner does actually matter to me, means something more than technique and iconography, something more than colour, tone and texture, something more than form and volume and composition, and that the part of human being it represents is threatened by these people. Little wonder that Kriegbaum, who is so much more serious than I am and so much more implicated in the hierarchy that menaces what he loves, looks a little green about the gills as he struggles to maintain the stream of platitudes his Führer requires. I decide to help him out.

You know, my dear, how fond I am of quirky homophones. What joy, when browsing through an atlas, to discover an area north of the Caucuses called The Manych Depression! Likewise, I cherish the neologism "septych," which sounds like putrefaction, but in fact denotes a work of art composed of seven panels. Kriegbaum is explaining that the two works in front of us now, *Saint Florian Leaving The Monastery* and *The Martyrdom of Saint Florian,* come from a septych by Albrecht Altdorfer. Unless you're interested in the history of art and the technicalities of colour, these are not Altdorfer's most interesting paintings, and Kriegbaum's making heavy work of it. So when Hitler mentions that Saint Florian is the patron saint of his hometown of Linz, I take the opportunity to "lighten" the atmosphere.

"Linz?" I say. "But that's in Upper Austria, isn't it? I thought you were from Lower Austria. Döllersheim or something like that was the name I heard."

This is more mischief on my part, but I do not anticipate the impact it will have. You remember Alois Hitler, the son of Maria Anna Schicklgruber and an unnamed father who was likely one of the Hiedler brothers? Well *he* was the one born in Döllersheim, not his son, who was born in Braunau am Inn. But there's a reason for my "mistake." I don't recall if I mentioned it, but during the thirties there was a rumour that Alois's father was either the son of a wealthy Jewish landlord called Frankenberger, who got the maid in the family way during a bit of Yiddish *droit de cuissage*, or that the progenitor was an even more illustrious predator, a certain Baron Rothschild of Vienna!

I never believed these stories. They were too convenient given the Nazi obsession with "pure Aryan pedigrees," a meaningless phrase but one that clearly couldn't accommodate a Jewish granddad, a Jewish granddad who just happened to present himself as the perfect boon to anti-Nazis, lazy-thinking Freudians, and scurrilous-minded fellows like myself. Moreover, in view of what happened afterwards, the subtext of the tale is plain distasteful, implying that six million Jews were murdered because some nameless Jew in the past had put a bun in granny's oven then buggered off. Same goes for the other persistent rumour that Hitler was pissed off because he picked up a dose of clap from a Jewish prostitute. At worst, the search for a Jew to blame is as anti-Semitic as that hogwash in *The Protocols of the Elders of Zion*. At best, it attempts to explain something that, morally speaking, is probably inexplicable.

Still, you can see why opponents thought rumours of Granddad Jude were rather fun and kept visiting Döllersheim in search of details. What I didn't appreciate was how seriously Hitler took all this claptrap. In fact, it upset him so much that while we were in Florence, the ancestral village in his recently annexed homeland was being evacuated in order to turn it into a firing range. Döllersheim disturbed The Flatulent Windbag so much that he wanted it blown off the face of the map and Granny's grave along with it.

"Linz?" I say. "But that's in Upper Austria, isn't it? I thought you were from Lower Austria. Döllersheim or something like that was the name I heard."

The effect is instantaneous. He spins round, penetrating little eyes trained on me, as friendly as a couple of nails hammered into a baseball bat. He stares at me with the fixed intensity of a dog trying to dominate a rival. Then he snarls. Himmler appears to be about to crap himself with panic. Goebbels scuttles about behind his master, like he's looking for something to stroke, a tail perhaps. Ribbentrop is slithering out of view. Dietrich is briskly rubbing the barrel of his pistol, warming it up in case anyone needs killing. Kriegbaum doesn't know where to put himself. As for the Italians, Mussolini has suddenly discovered how fascinating art can be and is poring over Saint Florian's pinkie with his acolytes.

The Führer is white hot with fury. There are no words this time, not like on the train to Naples. He doesn't need words. "Snarling" wasn't a metaphor. He's making a noise in the back of his throat, an angry gurgling, like broken glass draining down a plughole. "White hot" is wrong, though. There's something glacial about his inarticulate rage. There is heat inside it, but it's a heat that has gone so far it has turned icy, the opposite of blistering cold, a freezing heat, a passion so acute that it's cryogenic. I still don't know how to describe this. I said before that his anger was a tool. He works himself into a rage, uses the tool, then turns it off when the job is done. But sometimes the tool takes over. And sometimes, it's turned on by someone else. Yet he still knows where the switch is. His fury, his visible fury, probably only lasts thirty seconds before he gets a grip on himself, but it's thirty seconds too long for those of us who witness it.

Hitler turns back to *The Martyrdom*. Saint Florian's got a millstone tied to his neck prior to being tossed in the river. Goebbels pats down his hair, glaring at me, the twist of his lips suggesting millstones would be too good for me. Ribbentrop slicks himself back into position beside his master. Himmler tries to compose his face, a hopeless task with a face like that. The Führer is murmuring to himself. At first I can't catch his words, but then I realize he is consoling himself by quoting himself to himself: *"In this little town on the river Inn, Bavarian by blood and Austrian by nationality, gilded by the light of German martyrdom, there lived, at the end of the '80's of the last century, my parents: the father a faithful civil servant, the mother devoting herself to the cares of the household . . ."*

Bollocks! Mind you, I keep this to myself.

POSTCARD FROM THE PAST #27.

The lift. That's how I began this narrative. As it happens, there weren't just three of us, but I fancied that three-blokes-in-a-lift line for an opening. Set the right sort of tone, flippant and sufficiently hackneyed to hide something unexpected.

Hitler isn't exactly chipper after the Döllersheim gaffe, Goebbels is still glowering at me, and Mussolini looks more uptight than ever. The rest of the party are pretending everything is as it should be, except for Dietrich, who has left off rubbing his pistol while he tries to work out what's happening. Moments ago he was full of hope, persuaded he was about to be called upon to kill someone, but now something has gone horribly wrong and we're heading for the elevator. The Queen of Tarts is downstairs doing dubious things with icing sugar and The Flatulent Windbag needs something sweet to steady his nerves.

There are too many of us to fit in the lift, so I say I'll take the stairs, but as the doors open it's Goebbels who does the taking, of my elbow to be precise. He steers me in behind the tyrants and installs me beside Himmler, Dietrich, and Kriegbaum. Left on the landing, Starace, Bottai, and Ciano inspect a painting, pretending they never intended taking that particular elevator at all.

Why Goebbels gets me in there, I do not know. Perhaps he wants to keep an eye on me after what he saw at the Palazzo Vecchio, perhaps he has a presentiment, perhaps he takes a malicious pleasure from placing me in a sticky situation, and this is a sticky situation, very sticky. I mean, this is a lift we're in, that is to say a small, sealed box. Can you imagine what this means in the company of The Flatulent Windbag? Goebbels is a subtle man. He worships his master, but I wouldn't put it past him to exploit that master's digestive infelicities to discomfit people who find the man repellent.

It begins almost immediately. Kriegbaum presses the button, the doors shut, and Hitler farts. *Hey up, Rover!* The smell is indescribable. The farts are definitely worse than when he arrived five days ago. Kriegbaum glances sideways then concentrates on the panelling, like a dendrologist who has discovered a particularly interesting knot. The Constipated Prick appears to be trying to touch the roof with his chin. Himmler and Dietrich behave as if nothing is amiss. Himmler even has a little smile on his face. I'm not sure he isn't surreptitiously sniffing. Goebbels is watching me, like he's waiting for a sign. But when it comes, the sign is none of my doing.

The lift judders to a halt between floors. Kriegbaum presses the buttons. Nothing happens. Goebbels tries, then Dietrich, but there's nothing doing. The lift won't move and the doors won't open and there's no alarm and oh-my-god The Flatulent Windbag is flexing his knees! I suddenly possess a lively appreciation of the German people's need for *Lebensraum*. Living space is what we all need right now. Personally, I could do with a couple of stadiums of the stuff. The Duce stares fixedly at the lift doors, livid that modern technology should let him down in front of his guest. It's one thing for the human machines not to work like they should in a totalitarian system, but for the machine machines not to work is unforgivable.

"Otis," I say, pointing at the control panel. My words sound a bit strained. I'm trying to speak without breathing. "American company. Wouldn't happen with an Italian lift." And then, because I can't leave well alone and my magpie mind is stocked with all manner of trivia, I add: "First name

Elisha. Elisha Otis. Think it means 'God is salvation.' Elisha. Handy, really."

Mussolini turns his neck as if his collar is chafing, but he's pleased it's not an Italian lift that has failed. Hitler ignores me. Blond hair, blue eyes, and Aryan build notwithstanding, I've lost whatever cachet I had with him. Himmler's lips pinch tight in a prissy little moue, the Hebraic name far more repulsive to him than the effluvia filling the atmosphere.

There is a brief discussion among the minions about how to proceed. The dictators remain silent, above the fray. Dictators don't "do" domestic mishaps like jammed elevators. Dietrich touches his pistol. I think he wants to shoot the lift. I consider suggesting we fill it with fart gas so it rises to the top floor, but even the thought makes my eyes water, so I keep my mouth shut, which is by far the best policy in the circumstances. Kriegbaum's instincts for self-preservation are less highly developed than mine and he rashly opens his mouth to point out that our absence will be noted, that already they will be summoning the janitor.

This isn't good enough for Goebbels, though. He says it is intolerable that the Führer should have to wait for some factotum to free him. For once, I am inclined to agree. So when Himmler wonders whether someone could not climb onto the roof of the lift to seek help, I take one look at Hitler's jodhpurs and promptly volunteer. The thought of those trousers and what they contain and the havoc those contents could wreak in such a restricted space is too much for me. I feel a twinge of compunction about abandoning Kriegbaum, who has gone quite pale since making his reckless little speech, but the situation is critical and, in that great contribution made by the French language to the vocabulary of international diplomacy, it's a question of *sauve qui peut*. They're his countrymen, after all.

Climbing out is easier said than done. We're tightly packed and there's considerable shuffling about and excusing-me and would-you-minding before I can remove the lighting grill and open the trap accessing the roof hatch. We then have the tricky business of getting me up there. Dietrich is designated to make a stirrup with his hands. This isn't pleasant for either of us, not least me since I have to steady myself on his shoulders, like I'm about to give the blighter a kiss. But once my arms are through the hatch and I'm stepping up to pull my legs out, I manage to manoeuvre my cardboard shoe in such a way as to get the toe between Dietrich's teeth, which is good. I tell you, my dear, one has to take one's pleasures where one can in this life. I've still got that shoe. It may well be the only dental record left of Sepp Dietrich.

Everyone knows what the top of a lift looks like. We've all seen the films, know there's that moment when the car suddenly starts going up with the hero stuck on the roof and the shaft head fast approaching. But there is none of that drama in my case. Instead, I simply climb the ladder set into the sidewall and pummel the outer doors of the floor above. As Kriegbaum surmised, the mislaying of two tyrants is not an omission that has been overlooked and the museum's director is already on hand with the relevant keys. Once the power is switched off and the manual hoist set in motion, a jimmy does the rest and the captives are liberated, along with a small cloud of toxicity that makes those standing nearby quite dizzy. Nobody is harmed, though Kriegbaum is slightly unsteady on his feet and Mussolini looks a little pink. I would imagine any lingering doubts he had about the desirability of visiting museums have been put to rest in the minutes he was stuck in that lift.

A minor incident, nothing to speak of really . . . says I, modestly. Because it's now that it happens, now that I became "the hero." That little shit Goebbels arranges it. The instant he's out of the lift, he sends for Hoffman, and the next thing I know, I'm having my photo taken alongside a brace of Fascist dictators, and within hours the papers are reporting how the leaders were saved by a humble scholar.

This is Goebbels's revenge for my impertinent asides and ambiguous comments, the revenge that has caught up with me now, thirty years later. He identifies me with the people I despise. I don't suppose he foresees the end that awaits him and his hero. I don't imagine he foresees a future in which being designated as The Man Who Saved Hitler and Mussolini will be inconvenient in the extreme. He is subtle, but not that subtle. However, he knows enough to know that such public praise will piss me off no end. And I am duly pissed off no end.

So that's it, my dear. Basically, I became a Fascist hero because I was frightened of farts. Happily, that wasn't my only act of "heroism" that day. The second was less newsworthy, but more important. Less happily, it wasn't the end of Goebbels's plans for me, either.

POSTCARD FROM THE PAST #28.

I "saved" The Flatulent Windbag and The Constipated Prick. I also "saved" The Queen of Tarts. Note the inverted commas. The latter was riskier and a genuine choice, but it was still a very approximate sort of saving, trifling by contrast with the way she saved me from myself, lending me a slender grasp on self-respect that I have since frittered away. But that's another story. So, How I Won Your Mother. This is it.

This is it. Three little words freighted with a series of life's more intense experiences. One you know already, my dear, the exclamation mark *This-is-it!* that obsesses every young person, the frequently felt and more often frustrated *This-is-it!* of soul mates, true love, and all that delightfully intoxicating twaddle with which we distract ourselves in youth. Then there is the question mark *This-is-it?* of middle age, when one acknowledges that, yes, this is my life, these are my limitations, this is how it's probably going to be for the rest of my time here, this is what I am, what I am worth as a human being, what I am capable of achieving, a *This-is-it* that either entails acceptance of oneself, or leads to one of those foolish midlife crises, in which men rush off to remedy their fading virility by buying a big motorcycle or coupling with young women or sailing round the world to get back to where they began. Then, I would imagine, there is the *This-is-it* that hits us when we sidle out of life. I don't know what punctuation that involves. Probably a full stop. Maybe dot, dot, dot. A dash for believers. But the first *This-is-it* is by far the most exhilarating.

It's time for our refreshments. After the fury and the farts and the photos, my sugar levels are falling fast, and I need refreshing as a matter of some urgency. The moment Hoffman indicates he has finished, I'm off, haring down the stairs so fast that the others are left behind, so fast that I burst into the refreshments room before My Waitress has finished her preparations. Your Mum is pouring white powder from a twist of paper onto the whipped cream icing of her rum cake. You remember that cake? She always made it for birthdays, only without the special totalitarian ingredients.

My abrupt intrusion startles her. There is a flash of fear, a flicker of panic before she recognizes me and relaxes, proceeding to smooth the white powder into the cream with the blade of a knife. It is the final touch to a carefully composed recipe. Though short-lived, her alarm is enough to alert me. Instinctively, I understand that it's not just icing sugar she's adding to the cake. Nothing so anodyne. She's doctoring the dictators' delicacies.

I don't know what was on the menu that day. Sorbitol? Stachyose? Vebascose? Raffinose? Alumina hydrate? Calcium salts? I never knew the half of it. She had a whole pharmacopoeia at her disposal. As you know, she was a trained chemist. And, as on the previous occasions when she dispensed her wares, there are different cakes for different folks, one destined for The Flatulent Windbag, another for The Constipated Prick.

The whats spring to my lips, the what-ises and the what-are-yous and the what-do-you-thinks and the what-the-fucks, but before I can speak there is a flurry of activity behind me and the men for whom the cakes are intended come sweeping in accompanied by their entourage. The Führer is not best pleased to see me, but his face lights up at the sight of My Waitress. As for Mussolini, it's all the rest of him that lights up. Happily, neither of them notices the broad wink she gives me.

THIS IS IT! I'd give the rest of my life to live that wink once again. It's better than the one she gave me back on the train to Naples. That was just a bit saucy, but this time . . . THIS IS IT! There's complicity in it, a conspiracy to ridicule, above all promise and provocation, an invitation to play a part, to share in the charade, and take responsibility for whatever it is she is doing. And, I know, beyond any doubt, that what she is doing is not motivated by purely nutritional objectives.

THIS IS IT! She's dishing out the different cakes. They look the same. But different pathologies call for different therapies, costive on the one hand, carminative on the other. Dishing out the cakes with the white powder pasted into the icing and lord knows what else interleaved with the sponge and the vanilla cream and the ganache and *pasticciera*. She could be poisoning them for all I know. *Buon appetito*. I say nothing. I conceal the crime, take a chance, risk, I suppose, being carted off by large men with big coats, heavy hands, and small morals.

And so it begins. That silence is the first act of my career as a practising anti-Fascist. It is trivial, like so much else in my life back then, but in the ensuing years it will come to mean much more, indeed be much more, like so much else in all our lives back then.

She could be poisoning them for all I know. If she had known what was to come, she would have. She wasn't a woman for pussyfooting about. She wouldn't have hesitated, not like I did at the balcony or when they gave me the gun. If she had known about the *leggi razziali* that would be promulgated in a couple of months' time, about the consequences for her family, about all that would happen in Poland and points east after 1941, Hitler would have been swallowing cyanide seven years earlier and Mussolini would not have had to hang about waiting for a partisan's bullet. As it was, she was moved not by an impulse to murder but by her own peculiar brand of individualist anarchism, which was so very individual and so very anarchic that it needed its own unique form of expression. In this case, cake.

The way to a man's heart is through his stomach. And to the rest of him. Your Mum simply took that old adage to its logical conclusion. Confronted by tyrants, you don't tackle them head on, you don't turn tyrannical yourself, you don't deal out death and destruction. Those are their techniques. Instead, you make enquiries, you speak to journalists, diplomats, doormen, housekeepers, information mongers of all stripes, you wangle a job in the dispensary of a celebrated doctor, you find the weaknesses of your enemies and "encourage" those weaknesses. And if the weaknesses happen to be flatulence and constipation, so be it. You bake a cake. Two cakes, in fact. One for each variety of colon. And then you wait and you watch while bloating and impaction take their toll. It's not the conventional way of waging war. But, by God, it works. The curious thing is that the long-term consequences of those respective weaknesses in the digestive tracts of the dictators were the inverse of what one might have supposed. But I'll deal with consequences later.

That wink, though—THIS IS IT! I asked her once why she had trusted me. She was shocked when I caught her in the act, but as soon as she recognized me, she relaxed. You know what she said, why she knew her secret was safe with me? She reminded me of that day at the Palazzo Venezia when she first got close to the dictators and saw me saluting Goebbels as a pretext for escaping Hitler's halitosis. She told me that even then she had known I was an impostor like herself, known it perhaps before I did myself, and the reason why, she said, was because I looked too embarrassed to be a Fascist. That was why she trusted me. That was why she knew I wouldn't betray her. I won your Mum by means of mortification and discretion, qualities that even I would be the last to claim for myself. It is upon such slight intuitions as these that the patterns of our lives are played out. THIS IS IT!

I appreciate that if I am to exonerate myself in your eyes, I should romanticize my motives for doing what I did in the coming years, glorifying all the clandestine stuff your mother got me embroiled in against my better instincts. In a sense, I can do that, for what I did was done out of love. But I was not moved by noble sentiments. Never that. Noble sentiments have a nasty habit of persuading people to do unpleasant things that ought not to be done at all. You should bear that in mind with those fine friends of yours and their clamourous ideals. Remember what I said before, have fun, be kind, that's all that counts.

So, no heroic motives. I became a Fascist hero because I was frightened of farts. And I became an anti-Fascist because I fancied your mother. That's all. Then I ducked out of the one unequivocal chance I had to declare my willingness to go down in history.

POSTCARD FROM THE PAST #29.

I miss the signal, but there must have been one. My Waitress, Kriegbaum, the museum director, other assorted staff have already been dismissed. My own attempts to excuse myself were thwarted by Goebbels, who invited me to have more cake. In the circumstances, this seemed distinctly sinister. For one horrible moment, I feared he suspected something about the source of Hitler's farts. Well, not the source. That was fairly indisputable. But the reason they were getting worse. So I had more cake. Noblesse oblige. Only when the rest of the entourage leaves the room in response to some unseen prompt does it occur to me that, if there is something sinister afoot, its object might be me rather than My Waitress. Goebbels, Dietrich, Hitler, Ciano, and Mussolini remain behind—with me.

I don't know who set it up. Certainly not Mussolini. He's as surprised as myself. Nor Dietrich who doesn't have the wit for such refined cruelty. And Ciano wouldn't act behind his father-in-law's back, not yet. It may have been Hitler himself. He can read people, has perhaps seen my contempt, seen a secret desire inside me, secret even to me, and has been toying with me, more contemptuous of me than ever I was of him. But I suspect the principal agent is Goebbels with his nasty little novelist's eye and creative talent for skewering others.

He turns to me with a look of serpentine cordiality. I am wondering why nearly everyone else has left the room and wishing I could do so myself. My Waitress must be out there somewhere. She might want to wink at me. Mussolini is rocking back and forth on the heels of his boots, his satin dark eyes darting hither and thither, aware that something is up, but none too sure what it is and reluctant to betray his ignorance. Ciano is glancing from one face to another, equally mystified but interested rather than alarmed.

"Do you have any weapons?" says Goebbels.

"Why, do I need any?" I ask. I'm not being funny. Given the way Goebbels speaks, being armed seems like a sensible precaution.

"Nobody likes a neutral," he says, holding his upturned hand out to Dietrich. Reaching under the tail of his jacket, Dietrich unsnaps a fastening. "We all admire those who are ready to die for a cause they believe in," says Goebbels. "But dying for a cause is not enough. Killing is the thing, you see, the frontier to be crossed, the concretization of will. Because when you kill another man you make his will subordinate to your own." Dietrich gives Goebbels his gun. Goebbels continues speaking, the pistol resting on the palm of his hand, as if it is a rare flower he is displaying to the company. "You know," he says, "there are people who grasp reality with the incisive vigour of a bee sucking honey from a flower. I am indebted to Il Duce for the image. He understands these things. He also notes that others have to be crushed by truth before they begin to comprehend. In these ways, we come to master reality."

Mussolini is unprepared for this. He doesn't like surprises and he's doing such strenuous things with his chin that it's a wonder his neck doesn't snap. But he is clearly pleased to discover how quotable he is. He looks like he's tempted to try a little preening. If he could just get his head round and stick his nose under his armpit.

Goebbels lays the gun on the table beside the remains of the cakes. He steps back. Dietrich, too. Hitler leans forward, quivering with the rapt curiosity of a scientist awaiting the result of a delicately balanced experiment. He is at the far end of the table, beside Mussolini. Ciano is behind his boss. Goebbels and Dietrich several paces to my left. I am nearest the gun. One step and it would be in my hand. Hitler is staring at me eagerly. Mussolini is looking a little less eager. In 1926, he nearly had his nose shot off by Dublin born Violet Gibson. As far as he's concerned, the Irish have form with firearms.

"I wonder," continues Goebbels in his role as master of ceremonies, "do you consider yourself a man of the people, Mr. Colgan? Hegel declares that the 'people' are that part of the nation that does not know what it wants. Do you know what you want, Mr. Colgan? Because I think you do not like us. I have been told that you proclaim yourself an opponent of everything we stand for. But if I may presume once again to borrow the wisdom of the Duce: when one sets out from certain principles, one must not shrink from their logical consequences."

He nods at the table where the gun sits amid the debris of the cakes. He is offering me the opportunity to shoot the dictators. This can't have been improvised. Even if Mussolini has been taken by surprise, the German contingent know, have fixed the occasion to test me or to best me, in which case they won't have taken any chances. The pistol has to be unloaded. It is a game, rigged so they win either way. If I seize the gun, I go directly to the dungeons. If I don't, I am exposed as a coward.

Yet Goebbels's silky tones are peculiarly persuasive. And Hitler's intense concentration suggests there is something to play for, a possibility that the experiment might not pan out as anticipated. I cannot be sure there are no bullets in the gun. There's always a might-be. A moment's oversight, perhaps a genuine gamble on the part of risk-takers. And surely history compels me to take a chance, to grab the gun and squeeze the trigger, if only as a statement of faith. This is my second opportunity. I missed the first, but here . . .

Close your heart to pity. Act brutally. Those were Hitler's words to his generals a year later on the eve of war. I wish I'd heard them in Florence. I ought to have tried to kill the tyrants, bullets or no bullets. That I did not make even a token effort was not due to cowardice, though doubtless that is what they concluded. Rather, the moment Goebbels made his challenge, the instant he said that certain principles entail certain consequences, everything that I had been feeling in the previous days crystallized into a conviction that these people were totalitarian in one thing at least—they were utterly meretricious.

The movements they led were movements that appealed to the worst characteristics in their respective peoples. They were movements that exalted the cult of the trickster and glorified nihilism. They institutionalized the irrational and reactionary, sanctifying the odious congregation of belonging that defines itself by what and who it is not. They celebrated brutality, ignorance, cynicism, and incivility. Above all, they elevated violence as the validation for everything. They were the antithesis of civilization, for the defining quality of civilization is the relegation of violence to the remedy of last resort. And with the dawning of that conviction, it seemed to me that my best riposte to people like these was to incarnate the values they despised.

I am a mediocre man in a world of would-be supermen. When being a superman is the ideal to which one is supposed to aspire, being mediocre becomes an act of rebellion. *There are very few real men and the rest are sheep.* Mussolini is fond of Machiavelli's maxim, sees himself as a real man. Consequently, we mediocre men are duty-bound to embrace our inner ungulate. Sheep do not shoot guns. They butt heads in an inane display of obduracy, but they don't shoot guns.

To be an ordinary man when men are meant to be supermen, to refuse the counterfeit heroism and shabby hubris of self-proclaimed champions, to accept that one is full of doubt and fear, that one is weak and unwilling to destroy others to compensate for one's weakness, that is a kind of accomplishment. It is a small accomplishment, very small, one that will not be celebrated in films or novels or history books, but in extraordinary circumstances, ordinariness can claim victory of a sort.

Slowly, so slowly that it is quite clear how deliberate the move is, I put my hands in my pockets. Sometimes gestures can be more articulate than words.

I was wrong. I know that now. Holding you in my arms as a baby, I felt a love so strong I would have fought the whole world to protect you. Had I known that sensation then, had I known how many parents would lose their children, how many children their parents, perhaps I would have behaved differently, grabbed the gun regardless, done what they would have done if the roles were reversed.

Would it have mattered if the gun had no bullets? Even if it hadn't, on the off chance that I had survived the act, grabbing an unloaded gun would have been good for my self-esteem in the years that followed. It's not easy, knowing you perhaps had the opportunity to kill the people who were subsequently responsible for millions of deaths. The thought has haunted me for thirty years, the notion that there was a chance, no matter how slim, that the gun contained at least one bullet, that if I had acted differently . . .

It is absurd, verging on the solipsistic, but the sheer scale of what happened because of those two men, above all Hitler, magnifies the what-ifs so that even the most far-fetched speculation possesses a compelling legitimacy. On occasion, I have felt I should do what I failed to do then, to take life, only mine rather than theirs, a forfeit to compensate for that failure of judgment. But jokes make less mess.

You're in a room with a tiger, a poisonous snake, and a Nazi, and you've got a gun with two bullets. What do you do? Shoot the Nazi . . . twice!

Goebbels smiles. "I think you can take your pistol back, Sepp."

The Führer sniggers. That's a Hitler you don't see very often, the laughing Hitler, the gleeful little man delighting in the havoc he generates. It's not an image we care to reproduce because it makes what he did even more outrageous if that's possible. I only caught that one glimpse of him like that, but the laughing Hitler is there elsewhere, in the *Table Talk* if you can stomach it, chatting with Heydrich and Himmler, making arch comments about the "baseless" rumours being spread about the fate of the Jews. You can hear the smirking behind the words.

For all my ratiocination and rationalization, something died in me when Goebbels smiled and told Dietrich to take his gun back. But that doesn't matter. I mean that something died inside me. We all have to die a little in life if we are to grow and it is as well if this is done early while we still have the time and resources to get over it and get on with life.

I became a Fascist hero because I was frightened of farts. I became an anti-Fascist because I fancied your mother. And I became a mediocrity because it was the closest I could get to moral elegance.

POSTCARD FROM THE PAST #30.

consequences *n.* that which follows or comes after as a result or inference; effect: the relation of an effect to its cause: importance: social standing: consequentiality: (in *pl.*) a game describing the meeting of a lady and gentleman and its consequences, each player writing a part of the story not knowing what the others have written.

Bloke visits a Jewish friend in Germany in the 1930s, asks him what it's like living under the Nazis. "It's like being a tapeworm," says the Jew. "Everyday I squirm through all this brown crap waiting to be excreted."

I've felt like that anonymous Jew for some while. The Brownshirts were purged by 1938, but the blouses were still full of shit, and re-creating our encounter is like trying to construct a castle out of crap: it's messy, distasteful, and difficult to get the shape right. I always wanted to write a book, I mean a book about what happened back then. Not this book, but something pithy and playful called *Death—A Short Book About Life*. Gaiety is a form of politesse, a notably graceful form, and it seemed to me that, if one could imbue events with a little levity, the enormity of what we have experienced this century might be rendered less burdensome. But that book was beyond me. Instead, I made a triography, describing the meeting of a lady and gentleman, each player writing a part of the story not knowing what the others have written.

Consequence: your mother. She did wink at me again, winked and inveigled me into playing those partisan games that took me back and forth between the mountains and my curatorial duties for the next five years. And the winks continued for another decade after that until the day she decided I wasn't up to the mark. They only resumed during that last illness when she let me back into her life as a kind of nursing clown capable of making her laugh and easing her way out of the world with a smile on her lips.

Consequence: revenge *bis*. Goebbels let it be known that the Führer had been fascinated by my scintillating exposition of Italian art. This might not seem very vindictive, but it was a serious inconvenience to me. The scheming little turd understood that I had no desire for the spotlight, that I would be thoroughly put out by all the periodicals and clubs asking for my insights into the great man. Because that's what happened. I was deemed an expert on the *grosser Künstler* and everyone wanted to know what he thought of this painting or that and what a discerning eye he had and how proud I must have been to stand by his side while he dispensed perfectly structured apothegms of stunning perspicuity. The *nationalsozialistischer deutscher Studentenbund* were particularly importunate, pestering me to do a lecture tour, and for several months the editor of *Der schwarze Korps* was like a distant relative dunning me for money. I very nearly wrote an article just to get rid of him until your mother had the ingenious idea of sending him an extra-small condom instead—unused, I hasten to add. What he made of that enigmatic message, I do not know, but it did the trick, and I never heard from him again.

Consequence: my career as a partisan. The things I did for your mother! Actually, that's not true, pretending she bounced me into stuff. People thought I kowtowed, kept looking to her for my cue. Fact was I just liked watching her. Most of the time I went my own sweet way. Even going underground wasn't only for her. I was moved by another imperative. Comes to most of us sooner or later. The moment when we realize we are all responsible for our times, that one cannot remain a spectator of history forever, that standing at the window watching is morally untenable, and that no matter how comfortable the shadowy ambivalence of the onlooker, no matter how estranged one is from one's epoch, no matter how firmly persuaded of the futility of fighting, engagement eventually becomes inevitable.

Consequence: my career as a pundit. Once you've invented "facts" for Mussolini about the depth of the River Arno and bantered with Hitler about green grass and blue skies, pontificating on the TV is a doddle. It was in the course of those few days that I discovered the gift I subsequently coaxed into a career. I don't believe I would have become such a glib know-it-all without that experience. So that's one more crime of which those two were culpable.

Consequence: this is it. You know how people worry about life after death, does it exist, what does it consist of, how can we know, who's going to be elevated, who's going to be cast down, and all that guff? You know, too, how little I care for it. Well it's down to those days I spent with Hitler and Mussolini. Since then, life after death has seemed of secondary importance. It's life before death that worries me. How much, how long, how large, how wide, how bright. Besides these considerations, the afterlife pales into insignificance.

Consequence: you. Of the personal consequences, you are by far the most important. For a few years I lived in heaven with my small tribe of women: your mother, you, and Pooh-Belle, that irascible bitch we fished out of the rubbish bin when you were a babe. You remember her? I never knew such a bad-tempered dog, but we loved her nonetheless. You are all that's left of that idyll, which is why your withering contempt when you found that clipping was so devastating. Giving life to you I gave life to something inside myself that I hadn't known existed, but without which, I'm not sure I care to exist any longer. I still don't know whether what I have written here is enough to remedy the damage done by that cutting. I still don't know if I will even show you this manuscript. Perhaps it will linger in a bottom drawer to be discovered after my death, in which case you will have no right of reply, no chance to judge me face-to-face apprised of all the facts. If it does happen like that, it won't be out of malice. More my usual mix of vacillation and diffidence. You will be hurt, no doubt, perhaps even penitent, but those are the markers of mourning. Even without the disclosure of hidden stories, the death of someone near to us always reveals something in ourselves that engenders remorse. I am sincere in my doubts, though. I really wonder whether it is worth trying to explain. What is done is done and there are times in life when you cannot explain and must simply live with the consequences of being misunderstood, no matter how painful they may be, no matter how unjust they may seem. Sometimes it's simply easier to be unhappy than to be happy. You'll find this little by little. Life is an apprenticeship in sadness. The funny thing is, the sadder you get, the more precious life seems. I suppose it's like all apprenticeships, a training in appreciation.

Consequence: *Sturm und Drang 1*. Hitler went off to do what he always did after a visit to Italy, springing a nasty surprise on others, in this case *Kristallnacht* for the Jews and Sudetenland for the Czechs. Meanwhile, The Constipated Prick got his moment of glory and was able to pretend that he was the masterful broker of Munich. Then came the Germanification of Fascism and the serial humiliation of Mussolini, a five-year lesson in the eating of humble pie, as The Flatulent Windbag carried out one lightning strike after another, while The Constipated Prick dithered, then struck, got stuck, and had to be unstuck by his lightning chum.

Consequence: *Sturm und Drang 2*. I can't say for sure that your mother's cakes changed the course of history. Maybe Hitler went round the bend with tertiary syphilis or Dr. Morell's bulls' bollocks or was overcome by neurasthenia and

Parkinson's. But I can say that he ended up taking twenty-eight different medications for his nonstop farting, farting your mother had done her best to exacerbate, and I can say that Mussolini's faecal matter got so reticent that he ended up rolling round on the ground in agony. These things take their toll. As his health deteriorated, Mussolini became increasingly wraithlike and otherworldly, to the point at which it seemed he had very little engagement with reality at all. As for Hitler, he turned into a junkie. The more bound up one became with earthy matter, the more he negated the things of the earth. The more gas the other one produced, the less ethereal he became. The idea that this was your Mum's handiwork is not wholly fantastic. It was from this time on that Hitler's mood swings became increasingly unpredictable, his temper tantrums ever more operatic, his peculiar mix of self-regarding arrogance and paranoid insecurity more pronounced. She did make a very good cake, your mother. I wouldn't put it past her to have rearranged the world with her baking.

Consequence: these words. Appearances notwithstanding, my purpose here is not purely frivolous. We tend to deal with the horrors of history in two ways. Either we pretend they never happened and carry on as if life is a long musical comedy, or we go deep down inside them, immersing ourselves in the sheer bloody awfulness of it all. I wanted to do both, the second in the guise of the former. It is apt that the word *ecrire* incorporates both *rire* and *cri*, because writing is often a bark of laughter veiling a howl of despair. And I can assure you, all that scatology, no matter how coarse, conveys a kind of cracked morality. By treating him as The Flatulent Windbag, I am bringing Hitler down to earth. But in doing so, I do not aim to make him seem less terrible. The fact that he is risible, the fact that we *can* bring him down to earth, does not make him less terrible. On the contrary, that is when he is most frightening, when he is on earth, a human being. Real people are far more frightening than bogeymen and monsters because we cannot pretend they are something "other." They are people, like us. Worse, we might be one of them. You don't need me to tell you what these men did. Their crimes are enormous. And we have inflated the perpetrators to fit the crime, particularly Hitler. But he wasn't as big and bizarre when you met him, still less when you smelt him. He was one of us, a flesh and blood, farty little man. Was he mad? Well, he wasn't precisely normal. But it's too easy to say he was off his head, an inhuman monster. We can't just push him aside and pretend he has nothing to do with us. Because even if we do hive him off into some category of exceptionality (madder, badder, bleaker, sadder, sicker, weirder, freakier), we can't do that with the thousands of people who put his plans into action, the millions who compromised themselves, the tens of millions who shuffled by on the other side of the road looking the other way, the 90 percent of humanity who didn't do quite as much as they could have done.

In the end, this is the core accusation levelled against my generation by yours, guilt by association, the culpability of synchronicity, the fact that we were there when atrocity was transformed into an industrial enterprise. And you are right to do so. There's no escaping it. Blame has been a busy fellow these last few decades. Shame hasn't been able to keep up with him at all. There's no answer to this. *Mea culpa*. But beware, because you will have similar experiences of your own. You will live at the same time as terrible events, hopefully not so terrible, but bad enough, maybe next door, maybe on the other side of the world, but either way events for which you will have your own small portion of responsibility if only out of carelessness. It is the lot of humanity. In the case of our generation, the drama was more intense, the numbers greater, the dilemma more acute, but the guilt remains the same. Remember, it's not necessarily the big moments that count, the critical decisions taken in extreme circumstances. In moments of do-or-die, we often act on impulse and make the right choice. But the small moments, the cumulative minutiae of daily life, the interstices of opportunity, when things are ambiguous or penumbral, the results uncertain, the decisions and indecisions and undecisions reached almost unknowingly—how then? For my part, I feel tainted by failure, not by that silly photo, but by the inadequacy of my response to my times. The stain in my case is rather large. If you pass up the opportunity to rub out a couple of blots on the landscape as big as Hitler and Mussolini, your housekeeping credentials are seriously impaired. But we are all tainted by the compromises we make. These things happen. There's nothing to be done about it, except to do the best we can, to aspire to a little lucidity, a little courage, a little kindness, and to keep on keeping on.

POSTCARD FROM THE PAST #31.

At the station, Santa Maria Novella. The Flatulent Windbag is about to board his train. He is shaking hands with The Constipated Prick. His eyes are bright with tears. I'd like to think it's because of a particularly villainous fart, but I fear it is a product of genuine emotion. He really cares. The two men embrace then step back, still holding on to one another.

"No power in the world can come between us now," says Hitler.

There's a bit of elbow squeezing, some shoulder patting. They're almost stroking one another. I wouldn't be all that surprised if they embarked on a bout of mutual grooming.

"Henceforth, no force will be able to separate us," confirms Mussolini.

Leave them there. Let them go. We know what happens next. Somewhat less certain is what happens here, now, in this Parisian apartment. I can hear the elevator cage rattling to a halt, the latch being unhooked, the clack of the grill folding back into a concertina, footsteps on the landing.

There! The middle floorboard that gives and used to betray your adolescent outings. Sometimes it seems like I spent half my life lying awake listening for that middle floorboard. There's the sound of a key being inserted in the lock, a first turn, the pause for the tricky tumbler. Apart from myself and the concierge, who is on holiday, only one other person has a key to this place.

This much I predicted. What follows remains open to doubt. What sort of "why" have your brought with you, my dear?

Never mind. It must be confronted one way or the other. Like I say, you've got to deal with other people as they are.

Decision time. What's it to be? Show you the manuscript or tuck it away? In its own way, it is a choice between life and death. As a general rule, it is preferable to choose life.

Sehen sie, meine Herren.

H*EY UP, R*OVER*?* It was Charlie's story. You never knew Charlie. He died before you were born. He was a grand ungodly man with a gift for spreading life-enhancing mayhem. *Hey up, Rover* was his story, his sort of story. This is how it went . . .

Travelling salesman fetches up at a remote farmhouse late at night, asks if there's an inn nearby. "No inn," says the farmer, "but you're welcome to stay here." The man accepts gratefully. They settle down to supper. It's beans, a huge bowl heaped high with beans. The salesman has a delicate intestine, is particularly susceptible to wind when he eats beans, but out of politeness accepts the meal. Before long, he can feel a distressing distension building inside him. In the end, it gets too much, so he eases up one buttock to squeeze out a quiet one. Needless to say, it's not a quiet one. Nobody ever farts as quietly as they think they do. In fact, this one's more than just audible, it's bloody loud.

"Hey up, Rover," says the farmer, leaning over to look under the table.

Only then does the salesman realize that the farm dog is lying under the table. "Oh, thank God for that," he thinks. "He's blaming the dog." He's particularly pleased because he can feel another fart coming on. He holds it in as long as he can, but eventually there's nothing for it, and he lets rip, another mighty blast reverberating about the kitchen.

"Hey up, Rover!" says the farmer, a little more emphatically.

"Bloody hell, this is brilliant," thinks the travelling salesman, "he still believes it's the dog. I can fart all I like and he'll blame the dog."

So they carry on with their meal and before long the salesman is farting every few seconds, and every time he farts, the farmer leans over and says "Hey up, Rover," and the farts are getting louder and the salesman is becoming more and more cavalier, farting away like the safety valve on a pressure cooker, until eventually the farmer leans right over and says: "Hey up, Rover! Better shift yourself, the bugger's going to shit on you in a moment."

HE DID, TOO.

MAKES LESS MESS.

AFTERWORD

Any work of fiction based on historical characters, particularly such infamous individuals as Hitler and Mussolini, will inevitably make readers question the book's historical veracity. Of course, the novelist likes to pretend that fiction is truer than fact, but the niggling doubt remains: *Did that really happen?*

The events described here were inspired by the experience of the Italian art historian Ranuccio Bianchi Bandinelli (1900–1975), who was obliged to show Hitler and Mussolini round Florence and Rome in 1938. However, this is in no way intended as a retelling of his story. He does that well enough himself in *Hitler e Mussolini, 1938: il viaggio del Führer in Italia* (ISBN 978-8876412455). There is no English translation of this work, but it does exist in French under the title *Quelques jours avec Hitler et Mussolini* (ISBN 978-2355360503). Rather than being a template for the present work, Bandinelli's story is like a palimpsest, his experiences and observations intermittently visible to a greater or lesser degree behind the lines of my own narrative.

Among the more obvious borrowings are several anecdotes (for example Goebbels's story about Göring's marrons glacés), snippets of dialogue (like the dispute about architects), and some of the comments on works of art (Hitler's musings at the Piazzale Michelangelo). The narrator's initial dilemma (notably in the days running up to the visit), as well as his mixed feelings of contempt and fascination, also come from Bandinelli, as do the refrains *"Ein grosser Künstler"* / *"Sehen sie, meine Herren"* / and *"der alles weiss."* Above all, though, Bandinelli's experiences provide the situation and the chronological framework around which I have constructed my own story.

I have, however, tweaked the itinerary (both the bits described by Bandinelli and the parts of the programme in which he did not participate) when it suited my purposes. For instance, the dictators took different trains to Naples, Mussolini's arriving in the middle of the night, Hitler's the next morning, so the Führer's exposition of the works of Karl May could not have taken place en route. The exposition itself is far from implausible, though. Hitler's favourite novelist was a fascinating individual who lived a genuinely picaresque life, except that he had a depth and breadth of character usually lacking in picaresque heroes. The outline of his career here is a severely edited version of the original account. For anyone interested in discovering more about May, there's plenty of material on the Internet, but a useful starting point is www.karlmayusa.com.

I have also used some historical facts that would not have been known to an author writing in 1968. In particular, the Soviet autopsy (which is not necessarily to be trusted, being both a medical and political document) on Hitler's corpse wasn't released until 1970, Hitler's solipsistic line about Geli's death appeared in the police report into the affair but wasn't widely known until Ron Rosenbaum's (see below) investigations in the 1990s, the suppressed story of Mussolini's first wife, Ida Dalser (retold in the excellent film *Vincere* by Marco Bellocchio), didn't come to light until 2005, and Mussolini's description of Hitler as a *sentimentalone* appears in Claretta Petacci's diaries, first published in 2009 (*Mussolini Segreto* ISBN 978-8817043922). Likewise, the story (probably apocryphal, but too good to ignore) about a French minister asking what the English "did" with their Jews dates, to the best of my knowledge, from the 1990s.

Most of Hitler and Mussolini's words are their own, culled from Hitler's *Table Talk* (the R. H. Stevens and Norman Cameron translation of 1953, ISBN 978-1929631056) and Emil Ludwig's *Talks With Mussolini* (translated by Maurice Eden Paul and Cedar Paul in 1933), as well as interviews, speeches, monographs, memoirs, and conversations reported in diaries. However, I have edited and rewritten the basic material, in part to avoid translation copyright infringement (who actually "owns" Hitler's words is a wonderfully murky tale of itself, featuring fishy deals with shady businessmen that could have been lifted from a Graham Greene novel), but mainly because Hitler and Mussolini really did blather on mercilessly (Hitler, in particular, was like a perpetual motion machine of the verb), and if I hadn't rendered their pronouncements a bit more pithily the book would have been three times as long.

I have frequently used speeches and dialogue in contexts that differ from the original, sometimes even applying them to different events or people. For instance, Hitler's comment about Sepp Dietrich being slow on the uptake with jokes was actually about Franz Ritter von Epp, but I recycled it rather than multiplying references to people most of us have never heard of and can probably remain in total ignorance of without drastically impairing the quality of our lives. In a comparably opportunistic spirit, I have taken inspiration from things that took place elsewhere at different times. For instance, the episode in which Hitler "rehearses" his Sudetenland speech was based on pictures of him practising his rhetorical gestures. These photos, which are available on the Internet through the Getty collection, were taken in Germany in 1925 by Heinrich Hoffmann and published in 1955 in his memoir, *Hitler Was My Friend* (ISBN 978-1848326088).

As a general rule, any "fact" that sounds far too improbable to be true is true. By way of example, Hitler did have a chronic problem with flatulence (though it only got really acute later on), he did end up consuming a smorgasbord of drugs that would have disturbed the equilibrium of a far more balanced individual (though they weren't all directed at his digestive disorders), he was an adept and apparently amusing mimic, he did come from a very strange home, and on at least two occasions he told the story about defacing his school certificate. Likewise, Mussolini did suffer crippling constipation, did touch his testicles to ward off the evil eye, did stage stunts like wrestling with a toothless lion cub, would probably be behind bars as a rapist nowadays, and his regime did make suits out of milk and shoes out of cardboard. Moreover, the early history of Fascism was frequently characterized by fabulous incompetence, and the accidental decapitation and amputation referred to at the start did actually happen. The first British Fascists in particular were admirably inept. An historian with an eye for these absurdities is Roger Eatwell—*Fascism: A History* (ISBN 978-1844130900). All of which makes the movement's brief, but (at the time) apparently irreversible, success even more remarkable.

In the first draft, there were a lot more of these bizarre-but-true details, details to which I was dearly attached given their inherent potential for derision. However, the bits inside me that make shift as a novelist got the upper hand and a great deal of fun-but-superfluous history was weeded out in subsequent drafts along with the jokes that went with it. It's worth noting here that the thematic caricaturing of Hitler and Mussolini initially came about just by looking at them. Before I even began research, I had dubbed Mussolini "The Constipated Prick" on the strength of his photos (you've got to admit, he did look uptight and faintly phallic), and had Hitler down as "The Flatulent Windbag," partly because he clearly was besotted by the sound of his own voice, partly in counterpoint to Mussolini's constipation, and partly because of his diet. I was flabbergasted to discover that these capricious fictions corresponded to historical reality.

The "cetology" is all factual *or* has been widely believed to be factual (and not just by fruitcakes and the terminally credulous), in which case a proviso about its authenticity is incorporated in the text. If memory serves (which it may not, but never mind), with three exceptions (the first and last jokes in Cetology #2, and the thematic *Hey up, Rover!*), the italicized jokes were all told at the time, some with fatal consequences for the people who told them. For more of these, see Rudolph Herzog's *Dead Funny: Telling jokes in Hitler's Germany* (ISBN 978-1612191300). Hitler's favourite joke is cited in *Hitler's Last Witness: The Memoirs of Hitler's Bodyguard* (ISBN 978-1848327498) by Rochus Misch. Anybody taken with the Trichology sequence should read Rich Cohen's excellent *Vanity Fair* article, "Becoming Hitler," (available online).

The dictators' relationship was much as described, starstruck admiration on the part of Hitler (an admiration shared by many prominent figures prior to the war) turning to frustration and disappointment before gradually shading into weary clientelism moderated by a slightly demented fidelity. Certainly, after 1938, Mussolini was always running to catch up, and falling ever farther behind the harder he ran. I am willing to stand by the broader assertions about the two men's respective characters, even those that seem to aspire to sweeping generalization. In the first draft, I cited chapter and verse supporting these assertions, chapter and verse whittled out in subsequent versions as being redundant in a novel.

Apart from the Colgan family, all the characters actually existed. Experts in the field may feel that I have traduced one or two of them. For instance, I don't believe Karl Brandt was quite the idiot I portray him as, though he came close and there was definitely an element of moral cretinism in his behaviour, and Sepp Dietrich probably had more on his mind than petting the barrel of his gun. However, neither of them were very lovely people, and I suspect I can rub along well enough with any injustice I have done them. The snobbish condescension of the Italian court and the enthusiastic welcome of the crowds are accurate, though the latter rapidly waned after 1938.

The locations are all true to life, though I have taken considerable liberties with the episode in the lift. There was already a lift in the Uffizi in 1938, but I have no idea who made it, what form it took, how reliable it was, or whether it would have been used to get between the galleries and the refreshments room. One thing is certain, though. You really wouldn't want to get stuck in a lift with Hitler.

The narrator's particular tale, the temptation, the challenge are invented, though at least one consequence is taken from real life, in that Bandinelli was pestered for information about Hitler by fans eager to hear the Führer's brilliant artistic insights. The episode with the gun is invented, but not wholly implausible. The Fascist leaders were risk-takers and gamblers. As a general rule they preferred to take risks and gamble with other people's lives, but there was a degree of bravado and audacity in their spectacular rise to power that suggests my invention is not entirely beyond the bounds of credibility. Moreover, the writer Friedrich Reck-Malleczwen (see below) did once pass up an opportunity to shoot Hitler, an oversight he bitterly regretted in subsequent years, not least because he died with a bullet in the back of his own head at Dachau.

I read many books by way of research, read them with a growing sense of dismay that anything I made up would seem bland beside the clamouring lunacy of the times. I don't intend giving an exhaustive bibliography, the conventional biographies of the principals being well known anyway. However, I will mention A. N. Wilson's *Hitler: A short biography* (ISBN 978-0007413492). It does not supplant weightier tomes like Alan Bullock's long-standing classic, *Hitler: A study in tyranny* (ISBN 978-0060920203), nor does it aspire to, but it is written with wit and verve, and is an excellent introduction to the life. For obvious reasons, Mussolini has been less well-served by biographers and historians, but top of the field are R. J. B. Bosworth's two books, *Mussolini* (ISBN 978-0340981733) and *Mussolini's Italy* (ISBN

978-0143038566). Despite a slightly misleading subtitle, Santi Corvaja's *Hitler & Mussolini: The Secret Meetings* (ISBN 978-1929631421) (a good number of these "secret" meetings were plastered all over the newspapers) was very useful for filling in ancillary details of the dictators' trip, for instance Eva Braun's flirting with Ciano, Hitler calling room service "for a woman," and the near death-by-scenery of the soprano at the San Carlo opera house.

Special mention must go to the magnificently Olympian contempt of Friedrich Reck-Malleczwen's *Diary of a Man in Despair* (ISN 07516 30008). The dizzying hauteur of his disdain for Hitler is quite breathtaking and featured extensively in the first draft of the novel, but got edited out in subsequent drafts because I was enjoying it too much. It's usually a bad sign when authors are enjoying themselves too much. There's a tendency to forget the needs of the reader.

A book I read after I'd written the first draft and wish I'd read before (it would have saved me a lot of time; even a belated reading helped crystallize my own thinking and inspired at least one parenthetical phrase) is Ron Rosenbaum's masterful and very accessible *Explaining Hitler* (ISBN 00609 5339X). Possibly the single best book about Hitler, it is not so much a conventional biography as a metahistory of the conflicting interpretations that have been put forward for a phenomenon that Hugh Trevor-Roper, after fifty years mulling over the subject, could still describe as "a frightening mystery." Essential reading.

CPSIA information can be obtained at www.ICGtesting.com
Printed in the USA
LVOW11s2143070616

491655LV00001B/65/P

9 781579 624842